A RUINED LANDS NOVEL

SEA OF STORMS

LINDSEY POGUE

Sea of Storms
A Ruined Lands Novel

By Lindsey Pogue
Copyright © 2022 Roar Press LLC

All Rights Reserved. No part of this book may be reproduced in any form without permission in writing from the author, except as used in book review.

This is a work of fiction. Characters, names, places, events or incidents are products of the author's imagination. Any resemblance to actual people, living or dead, or to places or incidents is purely coincidental.

Cover Design by Deranged Doctor Designs

Isles of the Lost Winds

SHIP GRAVEYARD

HOMESTEAD

THE ISLAND

HOT CAVE

For my amazing readers!
You've followed me on my author adventure this far, so let's set sail for another!
Thank you to my Patreon supporters for contributing to Brynn and Killian's story. For helping me create the Reaper, and for helping me bring this tale to life.

Katie McGrath
Shelby Sanders
Charlene
K Webster
Conrad
Helen Mays
Fred
Tamara Pankonin
Laurie Keyser
Amanda Eide
Stephanie Edwards
Laura Price
Katelyn Bobbitt
Nicole Hartney
Sabrina Hatfield
Melinda Leininger
Julie Traina

Mindi Travis
Lee Alexander
Martha Brazier
Debbie Osterhout

AUTHOR'S NOTE

Dearest Readers,

    I can't believe this is my twenty-forth book published to date! And out of the many fantastical, weather-ravaged worlds I've created and written in, the Forgotten Lands world is my favorite yet!

    It started with sandstorms and lightning-scorched forests in the Forgotten Lands series proper, where drifters roam the lands and pirates hunt the open waters—a Victorian America reimagined after a climate shift decimated the world hundreds of years ago.

    But sailing overseas to the Ruined Lands—this sister series—has been the most surprising delight. It wasn't planned, and yet, it's been my most epic writing adventure. These are the books the little girl and scholar in me always wanted to write—fairy tale retellings, infused with history, timeless love stories, and epic adventures. Dystopian? Historical Fantasy? Call them what you will, but these are the imaginings that make me giddy.

    City of Ruin took us through secret passageways and haunted woods, to a land shrouded with secrets in my gothic, dystopian spin of "Beauty and the Beast." And now, we continue with *Sea of Storms*, a stand-alone but connected tale, intricately woven with pirates, Norse mythology, and island survival.

I hope you enjoy Killian's and Brynn's love story and adventure. I'm working on my Norse inspired "Snow White" retelling next! Stay tuned!

Until then, happy reading adventures.

Lindsey

GLOSSARY

Ægir - God of the sea; has nine daughters who represent the waves.

Allfather – The foremost god in the Norse pantheon, Odin was father to many, including Thor and Loki. Odin was often known as "Allfather," and the magnificent hall of Valhalla was Odin's home in Asgard, the domain of the Norse gods.

Berkano – Rune meaning: birth, sanctuary, becoming, life changes, shelter, liberation, sanctuary, secrets.

Draug – Norwegian term for an undead creature from Scandinavian literature and folktales.

Fadir – Scandinavian for "father."

Hel – Originally the name of the world of the dead; it later came to mean the goddess of death.

Hel's Hound – Garmr or Garm is a wolf associated with both Hel and Ragnarök, and described as a blood-stained guardian of Hel's gate.

Lokk – The "lokk" is performed in a high-pitched voice, as this carries better over long distances. Many varieties have sudden shifts from high to low notes. This form of singing is found in large parts of the world and is thought to be one of the earliest forms of music.

Njord – God of the wind, seafarers, coasts, waters and wealth; husband of Skadi.

Ran – Goddess and a personification of the sea; the underwater hall of Ran is where sailors would feast who died at sea; wife of Ægir.

Skadi – Goddess of winter and mountains - Associated with independence and self-reliance, especially for women. Skadi wanted revenge for the death of her father but was given a husband of her choosing as compensation instead; she "accidentally" chose Njord and their relationship was one of compromise more than anything—he wanted to be at sea, she in the mountains, so they split their time between both places; hence the changing seasons when she/he was away.

The Great Turning (also known as the Shift) – A climatic shift that changed the face of the entire world three hundred years ago. Every continent was altered, and those who survived were forced to brave a world far different than anything they'd known or experienced before.

The Web of Wyrd – A symbol/metaphor for fate and destiny derived from women's spinning. As the individual fibers turn round the spindle, or are woven together by the Norns at the foot of Yggdrasil, they become the thread of our lives.

Thrall – A slave or serf in Scandinavian lands during the Viking Age.

Tree of Life – Yggdrasil is an eternal green ash tree in Norse mythology. It stands in the middle of the world, with branches that stretch out over all of the nine realms. Each realm hangs on its own branch, but if the tree should shake or fall, so will all the realms.

Way Finder / Nordic Compass / Vegvisir – An eight-pointed runic compass with sigils for protection, strength, guidance and assistance with specific tasks or areas of life. They were drawn onto specific areas of the body or physical objects, such as the side of boats or buildings.

Woefuls – A Ruined Lands term for the poor/indentured populace.

LONG AGO...

Dark clouds reached far and wide, and the world began to wither. In the west, the skies blackened, the waters turned to poison, and the earth quaked. To the north, the land hardened to ice, winter stretched, unending, and old gods battled with the new. Cut off from the rest of the world by the unsailable seas, Norseland's Romantic Era was eclipsed in shadow and fell back into the Dark Ages. Rich or poor, young or old—there was no escaping the Great Turning.

Having no foreign merchants with which to trade, and with the overharvest of her land, Queen Sigrid, ruler of the dying Norse empire, struggled to maintain control amid chaos and despair. For discord was already brewing between two factions —those who followed the new Christian God, and those who prayed to the gods of old. Despite her distrust of men who would try to seize her power, the queen granted a select few the honor of becoming chieftain, and entrusted the kingdom to the men and women she deemed fit, allowing them their religious freedom in exchange for utter fealty.

In a country already unraveling, hunger and fear and religious persecution led to civil war and unrest. Brutality bore

LONG AGO...

fear. And while fear bore loyalty, it came at a price. There was no law. There was no justice. There were only brutes and their deep pockets as they grew fat off the queen's favor.

One man, however, a villain—who sailed the ocean no other man dared cross, as if he was made from it—brought the queen riches from faraway lands in exchange for able bodies to fill his ship. Every year, he returned. And every year, his name was whispered in city streets with far more fear than even the queen could muster. His name was a war cry as villages burned. Some called him Reaper, collector of souls. Some called him Hel's Hound, gatekeeper of the underworld. But only one thing was certain—he and his crew were relentless and not to be crossed.

To this day, there is no code in the northland. There is no honor. There is only violence, strife, and protection that comes at a heavy price. Cities fight cities, gangs roam the streets, and villages are raided.

Righteous and rich, or pagan and poor, no one is truly safe in frozen Norseland.

PROLOGUE
KILLIAN

There is no moon to guide me tonight, and the eerie cries of the woods follow me into the darkness. The more furious the storm, the louder the trees cry, and I run faster.

Why had I run away at all?

Because . . . Father says I am twelve years old now and duty-bound, like my brother.

But Father is not sending *him* away, only me. And I don't want to go to sea. To leave my family and life behind.

I run because, if they don't need me . . . then I don't need them.

I run because . . . Because . . . None of it seems important anymore as a chill cuts through my skin, making it hard to focus on anything other than the cold.

Mother always tells me to trust my instincts, but a fire will not save me tonight. It will not hold up against the storm, nor will it keep the creatures at bay or light the way ahead. So, I follow the creek bed, knowing it will eventually take me home.

I have played in these woods all my life, but it's different in the dark, and I wonder if ghosts cling to the shadows, because it feels as if I am being watched. Even if I know it is foolish—that no monsters lurk in the dark—I run faster.

I don't know how long I speed through the forest with only my satchel on my back, but my clothes are sodden, my hair matted to my face and poking me in my eyes, and I can no longer feel my feet.

When I see the creek bed winding its way around a garden of sandstone boulders, I practically leap for them. I don't care what hides in their shadows. I only know I must find shelter in them before fever sets in or I'm injured in the slick earth that slaps against my feet.

The wind howls with warning, but the last of its call is muffled as I crawl between stones, into a crevice within. There is no wind, only the drone of it above. And while a few drops of rain find their way in, I am safe.

With a whimper, I take a deep breath. *It is only rain and cold.* It is only a storm. Tomorrow the sun will rise and the clouds will part, and I will laugh at this, because the gods will not abandon me—I have done nothing to anger them.

Except for running away, a distant voice tells me, and I shudder. I *am* being punished. In turning my back on my family, I have angered the gods.

Lightning cracks through the sky, thunder shakes the ground, and tears form in the backs of my eyes.

I have never missed my mother tut-tutting me for speaking out of turn or missed my father's indifference more than I do now. At least at home, I have a comfortable bed and a fire in the hearth. I have my brother in the next room and a dry place to sleep.

Wet and shivering, I blow into my cupped hands to warm them.

I imagine myself in my bedroom beside the blazing fire, listening to my grandfather's voice, a low rumble I long to hear again, regaling me with stories of our homeland. About the threads of the Fates, which even the gods can never escape, and why we celebrate Skadi, goddess of winter, of our home, and reluctant bride of Njord. For it was Skadi's snowstorm that saved my grandfather when his village was raided, and Njord, the god of wind and seafarers, who blessed his journey across the treacherous sea to this prosperous land. But they are only stories. Still, I cling to them.

Alone, huddled in the stones, thoughts of home bring me as much longing as they bring me an unexpected ease. I am cold, but feel safe and hidden, and soon, my eyelids are too heavy to hold open.

Dampness seeps into my bones as my mind drifts, too exhausted to care about the tempest whirring around me.

The lull is comforting as I slide in and out of consciousness, until finally, it pulls me in completely. All desperation falls away and the heaviness in me lifts as I feel a sense of peace.

I'm light as a feather—all fears and torment forgotten.

"Killian." *A woman's voice meets my ears. It's rough, but sounds like a silky song that rouses my senses.* "Come with me, Killian." *The air cools around me, prickling my skin, and when I open my eyes and look up, she is standing there. A woman with loose, dark hair that catches the wind as she leans in, but I can't see her face.*

She reaches for me, her arm decorated with runes that glow up her forearm, and my heartbeat quickens. "Skadi?" *I breathe.*

"You must get up."

"Then . . . you have not abandoned me?"

"Come." *She beckons me, and her cool fingers brush against mine as I take her hand.*

A violent shiver wakes me and my eyes flash open. I am wracked with cold, no longer safe in the boulders along the creek bed as water rushes through the cracks and the crevice over me.

The creek is rising.

In a blur of frantic movements and racing thoughts, I crawl out into the cold. Rushing water splashes all around me as I scramble to higher ground. And as I climb up into the open arms of a beech tree, I stare down at the creek, nearly tripled in size as the valley floods.

Exhaustion gives way, and I sob as loneliness and fear consume me. And yet, as the tears fall from my eyes, the cool touch of winter caresses my face, and I think of her—Skadi.

I don't know how, but I can feel she is here with me. That I am not alone because she saved me.

As the cold wind brushes my cheeks and the rain drips over me, I think of the sea breeze in my hair, and suddenly, sailing away from this place doesn't feel so terrible or so lonely. It feels a lot more like Skadi has just saved me. That I cannot outrun my destiny.

1
BRYNN
18 YEARS LATER

Urine, manure, and a tinge of stale ale linger in the air, too pungent for even the frigid morning breeze to whisk it away as my sister and I hurry toward the fishing docks. The capital city of Northhelm is a sordid, depressing place battered by snowstorms. Its cobblestone streets are stained with blood, immortalizing the brink of an era that would never fully grow to fruition. A place where stone buildings with peaked roofs loom among log houses with grass-thatched canopies, all of them rotting or crumbling. Metal crosses hang from vaulted steeples, and carved totems of the Allfather and the old gods stand sentry at entrances to each faction of the city. Northhelm is a place stuck in a fragmented past with no real future.

The deeper we weave through the alleyways, the stronger the stench gets, and I brace myself for another day in this hell, forsaken by the gods.

Estrid trudges through the muddied streets just ahead. Her focus is on our job at hand, knowing it's the only way we'll eat well tonight. Perhaps not the *only* way, but "bartering" is the last thing we want to have to do, again.

Gripping the empty crate in my hands, I ignore the eyes on us as we pass the merchants, haulers, thugs, and prostitutes alike, all lining the dingy streets. With a sister who wields her beauty like a weapon, and me a knife-brandishing thief, I can't say I blame them.

With no family left, we might be the poorest of the poor in Northhelm, two sisters known to do just about anything for the right price if it ensures our survival, but not even ill repute can alter Estrid's mark on this city, for it is impossible to hide her beauty, a truth that is sometimes a blessing, but mostly a curse.

Perhaps it's not our reputation that garners wary stares of late, but who we are commanded by—Von Magnusson, Chieftain of Northhelm and debt collector to Queen Sigrid XII. A queen with an iron fist and cold heart.

"Brynn!" Estrid calls over her shoulder, just loud enough to hear above the fishmonger shouting to his daughter, as we walk along the pier market. "You coming? Our day won't get any easier if we have to collect debts and make Von's trades in a snowstorm."

Just like the gods have abandoned us, so have the seasons, leaving us in constant winter.

I nearly stop in my tracks, staring at the massive ship in port. "Es," I gasp, nudging her. It's not a fishing boat, like the others that swell with the crashing waves. It's giant and otherworldly. With Hel, goddess of death, carved into the prow and embossed on the banners snapping in the wind, I know instantly whose ship it is.

"Keep moving," Estrid whispers. She barely spares the thrall ship a glance. "No distractions. We have a task today." Two years older and more serious she may be, but Estrid isn't fooling me. I know her better than anyone.

We've been through agony together—being cold, subjugated, hungry, and having killed more men than I'm comfortable with to survive. We've done it all, and there's a barely perceptible pitch to her voice when she's wary.

But I follow without argument, though I can't look away from the ship as I sidestep a fish barrel. I might be impulsive with a blade, my boldness terrifying to some even, but that ship makes my blood turn to ice, and true fear grips hold of me.

I've only seen it a few times in my twenty years, but the entire *country* knows who it belongs to. And there's only one entity that frightens me more than the Queen of Norseland—the Reaper, collector of souls, and his horde of henchmen.

Despite having never seen the man himself, I know his reputation all too well—his moniker is whispered through the streets, and villagers avert their gazes when they think they've been overheard, as if merely mentioning his name is forbidden.

But I've seen what his men have done to villages—to *my* village—and I would not wish to cross them, even if my fingers itch to put a knife through the Reaper and each of his men. For the heartache I've endured at their hands. For the havoc they've wreaked in this country.

A man emerges from below deck as we pass the ship, and my steps falter. It's him—my crawling skin confirms as much. His features are scarred, his eyes dark and sinister. The brutal life he's lived is etched in every pockmark on his face, and I swallow thickly.

"Es—there he is," I whisper, chills rolling over the goosebumps already prickling.

The Reaper's eyes meet mine as he steps to the guardrail, peering down at me as if he can hear each nerve in my body blaring with alarm.

"Shit," I hiss, looking away. The last thing I want is to make eyes with a *draug* from the realm of the undead. Estrid and I have known the cruelest men in this city—I've felt the fiery tip of their irons, felt their lashings, and watched them stain the snow with my blood. And still, I would rather be struck dead, here and now, than ever be at his mercy.

I grip the crate in my hands tighter. Even the queen can't stop the Reaper from taking what he wants, and she is supposed to be the most ruthless of all.

Or perhaps she doesn't want to. The thought flickers, not for the first time. Still, I know what happens in Norseland in the Reaper's name, but where does he take the hapless souls he collects once he leaves this place? What does he do to them?

It's the unknown I fear most. At least in Northhelm, I know how to survive—how to fight. I am not a caged animal sailing toward an even bleaker future.

"You should know by now," my sister starts, and I can feel her eyeing the side of my face. "All men can be terrifying. Physical scars or not."

I meet her gaze, guilt burning in my chest. I might've had to kill to survive, but I would argue my sister has had it far worse and done unspeakable things in her twenty-two years to keep us fed and safe.

Without another word about it, Estrid and I turn down a muddied path of barely-exposed cobblestone. Life in the capital has always felt eclipsed by the shadow of what it would've been if not for the Great Turning.

Though pagans and Christians tend to keep to their own parts of the city, there is no denying the festering dissension that stalks the alleyways and fills people's eyes with malice. Von appoints thugs to maintain a modicum of peace in the streets, so workhouse production remains satisfactory to the queen. But still, the wrong look, the twitch of a scarred cheek, or a cough in the wrong direction could mean the next turf war or riot, so we keep our heads down as we hurry through.

"Don't get any ideas," Estrid tells me as we finally approach the outskirts of the city. "Keep your knives sheathed and your mouth closed." She eyes me carefully. "Don't make Von regret letting you out of the forge."

I roll my eyes. "Give me a break. I'm not a complete animal."

Estrid and I both chuckle at that because I'm not certain it's entirely true.

"We'll get Von's timber ordered for the forge fires this week," she continues, pulling her vest and tunic down, exposing her cleavage more. Von expects the best deals and the best wood in a land where forests grow scarcer by the day, and he also expects my sister to get it for him, no matter how much of her integrity it costs her. "We'll collect Von's debts once we're finished."

I nod and lift the crate that must be filled with coin and scrap metal to smelt for weapons by the time we return to Von's forge. "As you wish, oh beautiful one."

This time, Estrid rolls her eyes at me and settles her cloak over her shoulder, exposing her ample chest—though not enough to be completely obvious.

"Thankfully, the woodcutter is an old, fat man who just wants a good show. Anything else might send him to an early grave." Though I joke, I scour my memories for when, exactly, this became our path—or rather, the day we *accepted* this was our path.

The moment that horrible memory resurfaces, though, I almost recoil. Refusing to ever feel such desperation again, I force the thought of it away and pull my ratty cloak tighter around my shoulders. Having seen the Reaper's ship in port and then the man himself, I feel unsettled, and for the first time, Von's seal clasping my cloak together feels more like a shield than a curse.

But the Reaper is forgotten when the woodcutter's lodge

comes into view, and I swallow a new lump of dread. It's not the portly woodcutter in the yard with his woefuls today, but his son, Ivar. Ivar, who is supposed to be in the mountains, cutting down trees. Ivar, who never deals with the public and his father's business affairs because he is a barbarian of the worst kind, who terrorizes animals and children alike. Ivar, who has always hated Von and, in turn, despises us.

His powerful body swings his axe as if it's nothing more than a goose feather. Every flex of his arms is a needless reminder that he's a callous brute who only knows how to drink, fight, and wield a weapon. His gang of thugs aren't the worst this city has seen, but they are nothing to scoff at either, and my body coils with unease as he notices us approach.

Grinning immediately, Ivar straightens, and his blonde hair, loose from its ties, falls into his eyes as they skim curiously over me before landing on my sister. I feel her stiffen the moment she realizes her *preparation* for this conversation with the woodcutter was a very bad idea.

Ivar's golden eyebrows lift with far too much intrigue, and he crosses his arms over his chest, all with a kingly air, as if he's waiting for a royal feast.

I know nothing good will come of this discussion, and I have to bite back every single scathing word I have for him in warning.

"I'm here to speak with your father on Von's behalf," my sister says coolly.

Ivar smirks, his cold green eyes gleaming. "Lucky you. I'm the one you'll be *negotiating* with while he's up north, bartering for more lands to fell."

"Right, well," Estrid says, glancing around at the woodpiles behind Ivar. "What is the price this week? Von wants only the spruce."

"As always, Von sends you to manipulate my father, I see—the best wood for a shit price." Ivar's lip curls as he takes a step closer, only a small heap of freshly chopped fir is piled between him and us.

Estrid looks bored. "You speak as if I am the one who chooses forms of payment between men."

"Aren't you?" His gaze rakes over her cleavage and he licks his lips. While this is an exchange we have had often over the years, Ivar is one of the few I worry Von's status will not protect us from. Bad blood has run between them since Von and Ivar fought with sword and axe, only for Von to pull a knife from his boot when he was about to lose, leaving the hefty scar on Ivar's face.

The question is, what sort of mood is Ivar in today? Because Estrid's and my fates rest in his hands. A truth he's well aware of, by the looks of it.

Ivar steps out from around the woodpile. "You came here with an intention. If it's a deal Von wants, I'll be the one to broker it."

I take a step forward, my fingers itching to grab the blade at my hip. I could throw it and stab him between the eyes in a single breath. But Estrid reaches out to stop me, and suddenly, *I* am the one Ivar's attention fixes on.

"Ah, yes, Brynn—bodyguard and your sister's whipping post." Ivar laughs. "You're so tough, aren't you?" He appraises me this time, from my leather vest and pants down to my boots. Unlike Estrid, however, my figure is fully covered, and for good reason.

"I hear Von's *educated* you with your own hot iron so many times, you have more scars on that body of yours than the Reaper himself." He sniggers. "Funny, your sister is known for her wiles and looks. But you?" He pulls his bottom lip between his teeth. "All of that pent-up rage you must have. I bet you're the wild one—one I wouldn't mind mounting."

"I will cut off your manhood before I ever—"

"Brynn!" Estrid chides, her eyes never leaving the brute in

front of us. "Come on, Ivar. You know Von won't stand for this, not when his business with the *queen* is at stake. So, let's secure this week's allotment to keep him content—something *fair*," she specifies, "and we can all go on with our day."

Ivar's face narrows into something menacing, his jaw tightening as his features angle so sharply, I think he might truly be a monster. "You think I'm *afraid* of that cheating twat?" Though Ivar laughs, he is far from amused. He grabs my sister's arm, wrenching her closer with bruising pressure, and I reach for my knife.

Estrid puts her hand out to stop me, her eyes fixed on Ivar, and I freeze. I hold my breath, waiting for a single movement from him that might tempt me. I can't help how fast my heart pumps, or how much my blood whirs in my ears and through my veins, making every muscle in my body twitch with equal parts anticipation and fear.

"You don't want to do this, Ivar," Estrid continues. "You will start a war you won't be able to win. Von is too powerful, even for your crew."

"Oh, really?" he seethes. That was the wrong thing to say to Ivar, a man oozing with so much insecurity he would rather die than show a single sign of weakness.

"I hear the queen would bargain her own daughter for the right price. I could kill Von and take his spot, and she wouldn't blink an eye as long as she got her goods and taxes. Or—" He rips Von's brooch of ownership off my sister's cloak. Unpinned, it falls from around her shoulders, baring her supple skin and cleavage even more. "I could just take what belongs to Von and show him he is not as terrifying as he thinks he is." Ivar licks the side of my sister's face.

I'm about to slit his throat when the squish of footsteps in the slush—*many* of them—has the three of our heads snapping to the side.

"Gods," I breathe, though the word comes out in a puff of

white air. Three figures cloaked in purple march toward us. "The Reaper's henchmen."

Estrid wrenches her arm from Ivar's hold and takes my hand. "Come on," she rasps, tugging me into the bowels of the bustling city, away from Ivar and the Reaper's men as they approach him.

2
BRYNN

The forge is loud, steel clanking against steel throughout the longhouse. You'd never know it was snowing out, not with the heat of the fires five stalls deep on each side.

A gust of frigid wind accosts my sweat-dampened skin as the door to the workhouse opens, and Von strides inside. Phillip, Bo, and some of the other workers spare him a glance, and it's all I need to see the darkness in Von's eyes. He's been gone all day, but if I had to guess, he knows his timber for this week's steel production was never secured. No wood means no fires or weapons for the queen's ever-growing army, needed for patrolling the rebellions spreading throughout the country.

Snow falls from Von's fur cloak as he whips it off his shoulders, his plaited black hair falling long around his face. He's an imposing man, but it's his temper that stokes his reputation as one of the queen's most fearsome chieftains.

He tosses his cloak to the servant following behind him, and as Von looks at me, the scar stretching from his cheek to his bearded chin twitches with menace.

I turn back to hammering as a smug smirk pulls at my lips, wondering what Von will do to Ivar for meddling in his business affairs. I prefer imagining the gruesome possibilities rather than acknowledging the blisters on my hands stinging through my gloves.

Gripping my hammer tighter, I slam it down with more ferocity as I work out my pent-up anxieties of the day. Every muscle burns, and the sweat dripping off my nose and temples hisses and steams as it drops on the glowing iron rod. Another swing, another clank. I hit it over and over, imagining I'm pulverizing Ivar's face before remembering myself.

"Shit." I glare at the malformed edge of the thinning sword blade. "Well, that will cost me a meal," I mutter, wondering if it might still be salvageable.

Movement to my left catches my eye, and I glance toward the back of the longhouse as my sister is shoved into Von's living quarters behind the partition.

Clenching my teeth, I straighten. It's not unlike him to toss her around a bit, but after the day we've had, I hate to think what punishment might be in store for her part in disrupting his production. The queen wants her blades, and Von will do anything, including using my sister at whatever cost, in order to ensure she gets them. Today, we came back empty-handed and with no deal, and failed him.

"I know Estrid's his favorite," Bo says, and I startle to see him standing at my side. "But you aren't, Brynn." His raspy voice is thick with warning. Though Bo has warmed my bed on the long, cold nights, he's also the closest thing I have to a friend here.

His red locks, pulled away from his freckled face, curl with sweat around his temples, but there's no mistaking the kindness in his eyes. He is formidable in his own right, a toiling fisherman working off a debt owed to Von by his drunken father, an old blacksmith. But Bo's too soft to be here, even if his servitude is only temporary.

He worries his bottom lip, anticipating what I'll do. Yes, Bo's too kind, and his eyes are too innocent. "Best get back to work before he notices the absence of your hammering," he prompts.

"I could say the same to you," I volley, and glance back at the partition separating Von's personal ventures from his business ones. When I hear my sister cry out and Von's raised voice, my hot iron clatters onto the anvil, and I grip my hammer tighter.

"Shit—Brynn! Wait!" It's a whispered shout, but I ignore it.

Though I know Bo is right and I should stay on task, the pull to my sister is far greater than whatever Von might do to me in consequence, and I march to the back.

When I round the intricately carved partition, Von's coin counter, sitting at the table, freezes, the coins stacked in front of him glinting in the firelight. I barely see Estrid behind the shield of Von's thick body. But I see enough.

He has her pinned against one of the support posts near his bed, her face red and her eyes bulging as Von's hand grips her throat, choking the life from her. My sister's eyes flick to me with warning, but there's fear in them, real fear this time, and I won't be dissuaded.

"Get your fucking hands off her," I growl, and step closer, prepared to swing the hammer at him if I have to. The coin counter gapes at me as Von spins around, eyes wide and the scar on his lip trembling with rage when he notices my hammer.

It takes everything inside me not to swing at him, but I know maiming Von will cause more harm than good. It's all I can do to keep the hammer clutched at my side. I'm not strong, at least, not compared to him, but I am fast and far more determined.

"Out!" he commands his coin counter, who hurries gladly from sight. Even the hammering in the front of the workhouse seems to cease.

Von straightens, finally letting his hold on my sister's throat loosen enough for her to hit his hand away. She gasps a lungful of air, collapsing onto his bed.

"You stupid little bitch," he says, wrath fixed on me. He says it so low and angrily, I question if it's not a beating I'll receive but an ending. "You think a scrappy thing like you is anything against someone like me?"

"You want to be pissed at someone, be pissed at Ivar—*kill Ivar*," I tell him, because Von is right, I'm not nearly as strong or as seasoned as him, but even as I fear his wrath, I *refuse* to cower. "Ivar's the one who snubbed you for all to hear today, and said he would claim your status as his own. He's the one saying you're nothing, that he would take what's yours." I point to my sister. "Estrid tried to make him see sense. She was willing to do whatever it took to get your timber for you, but then the Reaper's men showed up. What were we supposed to do?"

Von's eyes snap to Estrid.

Oh no.

Von's fury upticks to face-reddening wrath, and he turns, making my sister flinch. "You saw the Reaper's men, and you said *nothing*?"

Estrid massages her throat, her chest still heaving. Brave-faced, she rises to her feet, her lithe body braced for whatever comes next as her blue eyes narrow. "I was going to, but you decided to choke me," she bites out.

Von's shoulders stiffen, and I hold my breath as he looks between the two of us. "Did he come for you?" he asks, and to my surprise, there's a pitch of concern in his voice as he meets my sister's gaze. "Because I won't let him take what is mine— fuck the queen," he spits. I know Von doesn't love my sister. A man like him could never love anything other than power and position, but a part of him cares for her, or rather, lusts for her. Desperately.

Estrid shakes her head. "I don't think so, but we ran. So I can't say for certain."

Von snarls and sucks a breath between his teeth. "So, there is no timber. Ivar's out there speaking against me as if that little shit has any claim over what *I've* built in this city. And you two," he says with a sneer. "You two are at the center of it all." All concern about losing my sister is gone as his brown eyes gleam fiendishly.

Von rips the hammer from my hand, pointing it warningly at me as he grabs my sister's neck again. "Don't you fucking move, Brynn," he says, eyes locked on me.

Estrid's hands fly to his hold, gripping at his fingers, ready to pry them away. But he doesn't choke her. Instead, his eyes linger on me as he weighs his options.

He's goading me. Von would love nothing better than to end me. I know this already. Even if he treats my sister like garbage, Bo is right. Estrid is his favorite pet, and Von knows she would be far less willing to do his bidding if he kills me.

His lips purse, a telltale sign he's battling between rage and control, but before he can decide what to do, a commotion in the front of the longhouse steals his attention. The hammering dies away and the workhouse doors close with a thud. Muttering and gasps reach our ears, and Von lets go of my sister, albeit reluctantly. "Stay here," he commands. And with a curse, he strides for the partition.

In two steps, I'm at my sister's side, checking her throat ringed with the red press of Von's fingers, and I take her hand in mine.

"You shouldn't have done that, B," she whispers. "He won't let that go—"

"Like you would've stayed silent?" I quirk an eyebrow at her and shake my head. "He can beat me all he wants. I'm used to it."

Her brow crumples at that, and I wave her worry away because it's true. Physical pain can be excruciating, but short of cutting off an appendage, one that Von needs me to use in order to work for him, there's not much he can do to me that hasn't been done before.

"And to what do I owe the pleasure?" Von's clipped voice meets my ears.

Ivar? I mouth to my sister.

She shrugs as we listen closely.

"I've come to take your workers," a man says roughly, but it's not Ivar. The dread plunging into the pit of my stomach is all I need to guess.

I grab Estrid's hand, clutching it tightly. A gut feeling I've learned to listen to over the years plants my feet in place.

"What—"

"Shh." I press my finger to my lips. My heart is suddenly pounding. Something unexplainable grips hold of me, and I point to the interlacing runes carved into the partition like a woven basket. Leaning closer, I peer through the slits.

All I can see is Von's back and Phillip watching in suspended horror far in the back.

"I don't care who you are," Von says. "These thralls are mine. All of them—their debts are mine to collect. But if it's steel blades you seek"—he holds up a nearly finished sword—"you may take whatever you like."

The Reaper takes a step into view, his face barely distinguishable in the shadow of his hood, but I know it's him, and I think my heart stops beating in my chest. I have to blink to ensure I'm seeing correctly.

The Reaper is here.

Whatever words are spoken next bleed away as I notice a dozen purple-cloaked figures behind him.

"It's him," I rasp as blood whirs in my ears and my vision blurs. Suddenly, it's all I can do to pull air into my lungs. I see fire and flames all over again. I see my world burned to ash and hear my mother's screams.

Estrid leans in to catch a glimpse of the Reaper for herself.

"What are the odds the Reaper and his men have come here by coincidence, after seeing us twice today already?" My question lets loose on a breath.

When Estrid looks at me, I see the same fear and confusion shining back at me. She's trying to discern a logical reason, but she can't. Because there isn't one. Like all men, the Reaper might've seen my sister and grown curious about her—he might want her for his collection of souls. Or perhaps I'd insulted him when making eye contact. "What if Ivar told him something?" I breathe. "Something to save his own hide when they came to him? Or to get back at Von?" Whatever the reason, Hel's Hound has come, and I know it's no mere coincidence.

"—by the queen's accord, I shall have them," the Reaper says. His voice is grave, his words patient, so certain of himself. *Because he has no reason to fear anyone.* That he would stroll in here with armed men is a testament to it. And I feel as if I might throw up.

I tug Estrid deeper into the back, where two goats and a roost of chickens mill about. It smells like manure, but it's far better than the front of the longhouse, filled with stinking bodies and the promise of death. "We have to go, Es."

"What? Brynn—we can't."

"We have to. I don't care what Von wants. He's no match for the Reaper and his men, and I refuse to let them take us."

She shakes her head.

"Estrid," I bite out. "Did you see how many of them there

were? If we stay, this doesn't end well for us. We *have* to go before they find us."

She searches my face, worrying her bottom lip. I know she doesn't want to risk losing what semblance of security we have here, but all of that disappeared the moment Von was targeted by the Reaper.

"I'd rather brave the winter and risk starving than the alternative. Wouldn't you? We're older now, Es—we're capable. We can do this. We can figure it out—"

"I will take what I'm owed by the queen. There's no need for bloodshed," the Reaper says, followed by the hiss of metal being drawn.

I grip Estrid's arm, forcing her to look at me. "We'll find Bo's father—stay with him until we can figure something out. He will want to help us, knowing we are Bo's friends."

"And risk his life?" Estrid counters. "Bo is working off his father's debt as it is. If Von *or* the Reaper finds us there, his father will be killed."

The goat nibbles on my boot and I shove him away. "Then —we'll stay in the stable, for tonight at least. We'll figure something out." As my sister hesitates, I say anything I can think of to sway her, leaving logic to worry about later. "I don't think we have a choice, Es." I glance frantically around, willing a different option to show itself. "We can go to one of the fishing villages and make our way to the Borderlands or one of the other cities where no one knows us." I clasp her hand in mine, willing her to agree. "I know it's risky, but we can do it as long as we're together."

I'm not a fool. I know the land is harsh and the weather is cruel. We would be battling for our lives if we left, trekking hundreds of miles to the next city. But I will her to see our imminent end in staying here a moment longer. "We could leave this place forever. We could find a little village along the way. Who knows—"

"You're insane," my sister breathes, but it's a yes. I see the hope she doesn't dare muster in her bright blue eyes.

Before another minute can pass, we steal two of Von's heaviest cloaks. I take the blade I know is hidden under Von's mattress, and Estrid and I sneak out the door toward the outhouse in the back. Out into the biting cold.

3
BRYNN

Deep cold settles into the shadows, promising a frigid night as Estrid and I hurry through the streets. In the snow, with others rustling about to get out of the winter wind, it's easy to blend in.

I grip my sister's hand tighter as we weave around villagers, our footsteps not so hurried it seems like we're running, even if my heart is pounding as if I am. We've just done something both very brave and very stupid.

"We didn't think this through," Estrid scolds, clutching her cloak tighter around her.

"As if we had the time," I toss back. My breath is white puffs around my face, quick and slightly labored as the adrenaline subsides and the weight of what we've done settles in.

"No one will shelter us," she rasps, the snow crunching loudly beneath our feet. The cold seeps its way in through the heavy pelts of our cloaks as if preparing us for a foreboding night. "They wouldn't risk angering Von—"

"If he's even alive. Besides," I say, stepping around a woman with her baby nestled to her chest. "No one can stop us if they don't know we're there. Right now, we need a place to stay, just for tonight." I've got it all planned out, sort of. We'll sleep with the livestock while we form a better plan.

"But who—" Estrid starts, and we lock eyes, realizing at once who will help us.

"Koll," we say in unison.

"He'll be at the Iron Horse and drunk," I tell her. "He'll let us sleep in the stables without saying a word, for a quick look at the goods." I glance at Estrid's ample chest. It's a small price to pay for the taste of freedom and a single night of rest. She nods without a second thought, and we hurry toward the tavern.

After a few more alleyways and road crossings, we reach the Iron Horse. Estrid and I stop outside to catch our breaths. We don't have a lot of time, but if we make it seem as if we are fleeing, everyone will know from whom, and they will never help us.

With a fortifying nod at one another, Estrid and I step into the tavern, standing side by side as we scan the patrons for the establishment's most reliable drunk. But while I see familiar faces, none of them are the droopy-eyed, face tattooed one we're looking for.

A man with dark, sea-blown hair, a scruffy face, and a wide smile sits in Koll's normal spot. The ladies flock to him as his laughter fills the room. He's striking in a not-from-around-here sort of way. Suddenly, a hand wraps around my arm, yanking me out the door.

Estrid curses beside me, and before I know it, we're in the cold and Ivar's pointed features look unsettlingly pleased. "The whore and the ball buster," he jeers, causing Estrid and me to take a step back.

Ivar elbows one of the two thugs flanking him, their eyes shimmering with drink as their gazes feast on us. Every fiber in me screams, *run*.

"Didn't get enough this morning, I see." Ivar takes a step

closer, reaches for my loose brown hair, and turns it over in his hand. His eyes, however, remain on my face—almost admiringly—and my stomach turns.

"Brynn," Estrid whispers, registering what I do. We're in no position to bring attention to ourselves right now.

As I reach for her hand, Ivar grabs hold of my arm, his fingers jabbing into my flesh.

"Let go," I grind out. I try to tug my arm away, but Ivar jerks me closer, relentless. Rearing back, I headbutt him, shocking us both, and though he falters a step, his grip on me tightens, his surprise shifting immediately to rage.

His thug friend, Nor, grabs hold of my sister, and feeling Ivar's lips against my ear, I cringe, instinctively shrinking away. "You're going to regret that, street rat."

A few people pass the alleyway, but they know better than to get involved in Ivar's business. They avert their gazes as Estrid and I are shoved behind the tavern, the shadows consuming us.

Ignoring the scent of piss and barley, I curse, trying to wrench my arms free from Ivar's hold so I can get to the knife on my hip. But his grasp is unyielding, and my head sings with pain as he slams me against the building, my skull smacking the wood. The world rings for a moment, my teeth grind in pain, and I have to catch my breath as I blink the world back into focus.

"I'll do whatever you want," my sister says. It's not a plea so much as a bargain. "You know I will. Just let Brynn go."

Ivar and his thugs laugh, making the hair rise on the back of my neck. "What's the fun in that?" he taunts. "Besides, gods only know who has been inside that nasty cunt," Ivar jeers at her. "But Brynn?" His hands travel up my thighs as he bites my ear. The sting and warmth of my blood on my cool skin chases away my lingering daze, and only then do I realize Estrid and I are pressed against the building, the three men at our backs. Though I can't see which of Ivar's thugs holds my sister, I can feel Ivar's breath hot against my cheek as he shoves my cloak out of the way and begins tugging at my pants.

"No!" I shout. Finding my resolve, my leg jerks, my knee knocking against the side of the tavern, smarting with pain in the cold, but I wedge my foot between me and the wall for leverage and shove backward.

Ivar loses his footing, too drunk to anticipate me, and stumbles as I spin around and unsheathe my knife. I stab Nor, still tugging at Estrid's clothes, in the neck and kick him away from her. He staggers back, falling into the snow with a curse.

"Come—" I reach for my sister's arm as a fist collides with the back of my head, and I'm slammed into the wall again as Ivar's arm shoves into my throat so hard I can barely breathe.

His eyes are crazed, unlike anything I've ever seen. "You fucking bitch," he growls.

Nor gurgles his final breaths in the snow as Ivar's other man apprehends Estrid once more.

"I'm going to kill your sister," Ivar promises me. "And I'm going to make you watch." He punches me in the face again, my cheek searing and head snapping back as my skull cracks against the building. White spots dot my vision, and it's all I can do to keep my eyes open.

Estrid's blonde hair and struggling form go in and out of view as my mind spins—every breath and blink and wince uncontrollable as I try to focus.

"Please," I rasp, because it's all I can manage. I can hear my sister's screams, distant in the wind, as my clothes are torn partly open, the cold air accosting me. My body feels heavy, and I think Ivar is all that is keeping me upright.

He slaps my face. "Stay awake," he growls. "I want you to see this." He slaps my face again, and my eyes fly open in time to meet Estrid's gaze. She's resolved. I barely register the blood on her face before I process Ivar shoving his thug out of the way.

"A gift for Von," Ivar spits out. He leans into my sister, marking the side of her face with his tongue before he shoves the blade up under her ribcage.

My sister.

My blade.

"No," I croak because I can no longer breathe. My chest constricts, my lungs won't work, and my eyes fill with tears. I want to be angry. I want to take that blade and slit Ivar's throat, but I can't look away from my sister as I fall to my knees. "Es," I whimper.

Only when Ivar steps away from her does Estrid tear her gaze from me. She grips the hilt of the knife in her chest and falls to the ground, choking as blood trickles from her mouth. It looks black in the moonlight.

"Estrid!" I cry as I force my mind and limbs to work. The world fades away as I scramble over and pull her into my arms. "Es—"

My sister blinks up at me, her eyes wild and shoulders lurching as she struggles to breathe. I can hardly see her through my tears. "I'm sorry," I mew, wiping her blonde hair from her face, smearing it with blood. "I'm so sorry."

Her chin trembles and I pull her closer, darkness dancing along my vision as I sway with her in my arms. *This isn't happening. This* can't *be happening.* I squeeze her against me once more, knowing the warmth of her body means none of this can be real.

But as I lean away, laughter echoes around me, and I see the life in her eyes dim in the faint light of the glistening snow. My sister is gone. It feels impossible, but deep down, I know it's true. I feel her absence in my soul like a ravenous, sharp-toothed kraken devouring me from the inside out.

I shake my head, the pain swimming through me like

shards of broken ice. *If* this is real, I have no reason to live. Not anymore.

"Estrid—"

One of the men grabs onto my arm to haul me up, their laughter booming. Without thinking, I pull the knife from my sister's chest and spin around. My vision is too blurry, but I make out his form well enough and feel when metal pierces flesh. I scream, stabbing him over and over again until the grip on me loosens and the form in front of me falls away.

Everything in me is hollow and numb, and I wail out a sob, falling to my knees once more. But my cries turn to screams as a blade sears through my arm. Knuckles meet my right temple, knocking me over, and finally—blissfully—the world goes black.

4
BRYNN

I'm jostled to consciousness. My body aches, and suddenly, I'm weightless. Warmth soaks into me, my body feeding off the comfort as my head throbs to near bursting. I try to open my eyes, but they're too heavy, the effort too much.

I hear a whimper. *My* whimper, and then it all comes rushing back.

Blonde hair. Blue eyes.
Snarling teeth and sour breath.
The warm drip of blood.
Ivar.

"No—" I croak, stirring against him, but I can't open my eyes—I can't force my body to move.

"Be still." A soft voice meets my ears, barely audible over the sound of my pounding heart. Finally, I pry my eyes open, just enough to see glinting snow in the moonlight and four crumpled bodies, one with pale skin and glowing blonde hair.

Another whimper escapes me, and I hear my sister's name on the wind. Then I'm dragged under once more.

Creaking wood.

Retching.

A cacophony of unfamiliar sounds echoes around me, and a subtle shift of the hard floor has me lurching awake.

"Ah—" I cringe, my body protesting with the slightest movement. My arm burns and my head pounds with the force of an anvil hammer.

Sucking in a lungful of air, I taste brine on my tongue, and the scent of bile assaults my senses as the world around me narrows to focus. I blink. Heaving bodies coalesce around me, hunched over and trembling. Everything feels cold but wet, moisture clinging to my cheeks and nose like a second skin. "What—" I suck in another breath as my side twinges.

"Brynn?"

I glance in the direction of a familiar voice, but I'm not certain if I'm relieved or more confused. "Bo?" He maneuvers around dozens of people huddled on the floor. It's only as he catches himself on a support beam that I realize he's struggling to keep his balance because the world is rocking. In fact, the wood is wet in some areas, as if the sea has sought a way in.

"A ship," I breathe. Panic enlivening every one of my senses, I peer around again, only to realize it's full of sickness. Some people convulse, others lay motionless, but if they are sleeping or dead, I'm not sure. My stomach lurches. I don't know if it's because of the motion of the waves or the stench in the air.

Bo crouches beside me, wincing as his knees hit the ground with another abrupt toss from the ship.

"What is this place?" I rasp, my throat parched as I wonder how long I've been unconscious. Or is it because I'm acutely aware I cannot swim? *Why am I on a fucking ship?* I want to shriek with the surmounting confusion, but all too quickly, unbridled desperation and dread fill me, and my blood runs cold. "Estrid." I feel the truth of what I dare not utter burning the backs of my eyes and twisting my insides tighter.

"I don't know what happened to her," Bo says carefully, and he assesses my body up and down. As the memories from the alleyway inundate me, my hand flies to my mouth, but not quickly enough. A sob escapes me. Bo might not know what happened to her, but I do, and he sees it plainly on my face.

"I'm sorry, Brynn," he says, but I barely hear him over the jangle of chains and the creaking ship. Someone retches beside me. The stench of bile hits my nose and my insides roil.

Gripping my stomach, I lurch forward. My cape falls from around my shoulders and a mess of matted hair slaps me in the face as I expel my insides into a pail of water beside me. My throat burns as I gag for breath, sobbing with another heave. The smell. The movement. The memories. The truth is that Estrid is dead.

All of it is too much, and I retch again.

Bo's hand is warm on my shoulder, his whispered warnings to mind my wounds lost in a maelstrom of agony as my body trembles and my life—every purpose for living—escapes me.

"Tell me he's dead," I finally manage through tears, spitting the sour taste from my mouth.

"Who?" Bo's palm flattens on the floorboards to steady himself as the ship sways again.

"Ivar," I seethe. "Did you kill him?"

"Ivar?" he gasps, and understanding dawns on him as his gaze rakes down my body again. I didn't know Bo's face could crumple more, but it does, and I bite back a scream. "I don't know," he admits. "Last I saw, you were gunning for Von at the workhouse. Then you were unconscious on this pallet in the corner when we all boarded the ship." He pauses, considering his next words. "Estrid wasn't with you."

I swallow another sob, beyond confused. "If you didn't bring me here, then who?" I glower at him—at the world—stuck between utter misery and bewilderment.

Bo shakes his head. "One of the crew members, I guess."

I peer around what I assume is steerage, at all the hapless unfortunates huddled together or lying on the floor. There was only one ship at port that could hold so many bodies. "This is the Reaper's ship." The words barely escape me as my blood runs so cold, I feel numb to it all.

Bo nods, and for the first time, I look at him. *Really* look at him. At his harried and grim features, his kind, green eyes shadowed with exhaustion and fear.

"How many days has it been?" I whisper.

"Just since last night."

I blink. *Last night.* Last night Estrid and I were trying to flee the Reaper, and now? My chin trembles. "It was all for nothing," I murmur. Overcome with a mixture of shock and apathy, I sit with the reality I've awakened to, though I'm not sure if my resentment, guilt, or grief is stronger. "I told her we should run," I confess, realizing the guilt weighs far heavier than the rest. "And," I say again, "it was all for nothing." I almost laugh, hysterical, as I realize I made it out of Northhelm after all. Just not the way I'd wanted. And alone. Before I can reel it in, a keening moan escapes my throat.

"Von is dead," Bo offers as a small consolation. There's a hint of triumph in his voice.

My unfocused gaze shifts to him, though his news brings me no solace.

"The Reaper's crew killed him when he stood against them. Even Von's guards were no match for them."

"Where is the Reaper taking us?" I'm not sure why I ask because I don't care—none of it really matters, not anymore.

"Across the North Sea."

My eyes dart to his. "No one sails to the Old Lands," I think aloud. I've always wondered where the Reaper takes his ship of souls, and now I'm about to find out.

My chin trembles again. My heart aches with unbearable sadness; I am nothing without Estrid. Not a sister or protector. I am no one. My hands move to my face again, and I wince. My arm burns and my ribs pinch with pain. I don't know what Ivar did to me after I lost consciousness, and as my fatigued muscles quaver, I glance down.

A rolling wave of relief soothes a small part of me when I see my clothes are torn, but no more than I remember. I'm covered in blood from a cut on my arm and a few other wounds I don't recall getting. My face is swollen, and the pounding in my head hurts beyond measure.

I inch my hand up to the base of my skull, reticent to feel the lump I'm certain has formed, then touch the tender flesh on my temple. It's impossible not to cringe as I relive the impact of every blow.

But it's my arm I stare at as I lower it back down. "Thank you for tending to it," I say, flashing Bo a grateful smile. It's watery at best, but it's all I can manage as my emotions bubble to the surface again.

"You were bandaged when I boarded," he admits sheepishly. "I've only checked on you a couple of times." He nods to the water pail beside me. "That was already here too." He grimaces when he looks at its contents. Bile and water slosh out as the boat lurches. "I can refill it for you, though."

I have a tsunami of questions, but tell myself none of the answers matter. Not when my heart is broken and I wish I was dead in the snow alongside my sister. Instead, I'm a captive on a ship, commanded by the worst of men who is responsible for everything I've ever lost in my life.

Bo's hand rests on my lap. "I'll get you some fresh water."

I nod, mouthing my thanks, and Bo staggers away with my water pail.

Feeling deplorable, destitute, and unable to hold myself together a second longer, I lie back, ignoring the pain as I cover my face with my soiled cloak and weep.

5
BRYNN

For two days, I am in and out of a fitful sleep. A woman's voice punctuates my dreams, but it's distant and indistinct, mixing with the sound of crying children and purging sickness. I don't touch the bread that's been left by my pallet, but my water pail is always full when I'm coherent enough to notice, and I have Bo to thank for that. Whether it's my head injuries or pure grief, my efforts to stay awake are futile. Then again, I don't care enough to try.

When I finally wake, my stomach is cramped and my bladder near bursting as I force my eyes to stay open.

Lanterns sway with the ship, casting moving shadows in the rafters above me. The sour stench of vomit permeates the air, and whispers fill the void between creaking beams and jostling chains, though most people seem to have found some respite for the night.

My body aches as I inch myself up to sit. My stomach stirs a little, and my cloak falls from around my shoulders into my lap. Though my head still thrums, and my face feels tight, it's not as tender as before. Licking my dry lips, I find they, too, are still swollen.

With a grimace, I dip the copper cup beside me into my water pail and fill it to the brim. Suddenly parched, I can't gulp it down fast enough. Only, it's not water at all, but a diluted spirit of some sort. Still, my body consumes it greedily, like the sun evaporates the melting snow, and I gasp when the cup is empty.

Despite my overfull bladder, I lick every last drop from my lips, and with a renewed urgency, I survey the crowded space. It's half the size of Von's longhouse, and with barrels and crates and sacks stacked along the walls, I don't know how I am supposed to relieve myself down here. No one is peeing in any buckets, and it doesn't smell like piss and shit like half the alleyways back home.

When I notice Bo curled up on the floor beside me, covered in his thick woolen cloak and soundly sleeping, I almost wake him to ask, when movement catches my eye.

An older man curses on unsteady feet as he stumbles out of shadows near the bow. He braces his palm against the low roof with one hand and continues pulling his pants up with the other.

I climb to my feet, certain I know where he's been. It takes me a few heartbeats to find my footing on legs I haven't used in days, let alone at sea. A sudden surge of unease threatens to send me spiraling as the thought of waves and water, surrounding us on all sides, plagues my mind. I try to exhale it away. It doesn't matter that I cannot swim because the ship will not sink. The Reaper's journeys are said to be blessed by the gods themselves. Besides, luck has always evaded me.

I will be fine. I will be fine. I repeat that over and over as I exhale another slow, steady breath and use the closest support beam to keep upright.

Everything hurts, especially hunched in the belly of this behemoth ship, but my muscles yearn for movement.

Someone retches in the mass of people clustered down

here. A child whimpers. But I'm too focused on relieving myself as I stumble my way toward the shadows.

The closer I get to the narrowing bow of the ship, the louder the sound of crashing waves becomes. When I see the large holes in the boards, I understand instantly and swallow the dread that accompanies it. Knowing what I must do, I suddenly can't move fast enough.

Necessities taken care of, I pause at the barrels against the closest wall. Popping the top off one of them, I study the salted meats, and guess that fish, ale, and dried goods fill the rest of the sacks and crates stored in here with us.

Why would the Reaper keep us down here with his provisions? It seems a dangerous gamble to allow us access to the sustenance he and his men need to survive the trip. But then again, noting the bread left by my bedroll, I guess we all need to survive off it too.

I scan the pallets and restless bodies spread out before me. There must be thirty people on this ship, but if we are thralls being taken as slaves, we are not chained. Then I realize most of the people down here are sick, some more than others, and save for jumping overboard, there is nowhere for us to flee. If I weren't more terrified of the sea than the Reaper, I might seriously contemplate the idea.

Still, how I got here—my bandaged arm . . . It's all so curious and rattles me with the urgent need to understand and explore the ship.

I notice a few familiar, sleeping faces from Northhelm as I head for the steps. Most everyone is clustered together in their own nest of limbs and blankets, sleeping or simply moaning with sickness. A few men from Von's workhouse are here, but

I've never spoken to them. It's only Bo and Phillip that I know well enough to consider friends.

As I draw closer, Phillip's graying mustache twitches in his sleep, and like the others, he looks ill. Though he's a drunken gambler, indebted to Von for a slew of things, he looks more ashen and sweatier than usual, even in the lantern shadows.

Collecting my cloak from my little removed corner in the space, I painstakingly wrap myself in preparation for the cold. I'm far too restless to lie in wait for whatever comes with the new day, now that I'm coherent enough to notice. And, more than anything, I refuse to let my mind drift to thoughts far darker than my uncertain future. Thoughts of my sister. My *dead* sister, and the guilt-ridden sorrow that accompanies them.

I eye the steps across the berth, leading above deck. Muted light filters down, and I want to see what's up there as much as I want to hide from it. It's only as I feel my fear getting the better of me that I shake myself free of it and force my feet toward the light.

I revel in the warmth of fox furs and elk hide crusted in blood, ignoring the aches in my limbs, only compounding with each step to the stairs.

Instinctively, I reach for my knives at my belt, uncertain who awaits me above, but my blades aren't there. With a silent curse, I hope they are lying with Ivar's *dead* body back home, and cautiously make my way to the upper level. I'm acutely aware that I'm a dead woman, whether it's on this ship or once we land wherever the Reaper takes us. Because if my wounds don't kill me, my apathy for this life I've woken up to will, and I would rather die fighting for my freedom than be indentured to anyone ever again.

Inky night, spilling in from above, illuminates the next level with moving shadows, and I pause halfway up the steps. There are more goods, including crates of fowl, fluttering and

SEA OF STORMS

cooing inside, and hammocks that rock with the motion of the ship. The men filling them snore, but the sound is nearly drowned out by the vehement crashing waves pounding against the ship.

Once again, it hits me that this is not a vessel from our world. It's a monstrous whale in the ocean, and we are what remains of its evening feast.

One of the crewmen coughs, and I hold my breath as he shifts in his hammock, oblivious as it sways. He drapes his arm over his eyes, and a snore passes his lips once more as he settles back to sleep.

My fingers twitch at my sides. Had I my knives right now, I could slit some of their throats before the rest were coherent enough to apprehend and kill me. Which begs the question of why the crew would put themselves in such danger?

I look down at the unrestrained passengers below, but as the ship sways and my insides roll a little, I have to grip the wall to keep myself upright. I file my curiosities away for now with the rest of the confounding things I've discovered since waking. And palms sweating a little, I climb the final steps. I stop tentatively at the top and close my eyes as the sea breeze accosts my face and whips through my hair. Then, I brace myself for the ever-stretching sea I know lays before me. With another roll of the waves, I open my eyes.

My heart hammers in my chest as I take in the terrifying, beautiful expanse. Waves. Glimmering. Swelling. Stretching as far as the eye can see. It's monstrous and breathtaking all at once.

Distant voices catch my ears, and I scan the moonlight deck to find two men hunched over a barrel in a protective alcove out of the wind across the ship. Their murmured laughter reaches my ears over the sound of thrashing sails and snapping ropes, but it's nearly consumed by the wind.

I squint up at the glowing moon. There are no snow clouds

to hide its grandeur, and before I realize it, it's drawn me to the edge of the ship where only the guardrail keeps the splash of waves at bay.

I could jump in and end this putrid feeling of guilt. I could protect myself from all that's to come. But a cowardly chill rolls over me as I imagine what it feels like to drown. I've come to terms with meeting my death at the end of a blade. But in the bowels of the ocean? I clasp my cloak tighter around my shoulders, staring down at Njord's breath, coaxing the ship onward as if he *assists* the Reaper's mission.

"You do not sleep with the others?"

I startle as a velvety voice catches my ear. A dark figure sits between two barrels lining a raised platform. Once again, I reach for my blades, the abrupt movement making me wince, but it's the absence of them at my hip that sends my heart racing.

The man doesn't move, only watches me with his arms draped over his bent knees, a glinting bottle gripped in his fingers. He is not below with the captives, nor is he sick.

"Same as you," I say, finding my voice. To sit with such ease, he is one of the crewmen, and though my pulse thrums with apprehension, I find the sea at my back far more terrifying than he is at present.

"Why not?" he asks. He's only a silhouette in the shadows, though he can see me clearly in the moonlight; I can feel his eyes on me, and unnerved, I turn to the water once more.

"I woke on the one ship I swore I would die before ever setting foot on," I say to the wind, forcing myself to watch the taunting waves. "Sailing to a place unknown to me, toward a future I did not ask for. That is why I do not sleep down below with the others."

If the man hears me over the wind, he has no reply.

A part of me knows I should fear the man behind me and not turn my back on him, and yet, I can't bring myself to care

SEA OF STORMS

enough as I stare at the sea. If my fear of it is the only thing keeping me from ending the sickness I feel breeding inside me—the remorse I know will eat me alive—I know I must conquer it.

I inhale the rush of the brisk breeze and allow my eyes to close for one blissful moment before my shaking muscles can remind me I am battered, miserable, and restless. Opening my eyes again, I lean forward, daring to look down.

"Are you going to jump?" the man asks.

My eyes burn with unshed tears as cowardice grips hold of me again. I want to jump—I don't want to live this life alone—but I'm not certain I can.

"It would be a shame after the crew took such care to tend to your wounds. Or," he says, as if it's an afterthought, "so I've been told."

Rankled by his jabbering, I wipe a tear from my cheek and glare over my shoulder at him. "Please, stop talking," I bite out.

"You came over to my side of the ship."

I glance around. "I didn't realize there were *sides*."

The crewman shrugs and climbs to his feet. "Most people would be grateful for a dry place to recover at sea," he adds.

I scoff, unable to help myself. "Is that what happened? I've been brought upon the Reaper's ship to *recover*?" I turn around, bracing myself for whatever comes next.

"If memory serves correctly, you were a bloody heap when Basher brought you aboard."

Basher. He sounds frightening. "Well, you'll have to forgive me if I seem unappreciative, but I know this crew isn't concerned about my care and comfort as much as it's worried about mending an able body. I know you take me to be a slave."

"If that's how you see it," he says. "But if you ask me, you're lucky to be alive."

"Am I?" My bitter laugh must surprise us both because the man's head tilts ever so slightly.

The whites of his eyes widen in the moonlight as he stops two paces away. "So, you do prefer death then?" He sounds more amused than admonishing.

As I ponder his question, I can't help but think blissful blackness would bring me peace. "I'm not sure there is a point to living," I say quietly, and turn my back to him. "Not anymore." I peer out at the swells, imagining them swallowing me whole. This time, however, I don't feel as much fear as I did before.

"What happened to you?" the sailor asks.

I huff, the wind tugging at my hair. "It doesn't matter," I tell him.

The ship dips and lurches again before the man taps my back with the mouth of his bottle. "Here," he offers. "Sounds like you need this more than I do." Though his words sound mocking, there's a soft edge to his voice that surprises me.

I peer back, and he takes a fumbling step to brace himself as the ship shifts beneath us.

The sailor shoves the bottle at my chest, forcing me to grip it with my good arm, and my cloak falls away. I've barely processed I'm holding the bottle when he grabs my wrist with bruising force, pushing my sleeve up all the way with sudden urgency.

"What is this?" he demands, but I tear my arm away, glaring at him as I cover my tattoos again.

"The mark of Skadi," I grit out, running my hand over my forearm protectively.

"I know that, but why are her runes on your arm?"

Hiding beneath my cloak again, I watch the sailor's shadowed features as close as I can. His eyes gleam, narrowed as they are in the moonlight. "It's none of your concern," I tell him. And it's at this moment I realize these markings are all I have left of my family and my past. Of home and of my sister.

The crewman stumbles back another step, and I'm convinced he's drunk this time. Then, he turns to walk away.

"Tell me," I blurt, clenching my hands into fists, bracing myself. "I know we sail toward the Old Lands, but the Reaper... Where is he taking us?"

The man straightens. "You don't know?"

"I've been unconscious for two days," I remind him.

The sailor is thoughtful for a moment as I hold my breath, dreading the answer. He runs his hand through his wild hair as he peers in what I assume is the direction of our destination. Finally, he speaks. "We sail to New London."

With a heavy exhale, I squeeze my eyes shut. *The Black Country*. Though I have never met anyone from there, I know its foul reputation is one that reaches long before the Great Turning. Poverty. Woefuls overworked and kept as little more than slaves to landowners, much like Norseland. I always pictured them sickly, having lived in a land that was poisoned by industry centuries ago.

"We're going to my own personal hell." The sailor's words are nearly lost in the wind, but I hear their discontent.

Hell? I take in his clothes—his cloak of plush furs, his white tunic practically glowing in the moonlight, and his leather pants and boots gleaming as he shifts. What sort of hell does he think he has lived through? Because I doubt he's lived on the streets or had to offer flesh and dignity in exchange for food. "But you are not a woeful, nor a captive on this ship."

The man's white teeth flash in the darkness as he smiles. I can barely see his face, but somehow, he seems familiar. "Aren't I?" Huffing a breath, he nods toward the ocean. "If it's death you prefer to this ship or the life awaiting you," he says. "Jump, because if the frigid water doesn't kill you, the waves surely will." And with those final words, he stalks toward the men playing dice across the deck.

Unfocused, I stare at his retreating shadow as his words circle through my mind, tempting me. If the waves consumed me, I would not have to fear my destiny, nor would I have to fight it.

A deluge of images crash over me as I turn back to the ocean—Estrid's bloody lips parting with her final breath, my knife protruding from her chest. The light in her eyes, the fear and resolve both fading to nothing in their dulling, blue depths.

It starts as a ripple at first. Then what's left of the numbness cracks like a frozen lake on the cusp of spring, yearning to break free.

We were on the run, trying to get away from *him*. And yet, here I am, in a callous twist of destiny, on the Reaper's ship.

Rawness tears through me, agony and misery and fear alive and gnashing like sharpened teeth against whatever parts of me remain.

Estrid is dead, and it's my fault.

Guilt consumes me like a bottomless void that cannot be filled, and my lungs burn so fiercely, I can't catch my breath. My hand flies to my chest, and I tug at my vest, gripping onto it, wishing I could tear it free. I don't want to go to the Black Country. I don't want to bear this burden of guilt for the rest of my days. I don't think I can survive it.

The Fates sober me with a gust of cold wind that blows through my hair with sudden ferocity, and I have to take a bracing step against it.

You are alive, they tell me. It's a strange thought, and I'm not sure where it comes from, but as much as it angers me that I am, it dawns on me that the very man we were running from is on this ship somewhere.

The man responsible for Von's anger and Ivar's wrath.

The man responsible for burning down my village and taking my parents and brother from me.

These are the Reaper's men. This is *his* ship, and if there was ever a way to seek revenge or put a stop to his brutal reign of the expansive sea, this is the perfect opportunity to do it.

And if death claims me in the end, so be it.

6
KILLIAN

I'm drunk. More than I thought. Because none of this makes the slightest bit of sense.

The wind in my ears is nothing to the booming, nonsensical thoughts that whir through me as I watch the woman from the shadows. I'd thought it strange she would wander about the ship in the middle of the night, but now I know it is far more than strange. Her presence is some sort of test—a game between the gods to finally claim my ever-loving sanity.

Her voice sounded unnervingly familiar when she'd first spoke, but I'd chalked the fuzzy memory up to the bottle of rum she holds against her chest as she nestles into the same spot I vacated below.

But her runs . . . Seeing them felt like an exhumation of old ghosts, and the final tipping of the scales that have been teetering for years.

"*I woke on the one ship I swore I would die before ever setting foot on.*"

Running my hand over my face, I will the fog in my mind

to clear, but all I can hear is the acid in the woman's voice and I'm more confused than ever.

When Basher brought her aboard, I hadn't thought anything about it. Workers arrive injured on every voyage. But this is different.

That strange, rain-soaked night eighteen years ago comes flooding back.

Who is she and why has she been placed in my path for what feels like the second time?

I try to pull myself together but as the sickening guilt in my gut churns, I head for another bottle of rum instead, desperate for the fog to return and numb the past away.

7
BRYNN

Tucked between the two barrels out of the wind, I watch the sunrise. It's not brilliantly colored and promising, but it isn't foreboding either—just another gray morning, something I'm used to back home.

I'm not sure how long I've been turning the bottle the sailor gave me around and around on the deck. I still don't know what's inside because I haven't taken a single sip; I want clarity as I contemplate how I will kill the Reaper, not for the world to blur. He is my purpose now, and I have a matter of days, perhaps a couple of weeks on the water at most, to figure out how I'm going to do it.

Glancing around, I see the ship as it is in daylight—a bustling city sailing the sea. A few people I recognize from below carry pails and dump the contents over the edge. While it is morning, and some might still be sleeping, I wonder how many are still feeling ill. It's seasickness, I realize now. Having never been on the water, I hadn't given it much thought, but as my stomach somersaults here and there with the movement of the ship, I've begun to realize it will be a very long journey for some. While I pity them, I don't look forward to going below deck again in the stench of sickness either. And yet, I can't remain up here forever, even if watching the waking crew perform their morning duties fascinates me.

A woman with ebony skin climbs down from the lookout at the top of the mast, eyes red with exhaustion or perhaps from the wind, though her hair remains neatly braided in long ropes against her back. An eye scope is tucked into her belt, her leather jacket clasped up to her neck, and she exchanges a few words with a crewman, hoisting himself to a crosstree to mend a sail. Another man with a shaved head hauls a barrel to its side, dumping the water collected on top before rolling it toward the other side of the ship. Despite the fact he appears to be covering a missing eye with the bandanna around his head, he's whistling as if it is just another day aboard the Reaper's ship.

A clank and clatter startles me, and a boy who barely looks old enough to be a sailor collects the pots he's dropped coming up the steps. An orange cat with three legs hobbles up after him.

"I'm fine—" the kid says, making another clatter. "Slops on in twenty." He waves everyone's concern away, though as I peer around, the rest of the crew only smirk to themselves and continue about their business.

"Still searchin' for your sea legs, eh, Tug?" A shaggy-haired deck swabber pauses, setting his mop aside as he bends down to help the boy. They're only a few years apart in age, but the young man swabbing the ship is missing all but two fingers.

Tug huffs with exasperation. "It always happens when we've just set sail. I'll manage."

"You better," the swabber says with a chuckle. "Captain wants his breakfast. And we know how he gets when he's hungry."

Tug meets the man's eyes, looking almost sheepish. "Don't worry. I know." Pots stacked haphazardly in one another, Tug hurries on clumsy feet toward one of the barrels on the other end of the ship, tossing a "Thanks, Scuds!" over his shoulder as he goes.

Tug is a scrawny thing, and I would say he is a thrall child on this ship, but there's something about the way the crew smiles at him, the way he bustles about as if he's trying to impress them, that makes me think he isn't one of us, but one of them. Or rather, he's trying to be.

Scanning the crew again, I shake my head. Whatever atrocities these people have committed, whatever reputations precede them, in the dull light of day, they appear completely normal. Their clothes are well worn, their hair slightly matted and oily from days at sea. Save for the weathered look of some of their skin, they appear like anyone else sailing from Northhelm. They are well adapted to this life at sea, which suits me just fine; their false sense of security will be to my advantage, and seeking vengeance will be easier than I thought.

As the sun breaks through the cloud cover, almost oppressive against my skin in its sudden appearance, I decide to see how Bo and Phillip fared the night. I want to know everything that happened after Estrid and I ran and why only some of the workers from Von's forge were brought here. Or worse, if the five of them are all of twelve who survived.

Emerging from my cocoon, I climb to my feet. My nose is frozen from the bite of the wind, though the sea is calmer than it was during the night. The ache in my muscles—my ribs and back and my head—don't go unnoticed, but I welcome the pain; it's a reminder of what happened and my task ahead.

Gripping the barrel for support, I find my sea legs again, something I'm still not used to. The water collecting on the top of the barrel ripples, drawing my attention to the appalling figure reflected in it.

Tired blue eyes edged with purple and green bruises blink back at me, bruises that stretch from my temple to my cheek.

My busted, chapped bottom lip curls in a grimace, and my bedraggled hair flutters in wild strands around my face.

I peer down at my clothes, taking in my sorry state in the light of day. Dirt and blood crust my hands, arm, and tunic. My fur vest is almost worse than my cloak, matted with dried mud from the snow. A quick scrub of my skin and change of clothes would do wonders for my mood, but that's the least of my concerns as my stomach rolls.

Squeezing my eyes shut, I exhale my nerves and exhaustion away.

I need to talk to Bo. I *need* answers.

Opening my eyes again, I meet the gaze of the whistling barrel man as he comes to a stop in front of me. He studies me closely, taking in my horrifying appearance. "What are you doing up here, missy? You should be below with the rest of them." There is no harshness in his voice, only surprise and a bit of apprehension.

"Since I wasn't chained down, I assumed I was allowed to walk the ship."

He smirks, eyeing the bottle in my hand. "Suit yourself," he says, as if he knows a secret, and he steps aside so I can pass. He dips his head, and when I glance at him in my periphery, he tips over the barrel I was standing in front of, and his whistling begins again. I mean to hand him the bottle, assuming he'd appreciate its contents more than me, but decide it's a weapon, if nothing else. The only one I've got.

Gripping the bottle tighter, I turn to head below deck.

I don't take three steps when another man sees me and stops a few paces away. His long coat catches the breeze, and like the whistler, he looks at me strangely. I glower at him, about to ask why the hell I'm not locked in the dungeon if I'm not supposed to be above deck. But I stop myself. My head tilts of its own accord before it dawns on me. I know this man from Northhelm. From the tavern the other night. I remember his bright smile and laughter as the women flocked to him.

Only now, his dark brown hair is combed back, curling behind his ears as it catches the sunlight. His dark beard is freshly trimmed, and his eyes glint a steely blue.

I examine him up and down as he does the same to me in my mangled glory. Though his clothes are just as sun-bleached and well-worn as the rest of the crew's, he's far less terrifying to look at than most people on this ship with scars, chipped teeth, and missing fingers and eyes. Me and my swollen face included.

His eyebrow lifts as he takes a step closer, nodding to the bottle gripped in my fingers. "That was meant to be consumed." His voice is a familiar velvet with a hint of far too much amusement, and all the pieces fall into place. His eyes narrow on my tattooed arm hidden beneath my cloak, and I'm certain it's him.

I grip the bottle tighter. "I prefer a clear head."

"If you insist," he says, and snatches the bottle back. He downs its contents in three gulps, as if he can't feel the effects of it fast enough, before he licks his lips on an exhale. "No need for it to go to waste," he explains.

"The last two times I've seen you, you've been drunk. Why make the third any different?" I deadpan.

His eyes shift to my busted lip. "Sober is no fun," he explains. The edge in his voice, however, belies his flippancy.

"Committed too many atrocities to sleep at night?" While I'd like to think I would not be so combative to all the Reaper's men, there's something about this man that emboldens me. Especially the way his gaze keeps shifting to my arm, as if he can't stop thinking about it.

He discards the bottle on a barrel top. "Are you always this pleasant?"

"Are you always such a drunkard?" I counter. But I can tell I've overstepped as whatever amusement I saw in him fades.

"You're hell-bent on being miserable, aren't you?" he muses.

I can't help a sneer, glancing to the empty bottle before meeting his gaze again. As if he has any room to talk. "Perhaps I wouldn't be so miserable if I wasn't on the ship with the very people responsible for this—" I gesture to my face.

His consternation narrows to a frown. "Explain," he commands.

Ignoring the voice that tells me the Reaper is only one of many reasons Estrid is dead, I square my shoulders. "If it weren't for all of you in your hoods, stalking Northhelm the other night and claiming *miserable* souls like me, I wouldn't have had to run. Ivar would not have found us, and my sister would not be *dead*." I want to seethe the words, but the painful reality that Estrid is gone resurfaces and my voice cracks before I can swallow it down. I know the man hears it.

His eyes are far too knowing, the blue mixing with the gray like churning storm clouds as he stares at me. It's only then I realize how close I've drawn to him, that my clenched hands ache at my sides and that my chin trembles. I take a step back.

I don't want him to see the tears threatening my eyes, so I brush past him and head below deck, praying Bo is awake.

Exhaling a torrent of unwanted emotions that make me feel far weaker than what I can handle right now, I make my way down the steps. My resolve is instantly forgotten as the stench of vomit assaults me, and it's all I can do to make it to Bo without losing what meager contents remain in my stomach. But as I approach, I notice Phillip isn't sick like the others, but wounded.

Both men look at me as my steps quicken toward them.

"Brynn," Phillip says. "I didn't know you were on board."

He swallows thickly, expelling his pain. "You weren't at the forge when—"

I shake my head. "Estrid and I fled," I softly explain, taking in his bloodied clothes. "Though it was for naught."

"Fled?" he breathes. "From Von?" Phillip glances around, looking for Estrid, and I answer the question I can't bear to hear.

"She's gone," I say, and my voice sounds far more detached than I feel.

Phillip's eyes widen as Bo has the decency to look away. "What happened?"

"Ivar," I whisper, and Phillip's surprise crumples, knowing all too well how it must have ended.

"I'm sorry," he says gruffly, wincing as he tries to control his breaths. There was little time for chitchat in the forge. Our days were spent toiling, and our nights were for sleeping, as long as Von didn't have special errands for me and my sister. But while Phillip isn't exactly a friend, there is an unexpected comradery, it seems, when you live under the same roof with a man like Von.

With some effort, I crouch down, concerned about the strange hue of Phillip's skin. "How bad is it?" I ask, nodding to his injured side.

"He'll live," Bo says. "If we can keep his wound clean." He peers around the berth of the ship. "I'll speak with the captain and see if he might—"

"Everyone above deck!" a voice booms, and when I look behind me, my heart shudders and stills in my chest. Behind one-eye bandanna-guy, who's addressing us, the Reaper stands with one leg propped on the bottom step, his gaze sweeping over the group of us. Having seen him on the ship the other day, his scarred face that people have whispered about over the years doesn't seem quite so jarring.

He squints slightly, like he's counting heads, but his expression gives nothing else away. Abruptly, he turns and stomps up the steps, disappearing above.

"We'll be right back," Bo says, meeting Phillip's cloudy gaze.

Bo offers his hand to help me up. With a grimace, I peer down at Phillip. Though Bo says he will live with such certainty, I can only wonder if that's true.

"I'll bring fresh water down when I return," I promise, hoping I can deliver.

He offers a tight-lipped nod of gratitude and lays his head back down, exhaling his pain.

Gently, I tap his foot with my boot. "Hang in there. I'll steal whatever's needed to get you fixed up." I wink at him, though I'm not sure he can tell with my face as swollen as it is. "You know I'm good for it."

Phillip huffs a laugh. "Don't get yourself into any trouble on my account," he says.

"Let's get a move on!" One Eye calls.

Filing toward the steps with the others, Bo and I make our way above deck. Only a couple dozen people come up, while those that are too sick remain below. The moment fresh air hits my face, I inhale a cleansing breath deep into my lungs. And it strikes me that, while many of us look worse for wear, there is an expression on the others' faces that confuses me. Concern, yes, but not necessarily fear, as they chatter among themselves, their eyes flicking to the Reaper, standing near the mast.

The half drunken sailor descends the steps from a second level, but I can only stare at the Reaper. At his pockmarked cheeks, his black eyes, and the pensive look on his face as he folds his arms over his chest, impatiently waiting.

The Reaper cups one hand around his mouth. "Quiet down, now!" he commands.

Something about this doesn't fit. I've never been on a ship

before, let alone met the Reaper, but standing here like an anxious crowd awaiting orders is not what I expected it would be like.

I elbow a man out of my way so I can see the crew clearly. The Reaper squints into the sunlight, peering out at us. "Quiet, now. The captain would like to have a word."

I frown, but I have little time to fully process his meaning as the crew parts and the *captain* steps through. He nods as his gaze sweeps over us all.

"What the fuck," I breathe.

Bo glances down at me, his arms crossed over his massive chest.

As the captain peers out at the crowd, my mind reels with utter bewilderment, and I have to close my mouth to keep it from gaping. "He's the captain—*he's* the Reaper?" I glare from the drunken sailor to Bo.

He frowns, confused as much as I am, as he dips his chin in a slight nod. Obviously, I should know this, that it's common knowledge. And yet . . .

My gaze snaps back to *the captain.* He's a smug drunk, not the scar-faced villain people have whispered endlessly about. Bo, with his thick, muscular body and floppy hair is more terrifying than him.

That's not true, my childhood-self whispers in the back of my mind. I know what the Reaper has done. The havoc he's caused. The people he's killed and the innocent lives he's taken. I've watched my own home burn to the ground in *his* name. Led by his hooded monsters. And no matter what our encounter has been, I would be a fool to dismiss him.

Regardless of why and how, he is the only sea captain known to cross the treacherous North Sea. And the only man with more clout in Norseland than the queen, and there is nothing more terrifying than that.

And I have been insulting him all morning.

8
BRYNN

"By Thor's hammer, I swear to the gods . . ." I mutter. Squeezing my eyes shut, I rub my temple a bit too harshly. With a wince, I try to recall all the things I've said to the Reaper between last night and now because I have no doubt I made an unwanted impression, which is the last thing I wanted to do—I'm no longer invisible to him.

"We've afforded you all the time we can for you to settle." The captain continues, surveying his passengers. "But this is a large ship, and the sea is perilous. With so many bodies and tasks required, there is much to be done—more than my crew can or should have to manage on their own. Norik," he says, nodding to the scar-faced man beside him, "is my bosun, and will speak with each one of you, take note of your skills, and assign you your duties while you are aboard the *Berkano*. He'll go over safety procedures as well."

Berkano? As in, rebirth and protection?

My gaze shifts to the woman carved into the head of the ship. Hel, presider of the underworld—of death. The more I try to understand what's happening, the more confused I become.

I look at Norik, trying to reconcile who he is in all of this. He's not the Reaper, and yet, he was the one collecting workers while the captain whored around, drinking in that tavern?

My temples throb, my headache burgeoning once more.

"We will be at sea for another two weeks," the captain continues. "And when I warned you before you boarded this ship that you may not make it to the Black Country, I meant it." His voice is grave, his gaze pointed—nothing like the man I spoke with this morning—and the passengers hang on his every word with rapt attention.

"I have only two rules while aboard this ship, and I expect them to be followed. Listen to my crew, and do not be a hero. The sea doesn't care what lives you've already lived, how tired you are—how hopeful. If you want to survive, you will worry about yourself and only yourself. Deviating from those two things puts my crew's lives in danger, and none of you are more important than them, not if you want to reach New London alive."

An evil smirk quirks his lips. "If you feel ill at the sway of this ship now," he continues, "you have not felt the wrath of the ocean yet. Njord has been with us these past three days, blessing our journey with steady winds, but I promise you, our luck will not hold out forever. The sea is vicious, and she would swallow us whole if we let her. It is why everyone *must* contribute to the safety and maintenance of this ship." His words brook no argument, not even a groan from those barely able to stand.

"Should you have any issues, seek out Norik. He will tend to your needs as best he can. And this," he says, gesturing to One Eye, "is Boots. Tug is preparing your morning meal below, and you are familiar with Basher, my quartermaster, who is with the rest of my crew, charting our course for the next two days."

Basher. The one who brought me aboard half-dead. I feel a pang of disappointment that I have not seen him yet.

"Above all else," the captain calls out, and Norik takes in the flock of green-faced urchins standing around them, "you will listen to my crew if you want to survive the journey to your new life—your freedom."

My eyes widen, and I tug on Bo's arm. His muscles flex automatically as he tears his gaze from the captain.

"Freedom?" I whisper.

"Yes," he says in a rush. "Freedom awaits us in the Black Country. Shh."

That's impossible. The captain continues speaking, and Bo hangs on his every word, but none of this makes any sense. The Reaper doesn't free people, and the Black Country is not a place of freedom but a land of death and decay, filled with nothing more than crumbling cities since the Great Turning. Everyone knows this.

I stagger back from the crowd. I'm not sure if my sudden lightheadedness is from lack of food, sleep, the multiple blows to my head, or incredulity, but I bump into someone before I find a barrel to brace myself on.

"Are you all right?" Bo asks, approaching when the crowd begins to disperse. "Are you seasick?"

I pry my eyes open, blinking up at him in the sunlight, too bright around his face. "What happened while I was unconscious, Bo? Why am I here?"

He crouches in front of me, his green eyes filled with sympathy. That he would be on this ship without his father makes no sense, not when he was slaving away for Von to pay off his father's debt. With Von dead, there was no reason for him to leave.

"And . . . where is your father? Why are you sailing across the sea—risking death—alone?"

Bo's brow furrows, and he runs fingers through his red,

scraggly beard. "My father is dead, Brynn." He takes a deep breath. "There is no reason for me to stay in Northhelm or any other place in Norseland."

I gape at him. "Dead?"

"I went to find him after the Reaper's crew came to Von's, only to learn Von killed my father weeks ago. Even with my working off his debt, Von wanted to make an example of my father." Bo shakes his head. "Slaving away for him . . . it was a fool's errand. It was for nothing."

"He was using you?" I want to say I don't believe it's true, but I do, and it's beyond heartbreaking. I reach for Bo's hand and squeeze his giant palm in mine. He could break my wrist if he gripped me too hard, but I know there isn't a mean bone in his body, which makes me all the more heartbroken. "I'm so sorry," I whisper, meeting his gaze. "You don't deserve all of this."

Bo blinks at me, and I can tell he hasn't had time to mourn his father properly, just as I haven't had the proper space to mourn my sister, but that is the life we live, and we both seem to understand that. "None of us does, Brynn. So, why *not* go to New London?" It's more of a desperate hope, though. A last resort to find a semblance of good in life. "Why not get away from tyranny and working my fingers to the bone?"

My heart aches for him, it really does, not only for the loss of his father but for the delusion the Reaper offers—freedom in New London. "And you really think life in the Black Country will be better?"

"I already know what awaits me in Norseland, Brynn. And like you, I'm alone—Von burned my father's cabin to the ground, so I have nothing left." The truth of his words stings, though I know they aren't meant to. "If I am to work tirelessly, let there at least be a change of scenery—a new life, whatever comes of it."

"Bo . . ." My words fail me. A man more feared than the

queen, who wreaks havoc across the country, does not offer freedom, not without a cost. And I fear it will be steep. But we're already on a ship with no place to turn, so I keep my thoughts to myself.

"Come," he says. "Let's go to Norik. I doubt they need bladesmiths while we're aboard, but we'll find something we can do to help. And someone must tend to Phillip."

I wave him to go without me. "I—I need a moment." Inhaling a deep breath, I rest my hand on my chest, attempting to tame my wildly beating heart.

Bo looks reluctant, but he seems to understand I'm barely hanging on to the thinnest tether of control, and he leaves me to my thoughts. Dangerous, unwanted thoughts. Heart-wrenching thoughts.

Estrid is dead.

We ran to save ourselves from a freedom ship?

Face heating, throat thickening, and bile churning in my stomach, I feel myself sway again. It's not possible. None of this can be true, because if it is, Estrid died in vain.

My fingernails dig into my thighs as they claw into fists. What have these men promised these people to make them so trusting? Decades of infamy would prove different, and now it isn't only my mother, father, and older brother dead because of the Reaper. Estrid is too, even if it is only because of the fear he's worked tirelessly to cultivate over the years.

"You look ill."

I squeeze my eyes shut at the sound of his voice. A flare of fear licks up my spine, but it's muted—only an engrained echo of what I've once felt about this man.

Instead, hate burns on the tip of my tongue, scathing words I wish were daggers, and I want to scream as much as I want to maim him.

"And angry," he adds, and I glare up at him. His cloak

snaps in the wind, but he stands there like a figurehead—a sentry on the ship, carved and unmovable.

Body coiled and quivering, I stand straight and sure, willing myself to control the rage and hate and fear. "Whatever you are," I grit out. "You are no savior to these people."

"I never claimed to be." He chuckles, and tilting his head, asks, "What is your name?"

Ignoring his question, my heart leaps as I take a step closer, gesturing to the poor souls chattering and walking about the ship. "These people think you are taking them to their freedom."

"I take them to a new life, one where they don't have to live in fear just to eat and stay warm."

I eye him up and down because, despite his promise of a different life, there is something he isn't saying. "But," I say, lip curling. "They will *still* be bound to you, will they not? We are going to be yours."

He measures his answer carefully. "Yes."

I straighten, jaw aching with tension.

"Whatever you think of me, I have not uttered a single deception to these people, neither has my crew. The people aboard this ship will have a better life in New London than what they had in Norseland. That I *can* promise."

Says the collector of souls. I want to say the words aloud, but I bite my tongue, glaring at Hel carved into his ship. "Forgive me," I say dryly. "But I find it hard to believe you do your bidding for the goddess of death, yet offer these people a more prosperous life in the process."

He glances toward the helm. "It is not Hel who blesses this ship," he says, hesitant. "But Skadi."

Absently, I grab my arm. I'm not sure what it means to him, exactly, but his interest in the runes marking my skin makes a little more sense now. And as the captain's eyes shift to me rubbing them with my thumb, my face begins to burn.

"And," he continues, "Reaper is only a nickname."

I shake my head. "Earned by your infamous reputation."

"That's the point."

"What is? Instilling fear in the hearts of innocent people who already breathe it night and day? Or hurting them instead?"

"Fear," he quickly clarifies, "in all men. It affords me a wide berth to do my duty, little Skadi."

I shake my head. "I am not your little Skadi. And I didn't ask to be on this ship—"

"And I didn't bring you aboard it. Your qualms are not with me, woman."

"Yes, Basher," I mutter. "So you say, but I have yet to meet him."

That makes the captain smile, though doleful shadows fill his eyes. "You *are* right about one thing. My crew calls me Kill, so *Reaper* is actually quite fitting." He explains it like it was a nickname borne of a drunken night among friends, and the lives lost amid his playacting are inconsequential. "And you still haven't told me your name—"

"Nor do I plan to."

He lifts his chin. "You're feisty, you know that?"

I scoff at him, unable to help myself. "This is all a jest to you," I rasp. My chest heaves, my body so taut it sings in pain, and I wish him dead as he stands before me, even if I know in my heart it will never be enough to take this desperate feeling away. This utter sense of loss and anger.

The captain lifts his head, almost defensively, and his shoulders tense. "People must fear the Reaper," he explains coolly. "Or there would be no freedom ship."

My eyes burn as I keep myself in place, torn between removing myself from his presence and penetrating glare, or risking it all here and now to kill him where he stands and suffer the consequences.

The captain's eyes narrow slightly on me as his jaw works beneath his beard. "You plan to kill me," he states, as if he can see my plan laid out before us.

In my surprise, I say nothing, and I feel my face pale as the Reaper chuckles, a bone-chilling sound that makes me stiffen.

"Little Skadi seeks revenge, just like her namesake," he utters to himself. "You're welcome to try."

As much as I want to end him and all he stands for, I can't. I don't have a blade. I have no weapon, only desperation and a racing, breaking heart. "Do not tempt me." It's only as his eyes widen slightly that I realize I've thought it aloud.

The Reaper assesses me up and down like he can see right through me. Every thought and regret. Every fraying nerve and splinter of guilt. "You will feel no better and will blame yourself no less for the role you played in what plagues you. Trust me in that."

I don't know what comes over me, only that white, hot, blinding pain and anger consumes me, and my fist meets his jaw.

I cover my mouth in absolute shock as the captain's eyes flare with ire and he reaches for his face. He glares at me as he straightens, his nostrils flaring. I should not have done that—for so many reasons, I should have refrained. My arm is on fire, and a new sort of fear I hadn't expected runs cold over my sweat-dampened skin.

The Reaper takes a step closer to me, his lip curling. "Feel better?" he grits out, and I can smell the lingering whiskey on his breath.

For once, my impulsive self remains quiet as I let my hand fall to my side. It sings with pain, and with no other option, I wait for whatever comes next.

"It's a long journey," he finally says, and takes a step away from me.

I inhale a much-needed breath.

"That's plenty of time to come to terms with your demons, little Skadi. The question is, will it be my life you will still want to claim by the end of it, or your own again?"

I open my mouth, but the words fall flat. Our eyes are locked on one another. His expression daring me to try something else.

"Killian?"

My attention darts behind him. The beautiful black woman from the crow's nest this morning stands with one hand on her scabbard, eyeing me cautiously. The captain's scowl, however, doesn't stray from me. When he says nothing, the woman's eyebrow lifts, delicate as it is on such a strong, well-honed body, and she tilts her head, amused and waiting.

Finally, the captain—Killian—looks at her. "Your feeble find is awake, Basher," he says, a smile in his voice once again.

I frown, taking her in, from billowy shirt and cinched fur vest to leather-clad legs and knee-high boots. "*You're* Basher?"

She stares between us, consternation furrowing her brow as Killian observes my surprise. His grin is slight, but it's there, twitching on his cheek.

"I think scrappy little Skadi means to kill me," he confides, rubbing his jaw for good measure. With his growing smirk, it's hard to tell if it's a gesture of discomfort or amusement. "I'd like to at least have my breakfast first."

I scowl as he turns and strides away.

With a hum of curiosity, Basher eyes me up and down. I can't tell if she's apprehensive or as amused as the captain seems to be.

"So," she starts, brow arched in question. "What, exactly, did I miss?"

9
BRYNN

Basher tilts her head, hands on her hips as she waits for me to explain. While I would normally toss a few choice words at someone who looked at me as if I owed them *anything* at all . . . I can't do that to Basher. I don't know her in the slightest, but she saved me, and even if a part of me wishes she hadn't, the other more reluctant part is grateful.

Instead of regaling her of my distressing encounters with the captain, I ask her the question that has been the fuzziest since I awoke. "Why did you bring me here?"

Basher's slightly perturbed expression softens, just barely, and she scans my body. No doubt she's remembering the pathetic physical state she found me in.

In a sudden jerk of movement, she steps closer and lifts the cloak off my shoulder so she can assess my arm. Her eyes dart to mine. "You're bleeding again." Without my cloak as a shield, the fresh blood sings against my skin in the wind. "And you need clean clothes." She cocks her head for me to follow. "Come."

Basher turns away, and in a spur of desperation, I grab her

arm, cringing as my ribs pinch with the movement, but I breathe through it.

Basher glares down at my hand, and though I know this woman saved me, I am not dumb enough to think we are friends either. Instantly, I drop my hand.

"There's a man below deck—his name is Phillip," I explain. "His wounds aren't doing well, and he needs attention." If she took pity on me back in Northhelm, maybe she'll take pity on him now.

Basher considers something, her eyes never leaving mine. "I'll have someone look at him." Though there is little kindness in her voice, it sounds like a promise, and when she nods again for me to follow her, I do as she says.

We weave through some of the passengers on deck as they speak with Boots and two other members of the crew I haven't seen before. The lines around their eyes and mouths etch their skin like the weather-beaten deck that creaks beneath my feet.

Eventually, Basher stops to speak with a woman with gray hair, long and stringy around her shoulders. Even with the shadow cast over her by the brim of her oversized hat, I can tell she's one of the oldest crew members I've seen on the ship. Still, the hard line of her mouth and the many hairline scars on her neck and arms, nearly enough to match the wrinkles on her skin, tell me she has weathered much in this life, far more than I have.

She looks from Basher to me, murmuring something that doesn't meet my ears.

Whoever these crew members are, they likely spend most of their lives at sea, and to what end? The landowners in New London must pay a hefty coin for their services. Or do they all work for the captain? He himself claimed we would be his in the Black Country. Perhaps these crew members are as well.

If what the captain says is true, he is a man of means to have such a grand ship. It might be weathered and well-used, but its rich, sorrel-swirled wood is better timber than I've seen in Norseland, and Von always required the best. Even the sails boast status, striped in purple and white. And Skadi, carved into the prow, would have cost more coin than I could lay eyes on in a lifetime.

The gray-haired woman nods at Basher once more, and we continue across the ship deck.

The waves and wind grow louder as she leads me up the steps to an upper level, to what I assume is the captain's side of the ship. I spot him in a room filled with maps and scrolls and books, his back to me as he speaks with Norik. Considering the bosun is only the scarred, menacing face of the Reaper's charade—not the man himself, as rumors would have everyone believe—makes me rife with anger all over again. *We ran from no one.* Hurt and guilt and far too much regret inch their way in alongside it.

Norik points to a chart of the sea painted across the wall of the room, little islands dotting the blue expanse. "The winds are pushing us southeast, toward the Isles of the Lost Winds," he reports.

The captain points to an area of the sea painted with crashing waves, his face pensive as he nods. "As long as we stay away from the Soundless—"

"In here," Basher snaps, waiting impatiently for me at an open door. It's only then I realize I've stopped to stare and scowl at the captain. Her look says, *Don't get any ideas because I'll kill you if I have to.*

Before either of the men can notice me, I leave my voyeurism for later.

"What happened to Norik's face?" I ask Basher as I step into the corridor behind her. It's a damp-smelling hallway I can barely fit through before we enter a small cabin with a faintly herbaceous odor masking the salt in the air. Save for the light that ekes its way through the cracks in the walls, it's dark.

"Smallpox," Basher finally answers, "from when he was little. New London boasts its reform and rebuilding, but it is far from sanitary and safe. Killian's father took Norik in as a teenager, after he purchased him in an orphanage, practically on his deathbed. Norik has been with the family ever since." Basher moves through the room, clanking around for a second.

An orphanage? Imagining how painful such a skin disease must have been, I allow a slight pang of empathy for the man.

Eventually, a lantern flares to life on the table, and the room blooms with flickering shadows. A bed draped in richly embroidered fabrics takes up most of what I assume is her cabin. It's quaint but a tight fit for the two of us.

A leather trunk adorned with silver medallions sits at the foot of her mattress, and a narrow path is all there is between the bed and the wall. A round table and chair are shoved in the corner where the lantern sits, and a collection of weapons is displayed on the wood-slatted wall. Scabbards, two different axes, a number of knives, and two pistols. Their hilts and grips and handles are all expertly crafted with embellishments that aren't like any I've seen forged in Norseland.

I watch Basher remove her leather jacket, imagining her wielding *any* of them in whatever exotic places she's been. The thick scar along her jaw glimmers in the lantern light, and everything about her boasts fierce determination and . . . survival.

"What was your life?" I ask, unable to resist.

She tosses her jacket onto her bed, her brow lifting quizzically.

"Before you joined this crew," I amend.

The threat of shadows whisks across Basher's face, filling her eyes as her long fingers find the delicate, silver crucifix hanging around her neck. On a ship carved with pagan gods, it seems a strange symbol to wear, and whatever solace it brings her is gone in the span of a moment.

Her eyes clear and focus on me again. "A wife," she says. "And a servant."

I can't help my disbelief. "You know what sort of lives we come from, and still, you work with the most notoriously loathsome man alive?"

Basher smiles, though it is not with the slightest bit of humor. "Despite the rumors, there are far worse men than the Reaper in the world, girl. I can assure you."

The glibness in her voice is maddening. "Perhaps you're right," I concede. "The men who burned my home, praising his name might be only slightly worse."

"That was not Killian's doing—nor was it any of ours."

I want to scream. "And that dissolves all of you of any fault? Because you weren't *there*? Never mind your captain is out there, boasting how important instilling fear in people is to allow him to carry out his duty—"

"Killian would never boast."

I scoff at that, cringing as my body spasms with the sudden movement.

Basher motions for me to remove my cloak. "Let's have a look at you." Her voice is softer than before, but the edge of irritation is far from gone.

Unclasping Von's pendant from my cloak, I scowl at it before tossing it onto the bed. My nostrils flare as I drag the cloak off my shoulder, breathing through the pain.

"Despite what you think," Basher says carefully, "we don't enjoy violence, nor do we condone it."

She takes the heft of my fur cloak in her hands, and I sigh with relief in its absence. Rubbing my shoulder, I eye all the blood.

"But," she continues, pushing up my sleeve, "some evils are necessary for the greater good."

My head snaps to her and tears prick my eyes like firewater. "Then you have never had your family burned alive in the name of *the greater good*," I grit out. "Your mother and father. Your brother."

Basher's hand stills at my biceps. "You know nothing of what I've suffered. Who I have lost. I, too, thought the Reaper the worst of men, but that was before."

"Before wha—"

"Before he saved my life," she snips. "Same as everyone else on this ship." Her brown eyes blaze in the lantern light as she stares me down, daring me to speak against her beloved captain again. But I don't. I *won't*. Whatever my feelings, they will not sway her, just as her words will *never* sway *me*. We both seem to acknowledge this and avert our gazes.

Basher unwraps the soiled bandages from my arm. Bandages she likely put there, I realize. "You're so full of questions—how about answering some for me?" she says. Basher's touch is slow and gentle. "Who were you before this, and what were you doing in that alleyway?"

Her question cuts deeply because the answer is painfully simple.

"Well?"

I force myself to look at her, though it's through the threat of tears. "I was a sister," I whisper. "And . . . a slave to survival." I glance around her room, seeing no similarities between us, though for some reason, I desperately want there to be. "It wasn't always that way, though." Blinking the tears from my eyes, I peer down at my hands in the flickering shadows, barely remembering my life before fleeing for Northhelm. And I hate that this woman, who I want to respect and trust, works for the person at the root of every malady I've ever known.

"And the alleyway?" she prompts.

"My sister and I worked for Von Magnusson, Chieftain of—"

"I know who he is." Basher looks at me through her lashes, balls up the old, soiled bandages, and tosses them by the door.

"We heard Norik in the forge and thought the Reaper had come for us, so . . . we ran, right into Ivar."

"I knew of him," Basher says. "He was not well-liked in Northhelm."

"Von or Ivar?" I ask with a little snort.

A smile curves the corner of Basher's full lips as she pulls a small trunk out from under her bed. "Both, I suppose, but I was referring to Ivar."

"Yes, well, he and Von have always hated each other, and Ivar wanted to hurt Von the only way he knew how." My throat swells with regret, and I worry it might close completely as I try to swallow the emotion away.

"You put up a good fight," Basher muses. "I'll give you that." She presses the tender flesh around my knife wound, and I hiss out the pain. Dabbing a tincture on a clean bit of cloth, she begins to wipe the dried blood away.

In our uncomfortable silence, I glance around her cabin again, ignoring the pain as best I can. Everything is timeworn and lived-in. And though it smells like brine and wet wood, there's a tinge of sweetness in the air, and I notice dried flower bunches hanging in the corners of the room.

"Wisteria," Basher says. "Just because I live with a bunch of crude men, doesn't mean I have to smell like one." She pulls out another tincture bottle and tears some clean cloth from a roll she has in the box.

"Sit," she says, and motions to the bed. "Remove your vest and shirt. I'll be right back."

It's not a suggestion but a request, and Basher steps out of the room, closing the door behind her.

As I unbutton my blood-crusted vest, my body heaves with momentary relief. Chills roll over me without the weight of my cloak. But sore as I am, as I peel my vest and woolen shirt away, it's as if my body is able to breathe for the first time in days.

My breath catches when I see my torso. Bruises cover my sides, and squeezing my eyes shut, I try and fail not to think of the alleyway again. Of Ivar's tongue against my sister's face. Of the look in Estrid's eyes as she took her final breaths.

I hate myself for being alive when she is not, but more than anything, I hate that I will have to live with so much regret for the rest of my life. And I *hate* that if Estrid were still alive, she would tell me to use this chance I've been given—because that's what it feels like, a chance. Even if I don't trust it, or the captain, in the slightest. Even if it goes against *everything* I've ever known.

The door opens again and Basher steps inside. She stops in the doorway, water sloshing onto the floor. I glance back to find her standing with a bowl in her hand and her eyes fixed on my back.

Ah, yes. "They are old," I assure her.

Basher's eyes meet mine as she kicks the door shut behind her. And after another quick scan of my bruised and mangled body, the furrow in her brow vanishes and her face is a beautiful mask of stone once again. "I assume nothing is broken?" She scans me up and down as she sets the bowl on the table and submerges a clean cloth.

"A rib may be cracked, but it will heal." Now that my mind isn't racing with chaos, my body aches tenfold.

Basher offers me the rag. "For your face," she says.

My lips purse, knowing how horrible I look. "Thank you," I mutter. Bracing myself, I scrub what I can off my cheeks. The cleaner I feel, the quicker I scrub, moving to my forehead and around my ears and neck with my good arm.

"It looks better," Basher says as she dresses my arm wound again. "Most of the blood was old." She ties the clean gauze at the end and steps around me, to the chest at the foot of her bed. Dipping my washing cloth in more water, I scrub the rest of my exposed skin. My entire body recoils from the cold as it drips over my arms and chest, but I relish the feel as much as I dislike it.

"You'll feel a little better," Basher says without looking at me. "Once you've cleaned what remains of Norseland from your flesh." She drapes a clean tunic across the bed. "I don't have enough to wrap you, but this will help with your ribs." She tosses a corset on top of it.

I watch her closely, wondering what has happened in her twenty or thirty years that would make her equal parts tough and tender.

"Why did you save me?" I ask, because people aren't kind for no reason. They don't save people the way she saved me. They mind their own business and keep their heads down, never certain who might be offended and retaliate against unwanted meddling. "Your captain said he has nothing to do with me being on this ship—that you brought me. I—" I shake my head, my mind stretching back into a murky memory. "I remember you carrying me."

Basher doesn't look at me as she closes the trunk, and as I fumble with the corset, she gestures for me to turn around. Her fingers are cool as they brush against my skin, cinching it closed. "I helped you because I despise men like Ivar. Because the world is cruel enough," she finally says. "Inhale."

I do and hold my breath as she tugs firmly against the stays. Pain shoots through me, and it feels as if my insides are being wrung to nothing.

"I could not leave you in the hands of that cretin," she admits.

I exhale slowly, and opening my eyes, I notice my sudden cleavage and almost laugh. "I can't remember the last time I dressed like an actual woman." I wince as she cinches me tighter.

"Done."

"Thank you," I say with another exhale. I appreciate the

pressure around my torso, helping to hold everything in place, and run my hand down the front of the thickly woven cloth. What would Ivar have done to me had Basher not come? "I've always hated him," I whisper.

"Well, I slit his throat," she says, dropping her hands to her sides. "He won't be skulking in any more alleyways or hurting any more women."

That Ivar is dead should give me peace, but it doesn't. At least, not as much as I was hoping for.

"Killian found me in much the same state," Basher offers, her gruffness gone. "Three years ago, in the withered lands outside of Talon Bay. I'd lost everything, didn't care much about living anymore." Basher opens a canister from her little box and scoops some salve on her fingers.

"Were you with them?" I ask, my voice only a whisper.

Her ministrations pause on my tender cheek. It dawns on me she's using her own private supplies on my wounds.

"When they came to Von's forge?"

Basher shakes her head as she finishes spreading the herbaceous ointment over my skin. "I don't collect passengers."

"Then what is it you do, exactly?"

"I'm the quartermaster. I take care of the crew, and of Killian—I do whatever he needs me to."

I watch her closely, wondering what sort of relationship they have, exactly. "If you didn't know I had run from your crew, how did you find me?"

"I didn't know you were from the forge at all. I was securing the last of our provisions for the trip home when I saw you needed help, and that was the end of it. But now," she continues, "you want to kill Killian." She sounds slightly bemused by that.

"I never said that," I admit, which is true.

"You don't have to. Your lust for vengeance gleams in your

eyes." She pauses a moment. "And that is problematic." She caps the ointment and drops it back into her chest.

A snide comment nearly passes my lips when she glares at me, all her kindness vanished. "He is the captain of this ship," she warns. "Nearly every man and woman on here owes Killian their life—crew, passengers, even you. You would do well to accept and remember that. I know my words cannot change what has happened to you in the past. So, hold grudges, if you must," she continues. "But any act against Killian is an act against me and the rest of us." Her words are sharp, like the fangs of a wolf, and while I don't cower easily, I believe she would kill me right here and now if it meant keeping Killian safe. "Whatever life you've come from in Northhelm is gone, Brynn. You may not grasp how lucky you are to be on this ship now, but you will soon enough."

I'm not sure why that sounds like a threat, but it does, and Basher stares at me with fierce brown eyes that gleam with challenge.

"How do you know my name?" I ask her, and grab the tunic to pull over me, wanting nothing more than to get out of here.

"I know everything about this ship and all who are on it," she replies. She nods to my arm. "Let me know if it gets worse. And in the meantime, I would stay out of trouble, if I were you."

I can promise her nothing, but I don't have to as the door to Basher's room swings open. I drop the tunic, wincing as I turn toward the sound too quickly, and find the man himself standing in the doorway.

Killian's eyes widen when he sees me standing there. His gaze slides over the front of me, taking in my corset, and I frown.

"I'll come back," he says, finally dragging his gaze away. He nods to Basher, and with that, he turns and walks out.

"Blow out the flame when you leave, and be sure you eat." Basher's eyes shift over me anew, then she makes her way to the door. "Tug's a horrible cook, but it's better than starving, and I've been told you've eaten next to nothing since arriving." Her gaze hardens. "You're no good to us if you're weak."

There it is. My worth laid out before me.

Basher shuts the door, leaving me in her room with all of her weapons. But as I painstakingly pull the clean tunic over my head, I'm aware of how ridiculous the idea of vengeance is at the moment, and it flits away as I wince again and blow the flame out behind me.

10
BRYNN

Sitting below deck on our pallets, Bo and I tend to our assigned tasks, fixing nets and braiding ropes, though my mind isn't focused. It spirals in too many directions all at once, and I can't tell if I'm relieved or resentful to be on this ship.

"Bo," I say, watching him burn the end of the rope he's binding with a flame. He dips it in hot wax when he's finished. "How can you be so . . . accepting?"

He glances up, a strand of red hair falling into his eyes. "What do you mean?" He rakes it back into the knot it fell from with his fingers.

"We're on the Reaper's ship," I say slowly. "Years of fearmongering and terror, and then one day, his crew shows up, tells you they can offer you a better life, and you just shrug and jump aboard."

Bo grins, holding up the end of the rope to examine his handiwork. "It didn't go quite like that," he says with a chuckle. "But it's different for me than it is for you, I think." His soft, green eyes meet mine. "He has not played any part in my life until now. Not like he has yours."

I think on that, realizing that is likely the case for many people on this ship. Even if my terror of the Reaper lessened the moment I learned he was actually Killian, the Reaper was —*is*—still an infamous villain, far worse than creatures conjured in my nightmares, because the Reaper isn't made up. He's real, and he has haunted my dreams for years, leaving as many scars on my soul as his name has left trails of blood and fire throughout Norseland.

"These people can't be monsters *and* freedom fighters, Bo." I shake my head. "The havoc and death, even if they weren't a part of it . . ." I exhale my exhaustion. "They let the fear and chaos enflame, using it to their advantage, and the blame has to fall on someone."

Bo looks at me, more concerned this time. "Don't do something stupid, Brynn."

I smirk. "You think you know me so well."

He stares at me, and I roll my eyes. "Since I'm struggling just to use my arm, I'd say my impulsive tendencies are low at the moment."

Bo smiles again and coils the rope to set aside with his others, while I finish mine.

Phillip stirs beside me, sucking in a pained breath. Forgetting my rope, I move closer and crouch next to him, lifting his sweaty tunic to assess his wound. It doesn't look well. It's irritated and red, and I worry it is festering.

"It will heal up," he says, though his voice is hoarse, and the sheen in his eyes belies his pain. "It just needs some time."

"Did Basher not send someone to tend to you?" I ask, brushing the matted, graying hair from Phillip's forehead.

"Aye." He lets out a deep breath. "Don't fuss over me, girl—"

"Hush," I tell him, and ball up my cloak for him to use as a pillow. "I don't need this right now, but you do." I lift his shoulder a little, trying to make him more comfortable.

"Are you certain?" He scans me up and down. "You look a bit worse for wear. Even for the likes of you." Phillip smiles, but it doesn't reach his eyes.

"I've seen better days," I mutter. "I'll give you that."

"Are you Brynn, the captain slayer?" a rough voice asks behind me, and rolling my eyes again, I pivot to look up at Norik. My gaze must say it all because a smirk tugs at his lips. "The captain would like to have a word with you."

I'm not sure why my heart palpitates slightly.

"Now," he prompts, and signals for me to follow.

I glance at Phillip. "I'll be right back."

"I'll be here . . . captain slayer."

As annoying as the moniker is, it's more inconvenient than anything, seeing how the element of surprise is no longer in my favor.

With a wince, I rise to my feet and follow Norik through the underdeck and up the steps.

"His cabin's this way," he says the moment we reach the open air. We head toward the stern.

The sea is relatively calm given the stormy afternoon clouds, but that only puts me slightly at ease. Somehow, the sea frightens me more in the daylight—the open expanse without end. After a few days, it still sends a chill over me. There is nothing out here. No rocks or icebergs. No land on the horizon. We are utterly alone and at the mercy of the gods.

I force myself to look away from the rolling blue, taking in the extra deckhands instead. They help with the barrels and swab the deck. There are a few people clustered in a circle under one of the balconies, cleaning dishes with the few children on board.

The kids laugh and play now, but what will life be like for them in New London? What will it be like for all of us? If what the crew told Bo is true, we will all be given food and shelter, even a day of rest, in exchange for our labor. Still, I can only imagine the Black Country as a bleak place, one which inspires no hope, only dread.

A swabbie calls Norik over, but he holds up his hand, telling the man to wait. Norik halts and looks at me, eyeing me closely. He doesn't trust me, that much is obvious. Nor should he.

"It's just up there," he grumbles, and I glance at the cabins and navigation room. After another moment of hesitation, Norik eventually walks away. Despite his distrust and the rumors apparently circulating the ship, Norik must not think me too dangerous if he's leaving me unguarded.

The truth is, as resolved as I was before, I'm not anymore. I'm angry and vengeful and I want the *Reaper* to pay for everything, but I know hurting Killian will not give me the peace I seek, even if I wish it would.

Anxious to be done with him, I climb the steps to the upper deck. The navigation room, where the chart is painted across the wall, is empty. Next, I head for the officers' quarters Basher took me to and notice a door with a glass window I remember from before.

Peering inside, I find Killian, poring over papers on a desk in front of a large window. His expression is one of consternation as he writes in a ledger, deep in thought. I don't know what he wants from me. To taunt me and make me squirm, knowing how much I despise him?

Just as I'm about to reach for the handle, I stop myself. Curiosity gets the better of me and I stare at the infamous captain. His brunette hair is pulled back. His trimmed beard is well kempt compared to the other boatmen. It even shimmers a little in the gray daylight, filtering in through the window behind him. His jacket is draped over the back of his chair as if he's settled in for a while, and dried wax covers portions of his desk.

He dips his quill in the inkwell and continues writing.

So, by night he is a drunken sailor, and by day, a captain, sitting in his grand room with his luxurious bed draped in richly colored fabrics, and walls lined with books.

There's a clatter on deck, and someone whistles a merry tune as they draw closer, so I rap my knuckles against the door before I'm caught spying.

Killian doesn't bother looking up as he motions for me to come in.

The door is swollen from the moisture in the air, and with a nudge of my hip, I force it open and step inside.

"Close the door," he commands. He's all business; his cocky humor and taunting vanished. The edge in his voice, the seriousness of it, gives me pause.

I'm standing there like a half-wit, I realize, hands gripped on the back of the chair, when Killian peers up through his lashes. He glances at the empty seat. "Sit."

Uncertain how long this conversation will take, I do as he says. I notice the jug of what I can only assume was or is a fermented libation of some sort and wonder if he's already started drinking again.

"I have need of your services," Killian starts, finally closing his ledger.

"My services?" I tense in my seat. "And what are those, exactly?"

He uncorks the jug and pours a rich, red liquid into a crystal goblet. "Your friend, Bo, tells me you're the best ironworker between the two of you."

"Three," I correct, and Killian takes a sip from his fancy glass. "There are three of us, though Phillip is unwell."

"Yes, well, out of the three of you, then."

I shrug. "I'm not certain I would say I'm the best, but I've been doing it the longest."

"Well, we are in need of new bracings for the bowsprit and

boom. I'd like to commission your services when we arrive in New London. Before you leave for the country."

"The country?"

He nods.

"And what if I don't wish to go to the country?"

Killian shrugs. "Then don't, but you will not have guaranteed food or shelter. And you will have no protection."

"Protection?" I say skeptically. "I thought you were taking us to a better life."

Killian sits back in his chair, clasping his hands in his lap. I can't help but notice the ink staining his fingers or the exasperation in his voice, as if he was prepared for me to argue with him. "In many ways, yes. But while New London is not as harsh a place as Norseland, it is just as vile."

I refrain from my cynical remarks that yearn to be spoken and wait for him to explain.

"Women are breeders there," he says carefully.

"What?" My breath hitches a little at the thought.

"Yes, breeders," he repeats brusquely. "Kidnapped frequently and worth more than any goods from any land. It would be foolish not to go to the country with the others." He waves his words away. "But I won't waste my breath convincing you. The choice is yours. I do, however, require your services."

"I will only consider it," I say, "if you will tend to my friend's wounds. He needs more than mint salve and clean bandages. Do you not have a doctor on board?"

"Of course, but what's happened to your friend?"

"Phillip was injured during your *collection*. One of Von's men tried to stop him from leaving, or so I've been told."

Killian's brow furrows. "That's unfortunate." He says it as if it's an inconvenience that one of his newly acquired workers is lame. "I was told he is a very skilled woodsman."

"Yes, he is, and should he get worse, he will be no good to you at all."

Killian's eyes move over me—far too thoughtfully to be lascivious. The longer he remains silent, the more I begin to fear what he might be considering, and shift uncomfortably.

Refusing to renegotiate my trade, however, I straighten my shoulders. "Well?"

Killian strums his fingers on his desk and takes a deep breath. "Of course I will have Doc see to your friend," he finally says, running his teeth over his bottom lip. The scruff there glistens with moisture, and I meet his gaze.

"Then I will help you when we dock in New London, in exchange."

"You do not need to *exchange* services with me. I will have Doc look at Phillip, regard—"

"No. Basher has already helped me," I tell him, and Killian's eyes flick to my chest. I know he's thinking about the corset my tunic is cinched over, and my cheeks flush. "Nothing in this life is free. I learned that long ago." I clear my throat. "So, I do it in exchange."

Killian shakes his head, but I ignore it and I rise to my feet. "As you wish," he grumbles. He opens his journal with a sigh as he goes about his business.

Taking the hint, I turn and leave, but I feel his gaze as I shut the door behind me.

11
BRYNN

The night is long, cold, and wet as a storm surges around us, tossing the ship in and out of the waves. The lanterns swing from their hooks, and the swaying shadows make my stomach churn along with everyone else's. Water spills down from above deck as we cower inside the berth with the stench and sound of people retching. Again. And as night gives way to day, the storm only worsens.

Fleetingly, I wonder where the three-legged cat hides during storms, assuming it's a warmer, dryer place than this.

Wrapping my cloak tighter around me to stave off the cold, I silently thank Basher for giving me the corset. It feels like the only thing keeping my sides from splitting as the ship lurches.

I check on Phillip, nestled between Bo and me to help keep him from sliding around, like one of the barrels I can hear on the level above. With every thump and clatter, I find myself holding my breath, and it's all I can do to keep from looking around for something to float on should the ship sink.

My stomach rolls at the thought, and I wipe my sweaty brow with the back of my hand.

I'm not the only one. A young boy with wide, tear-filled eyes looks like he's about to lose all of his resolve as he cowers a few people away from me. I haven't gotten to know any of the passengers. Not well, anyway. We haven't conversed more than what's been necessary because nothing has changed since boarding the *Berkano*. People are still distrusting and standoffish, especially when no one is completely certain what awaits us on the other side of this journey.

But seeing the child is alone when he wasn't before gives me pause.

"Bo!" I bark over the creaking ship. He looks at me, his face nearly as green as his eyes.

"Who does that kid belong to?"

Phillip's lashes flutter, weary and feverish, as he looks at the kid.

"And where are they?" I add.

"That's Surg's boy," Bo says, peeking around me. "But I haven't seen him."

Ah, yes. The tall man with a shaved head and braided beard the kids were doing dishes with yesterday.

When I look at the boy again, silent tears glisten on his cheeks, and his gaze is locked on the steps. I tell myself the boy isn't my concern. That it doesn't matter if he's shivering from the cold or if he's afraid.

But I know what it's like to be frightened and alone without your parents to comfort you, and I can't ignore that either.

"Where's your pa?" I call over the roar of the water and wailing wind.

"My *fadir* went—out there." He gestures and nearly falls forward with a surge in the waves. "He was help—helping secure the barrels."

I've already seen a few people get knocked around by rolling canisters and sliding crates down here, so I can only imagine how bad it is above deck, and my heart heavies for the boy. "Then he's with the crew. They will keep him safe," I try to reassure him.

Movement at the stairs catches my eye, and Basher hurries down the steps as if the ship isn't thrashing us all in different directions. Her expression is grim and exhausted, but she isn't pallid or sick. She only looks slightly concerned, and I think it's for us.

"Tie down what you can!" she commands over the storm. "This hurricane will worsen before it gets better." She disappears behind the steps, then comes out with a bunch of coiled rope and heaves it in our direction. "Tie everything up, so it doesn't roll around!" she instructs.

She looks at me and then at the other able bodies who can afford to move around.

Bo and I help Phillip wrap his arm around one of the support posts, tying him as snuggly as we can in place. You can't tell Doc, the older woman with the hat, was down here tending to him yesterday, because Phillip's clean shirt is sweat-stained and dappled with blood again. In my gut, I know it's blood poisoning from a dirty blade, but I don't dare say it.

"You'd do well to tie yourselves in too!" Basher calls, and she disappears up the steps again, bracing herself as she goes so as not to lose her footing.

I lose mine though, a few times, as I help Bo tie off the area. I have to hold on to the rafters and ropes to keep myself upright, but finally, we have the sacks and crates in our area secured as best we can.

When I glance at the boy again, he's sobbing. "Come here!" I call to him. "You can tie up here with us." He can't be more than seven or eight years old, and while we had blizzards in Norseland, nothing came close to the angry sea hurtling the ship around. "Hurry!" I tell him, reaching for his hand. "Grab hold of this rope, and I'll tie you in."

As the boy comes toward me, his eyes widen on something behind me, and relief washes over his face. "*Fadir!*"

I turn around just as the ship lurches up in a wave, and a pair of feet fly up with it and out of sight.

"*Fadir!*" Water rushes down the steps with another jolt and no sign of his pa.

The boy scrambles toward the steps, and I lunge for him.

"Wait!" I rush up the stairs behind him before I realize it, colliding into the wall as the sea tosses us like a pair of dice. I brace myself as I grab for the boy's foot that's just out of reach. "Kid—stop!"

The ship dips, water sprays over me, washing down the steps, and I nearly lose my footing as it lurches up again. When I look up, the boy is gone.

"Gods—" I curse, and scramble to the top, my lungs burning and legs weary from straining against the storm. A deluge of saltwater rushes me, freezing me to the bone and stinging my eyes as I gape, nearly paralyzed, at the sight before me.

Furious waves swell higher than the ship as it dips in and out of them—the mast and rigging clanking and creaking against the brunt of the turbulent winds. The deck is taking on so much water, it seems impossible we haven't sunk yet.

The ship veers toward another surmounting swell that roars in the wind, and I see the boy and his pa, gripping the ropes wound around a group of barrels at the mast.

More water crashes over the ship and pulls at my feet.

The wind tugs at the boy. He's too small to hold his own against the waves.

His father clutches him.

I call to them, knowing there is no possible way they could survive out here.

The water recedes, and the instant Surg sees me, I beckon the two of them over. "Hurry!" I shout.

But just as they see an opening, the rope around the barrels snaps. Surg is knocked off his feet by tumbling casks and he slides down the sloping deck toward the railing. The boy slips with him, clawing at the deck for something to hold on to.

It's all I can do to keep myself from losing purchase as I watch a ravenous wave crash over them, pulling them out to sea as if they were never there at all.

"No—"

A blurry visage appears in front of me, shoving me to the stairs and into the interior. I stumble down half the steps before landing on my knees in the berth. There is no more wind in my hair or water spraying my face. All I can hear is my heart drumming in my ears. All I can feel is the searing pain that wracks my body. And all I can see is a furious Killian.

"What the *fuck* were you thinking?" he shouts over the howling torrent above.

I wince in both discomfort and surprise. "He was going to die!" I shout back.

"He *did* die," Killian growls, water dripping off every inch of him. His eyes are blue fire in the storm's ominous light. "And you nearly did too!" It's a roar, and it unnerves me as his words rake over my skin.

My trembling body slumps, and my heart races so fast, I'm not sure I can breathe.

The boy and his pa are dead.

"*Never* risk your life for someone else on this ship, do you understand? That's how you die."

I blink at him.

"Now tie yourself off with the others," he orders.

I can't bring myself to argue because all I can think about is the boy and his pa and the looks on their faces as the sea swallowed them whole.

12
BRYNN

I stare at the ocean, at the water as flat as a frozen pond, and bluer than the cloudless sky above. The sea is so calm and tranquil, as if it has feasted well enough for one day. As if it's sated. For now.

But even as the boy's terror flashes to mind, it's Killian's anger that warms my cheeks with shame and fills my thoughts. I don't know what I was thinking helping that boy, only that I couldn't bear for a kid to die. To watch *anyone* else die. Not after Estrid. Not so close to supposed freedom.

I'm not sure how long I stare at the great expanse, but my face burns from the sun, and I lick my lips. It's only when someone coughs beside me that I remember the others, standing in silence along the ship, paying their respects to the lost boy and his pa.

Squinting, I take in some of their contemplative faces, crew and passenger alike. Not one of them is weeping—they don't even look distraught or affected, so much as solemn and resigned. Having lived in Norseland, a place of violence and death, no one wears their heart on their sleeve, but I'm sure they feel the loss keenly. Strangers or acquaintances, Surg and his son are an unnecessary reminder of how unforgiving life is and how quickly everything can change. Does it make some of them warier of their futures? Or are they anxious to once again be on land, whatever fate New London brings?

The sun glints blaringly in the distance, and shielding my eyes, I see Killian on the top deck, peering out at the sea. He's not gathered with the rest of us, but remains at the helm, alone.

A horn blows, startling me, but I don't take my eyes off the captain. He just stares and stares, his hair escaping its knot, blowing in the breeze as he grips the ledge of the ship. Eventually, he shakes his head, looks down at his feet, and pushes off the balustrade.

Basher walks up behind him, stopping only inches away. She rests her hand on his shoulder, and I hold my breath as I watch something protective and fierce transpire between them. And something tender as well, because whatever conversation they have seems to soothe Killian the slightest bit, and Basher runs her hand down his arm. Basher leads him into his cabin, the door shutting behind them.

While I don't know the captain like she does, I'm familiar enough with Killian to guess that tonight, no matter what comforts Basher offers, he'll be drinking as much as he can to forget his demons. Again.

13
BRYNN

"It ain't fancy," Tug says, a bit sheepishly as he and two of the passengers make their way through the lower deck. He can't be more than twelve or thirteen but the shadows in his eyes age him beyond his years.

Cat, his three-footed feline, follows him, though it might be for the pots of stew the three of them carry instead of the company. The orange mouser's tail snakes back and forth as he limps his way along, and between the two of them, the cat and his human are quite the pair.

Tug's shaggy brown hair sticks out from under his cap, and though he dresses every part the roughneck sailor in his leathers and stained linen top, his pants hang off his lanky body despite the cinch around his waist. And his boots and tunic look two sizes too big for him.

He offers me a wooden bowl. "It might be a bit salty," he adds. "But the potatoes will stick to ya well enough." His lips purse as he ladles brown sludge into my bowl. "Go ahead." He nudges it closer to me. There's an unexpected sympathy in his eyes, though I'm not sure why. "Don't listen to the guys," he says sheepishly. "I promise it's edible."

"I'm not worried about that, Tug," I say, bringing the bowl to my lips. It's definitely salty, but I've never been one to complain about a lukewarm meal.

"It's good, thanks." I force a small smile and he beams a little.

"Good." With a dip of his chin and satisfaction written on his face, Tug and his helpers move along, skipping Phillip who is in and out of a fitful fever sleep. Cat lingers by me, as if he knows I don't have much of an appetite tonight.

I lift an eyebrow and grunt at him.

When he seems to realize he's not getting a lick of my stew, he twitches his tail and with a wide-eyed, beseeching look, the three-legged beggar limps onward to the next potential sucker.

When Bo peers down at Cat with a grin, I roll my eyes and laugh. Bo's a *total* sucker.

As the night progresses, I coax Phillip to have a few bites of what's left of my stew as he comes to. He fights me on it, and eventually, I leave him be, knowing he's not likely to make it much longer, even if I know his body could use the sustenance.

When I become too restless to stay below, I finally head up for some fresh air and to stretch my legs. I'm not used to being cooped up, even if I know I should let my body rest. And without Estrid to talk to, I find the minutes feel more like hours the longer I sit with my thoughts and uncertainties.

Fourteen years ago, an eight-year-old Estrid promised me it was her and me. That we could survive anything. That it would always be the two of us. That was the day she pulled me up from a sobbing heap in the snow.

I don't know how many hours she'd let me lie there, inconsolable after we'd come back from hiding in the woods to find our family dead and everything we knew burned to all but ash.

"*Come on, Brynn.*" *Her voice was soft and grief-stricken.* "*We must go.*"

I shook my head, staring blankly into the inky night.

"Yes. We have to find shelter."

I said nothing, only dug my numb fingers deeper into the snow.

"Please," she whispered, and I could hear her shivering. "We will freeze if we stay out here." She choked on a sob of her own. "I have to take care of you now."

That Estrid had to fight through her own fear and worry about me; that we had to worry about freezing when our family was dead . . . That was the first time I felt anger. The first time I ever felt the burning need to hurt someone else.

I got up and took her hand, squeezing it in mine. Together, we cried and walked toward the village, assuming we'd find safety there. Estrid looked at me, trying to be brave. "It's just you and me now."

Gripping the rim of a barrel at the top of the steps, I wipe the tears from my eyes. She was right, it had been just the two of us for many years, but now, it's only me.

Lifting my face to the crisp night air, I let it chase the past away. Let it soothe the heat of anger and heaviness of grief.

Rolling dice and laughter meet my ears, and I'm not surprised to find Boots and Norik huddled under the stairs across the ship, passing the time while they are on duty. Another roll of laughter echoes, and it's whisked away by the steady breeze just as quickly.

Above, the moon is full and bright in the cloudless sky, and surrounding me, the sea is still calm and sated from yesterday's tempest. I'm growing used to being out here, with the ever-present wind in my hair. I can practically feel Njord, god of the wind and waves, all around me—whipping over me and kissing my cheeks. It's like he's real out here, unlike in the city, where it seems as if we've all been forgotten by the gods and left to rot in our sins.

I hold my face up to him. I've never felt such an . . . aliveness. Maybe it's because there has been so much death lately. Or because I miss Estrid so badly, sometimes I can't breathe. But I'm keenly aware I am alive while others aren't, and though I'm reticent to admit it, perhaps the gods haven't completely abandoned me yet.

Footsteps creak on the deck behind me, and the moment I hear the swish of a jug, I know who it is.

"Captain Killian," I breathe, licking my cracked lips.

"Captain Blackburn," he corrects. "If we're being proper about it."

Blackburn. I'd never thought of what his surname might be. It sounds almost as ominous as the Reaper. "All right, then," I say, my eyes fixed on the sea. "Captain Blackburn, have you come to scold me again? Because I promise you, there is no need." There's no real venom in my voice, only exhaustion.

When he doesn't answer, I pry my gaze from the rising moon to look at him.

He's scruffier and looks weighed down in the night shadows, despite his smirk.

"The question is, little Skadi, what do *you* want?" He nods to his perch between the two barrels. "You've found your way to my thinking spot."

Now that he mentions it, I don't know when I wandered here, or why. "I didn't realize it belonged to anyone."

He shrugs. "Well, it does, and while I don't normally like sharing," he says playfully, "I don't feel like arguing with you either."

I eye the jug in his hand, noting how predictable he is. Killian takes my curiosity as a silent request and offers it to me.

Lifting a wry eyebrow, I shake my head. "I thought you don't like sharing?"

He grins. "Trust me, it helps."

"With?"

"Everything you don't want to feel or think about," he answers, and walks over to his alcove, exhaling what sounds like a lungful of woes as he lowers himself down. "At least for a little while."

Even though I want to numb all the raw parts that burn inside of me, I can't bring myself to do it. "No, thank you," I murmur, and I wonder if I'm not more messed up than I thought.

"Suit yourself." Killian takes another swig as if he's doing so on my behalf, and I turn back to face the rolling sea, leaving the captain to his thoughts.

The more I stare at the water, the less frantic my fear of it becomes, and I make myself stand there a little longer. Its scent is indescribable as I inhale it so deeply, my lungs burn. It feels unexpectedly freeing, like I'm breathing for the first time in as long as I can remember.

Estrid would have something witty to say about my need to let things go and not hold on to so much anger. That it's only taking years off my life and adding lines to my face. But I don't want to think of her or my past in Norseland.

A remnant of my tears escapes my lashes, and I quickly wipe it away.

"I warned you the sea was dangerous," Killian says, mistaking my tears for the boy and his pa.

I stare up at the moon. "Everything in this life is dangerous," I counter.

"Of course that's true, and yet, knowing this, you mourn the loss of those who have died."

"As do you," I say tersely, glaring over my shoulder at his bottle.

"Yes, which is why I drink." Killian's eyes glint in the moonlight.

"Unlike you, I want to feel my regrets," I say, turning toward him. "Otherwise the sacrifices were for nothing."

"*Unlike me,*" he parrots with a huff, and there's a sad sort of amusement in his voice. "You're right." He leans his head back with a sigh. "I lost my first passenger on my first voyage with Norik, before I was even twenty. And for the last nine years, I've warned everyone who steps foot on this ship that it is not a promise of anything, only an opportunity. Even my crew takes their lives in their hands every time we set sail."

"And yet, you keep sailing."

Killian takes a swig of his drink in answer.

"How long have you all been at sea?" I ask, leaning my hip against the ledge. It's strange to think this is his life. That this city on the sea is where he spends months and years of his life.

"This time?" Killian scratches his beard, ruminating a moment. "Eight months, give or take."

"And your crew, they have no qualms staying at sea most of the year? No families to go home to?"

Killian takes another drink and runs his teeth over his bottom lip as he contemplates. "We do what the weather allows," he explains. "We stay in port and camp where we need to, because there is no one home to go back to. What binds us is our one shared goal, and that's the *Berkano*." He glances up at the sails snapping in the night. "The crew is from all around—Old France, Norseland, New London, the Americas—"

"The Americas?" I ask, having only heard of them in stories. "You've been there?"

Killian frowns. "It might be the most dangerous place I've been yet," he says gravely. "It's the most unpredictable. I was on the coast not even a week, and I'm not certain what's more terrifying, the lightning storms or the near constant rain." He says the last part with a tone that sounds almost afraid.

"You don't like the rain?" I ask, amused by him for once,

since it always seems to be the other way around. "You, captain of a ship through tempests and hurricanes."

Slowly, his eyes shift from somewhere on the horizon to me, and there's a look in them that makes me anxious. "Floods," he clarifies. "I don't like floods."

Unease ripples through me as I once again consider my disadvantage of being unable to swim. "No, I guess I wouldn't either."

"It's where I found Tug," Killian murmurs, and my unease is forgotten.

"*Found* him? Where? The Americas?"

He nods. "In one of their fallen cities, four years ago. I hadn't been in port a single day and the rains were relentless. I'm not sure why I came above deck," he says, his voice distracted and faraway. "If I was in my right mind, I would have stayed in my cabin. But I was far from sensible that night." There's shame in Killian's voice, like something I've felt in my most desperate moments. And though I yearn to glean another grain of truth about this man, it feels wrong to linger in whatever black thoughts plague him.

"But you were out," I hedge, "in the rain and found him?"

"More than that, I walked across the entire ship without a reason I can remember. Another game of the gods," he mutters. "I peered down at the docks, crashing against the rocks in the storm." Killian huffs with disbelief and picks at a fraying rope tied around a barrel. "I saw him in one of the fishing boats. Skin and bones. Freezing in his clothes that were seven sizes too big for him at the time. Gripping onto a box."

"What was in the box?" I breathe, my eyes burning as I imagine a younger Tug, scrawnier than he already is.

Killian's lip twitches and his face softens a little. "A mangy, three-legged cat."

I can't help a laugh, choked as it is, and I shake my head.

"So you brought them aboard," I realize. "You saved Tug."

Killian looks at me, guilt ridden. "That particular night . . . he saved me." Killian takes a long pull from the jug, downing one gulp and then another as if it might chase away the past. Then he gasps for breath, finally finished.

"They're his pa's clothes," I realize, recalling the way Tug's pants hang on him.

Killian stares into the darkness again. "Tug's never spoken about his life before. And I won't force him to. But I often wonder about it."

Four years without speaking of his past makes me sad, and yet, using my own suffering as a shield, I can imagine Tug isn't ready to let his barriers down just yet. "Perhaps he will tell you when the time is right."

Killian turns the jug around and tilts his head. "I'm assuming you believe in the Fates, little Skadi?"

I snort. "Depends on the day, I guess."

"And yet, you are marked with your goddess's namesake."

I fold my arms over my chest. "Skadi is not my namesake, at least not to anyone but you." I absently trace the runes running the length of my forearm. "I can barely recall what this name used to mean to me. Now, it serves only as a reminder that the Fates, if they have not abandoned me, are the worst monsters in the games the gods play."

"Hmm." Killian swishes the jug in his hand. "For once, we might agree on something."

We both seem surprised by that, then he takes another gulp.

"Shouldn't you be sober," I ask, clearing my throat, "in case another storm comes?"

"Why?" he quips. "Would you listen to me if I told you to do something this time?"

I don't gratify him with a reply, despite the presence of one at the tip of my tongue. "How is it," I start instead, unable to fathom the man before me, "that you can be drunk with nearly every waking breath, and yet, you are the most feared man in Norseland?"

"Ignorance is the cause of fear," he says simply. "Not me. And the longer Queen Sigrid keeps her people ignorant of the world around them, the more I'm able to use it to my advantage. Ignorance breeds ignorance. It's a spark, and I only need stoke it for it to catch flame."

I shake my head, suddenly vehement. "There are so many things wrong with what you just said."

"The fact remains, the queen and her warlords fear the scale tipping out of their favor, so they do little to question what the Reaper demands." He shrugs. "Mostly. Though, I admit it's all gotten a bit out of control—"

"A bit?" I snip. "Is that you acknowledging *a fraction* of the part you and your crew have played in the utter chaos that is Norseland now?"

"I am not responsible for the acts of other men," Killian clips out, but he's far too defensive to believe that entirely.

"No?" I fume. "If all you say is true, then people have been burning villages in Norseland for *years* in your name. By ignoring it—no, by *using* it to your advantage—you've all but slain innocent people with your own hands. You and Basher, you brush it all aside as if innocent people dying is a necessary evil. As if *my* family dying—my brother, my mother, my father, and now my sister—are not dead because of the fear so proudly spread about the Reaper."

Killian's entire body tenses and he springs to his feet. "You think I want this life?" he practically growls, and his final show of something other than indifference unnerves me. "I'm a pawn in this life, same as you." He drops his bottle against the deck and it shatters. Though I'm shocked to hear such resentment, it's hard to feel sorry for him.

Without another word, the drunk, infamous sea captain stalks away, another curse catching on the wind.

14
BRYNN

As the storm brews above, most of us are crowded below deck, huddled in groups, working on our new projects assigned by the crew. But it's all I can do to remain focused on mending nets while Phillip is in such bad shape.

His face is ashen, his eyes gleaming with fever when he manages to open them, and his lips are nearly blue. But it's the strain in his features that worries me most. It's getting worse, and pulling his shirt up to assess his wounds, I notice the discolored veins outstretching from beneath the bandage.

"How is he?" Bo whispers, crouching beside me. His green eyes are full of sorrow, and his voice is soft—he already knows the answer.

I shake my head in exhaustion. "Why is everyone dying, Bo?" I hate how weak I sound, but I can't help it. I don't understand why the gods would uproot these people and promise them a better future—giving them hope they've never dared to have before—only to be met with a fate such as this.

I don't realize I'm shaking until Bo places his big, warm

hands over mine, stroking my wrist with his thumb. "We'll do what we can for him," he promises.

Numbly, I nod, lost in the softness of his gaze. Over the days, a fondness has formed between us. A friendship—a real one that wasn't there before. And though I've sought comfort in his bed before, that's not what his presence offers me now. It's something far more intimate and terrifying. At the pinnacle of so much anger and fear, I realize how much I *want* his friendship. How desperate I am for it.

As his fingers lace reassuringly with mine, it's all I can do not to fall into him, just for a little while.

A throat clears, and Bo and I peer up into Killian's tumultuous gray eyes, shifting between us. "Boots reports you haven't finished all the nets." There is no doubt Killian is angry, but whether it's about our conversation last night or the nets, I can't be sure.

Bo rises to his feet. "I'm nearly finished. Brynn and I have been—"

"I don't need excuses," Killian says, glaring at him. "I need nets for fishing and ropes for rigging the sails that are battered from the last storm. Preferably before the next one arrives full force." His voice has a sharp edge that's unfounded, at least toward Bo, and I don't appreciate it.

I stand, though far less gracefully than Bo, as my healing arm hits the post. "Killian—"

"It's *Captain*," he commands. "And everyone has a job and contributes, or you don't deserve to be on this ship."

"A man is dying," I grit out.

"And so will the rest of us if we aren't prepared. Have you learned nothing since the last storm?" He stares at me, and his words cut so deep, my hands fist at my sides. This is more like the captain I'd imagined. A different Killian. One that isn't lost in a haze of indifference.

"Do your job," he orders, and verbal blow delivered, he stalks up the steps and disappears above deck.

Only when the passengers begin chattering again, do I realize they all heard our exchange, but I don't have it in me to care. "Gods save me, Bo," I grumble, meeting his gaze. "Because I don't know how I'm going to make it another two weeks on this ship with him."

15
KILLIAN

Gripping the edge of the window in my cabin, I watch the sea churn, a worrisome roiling blue that begins to swell as if Njord is warning me of the night to come. I knew we hadn't seen the last of Ægir. I'm not that lucky, and despite how blessed our journey has been so far, no good will come of staring at the impending storm.

My cabin door opens, and by the slow, familiar cadence of footsteps, I know it's Basher.

"Has Doc seen to it, then?" I ask, hating that the hot breath of death never lessens.

"As you asked." I can imagine Basher perfectly. Black eyebrow lifted as she crosses her arms over her chest, leaning against my desk as she stares at me. "I've never seen you so distracted, Kill. Even for you, this seems . . . excessive. Is this about Surg and his son?"

"Among other things," I say, which is true. I hate losing anyone on the ship, especially passengers we're all risking our lives to keep safe. Though I guarantee them nothing, it doesn't mean I don't pray to Njord and Skadi, who always feel the closest during each journey, for a safe voyage we can all drink to when it's over.

My head throbs from drinking too much rum last night, and it's putting me on edge. So are little Skadi's scathing words: *"You've all but slain innocent people with your own hands."*

"Killian?" Basher prompts, and as the clouds darken in the sky, I push myself away from the window.

"What of the sails?" I clip, striding to the rolled maps on my desk.

"The men are raising them now." I can feel Basher's eyes on me as I riffle through the scrolls in search of the charted isles we're about to pass.

"If we can outrun the storm," I tell her, "we stay to the west, as far away from the sandbanks as we can get." Unrolling the well-worn map, I stare down at the warren of isles that cluster in this part of the ocean, islands that were never on any map predating the Great Turning, before the world fell into darkness. Only a dozen of them have been mapped by my family through the generations, but in my gut, I know there are more; what knowledge we have of them is often in our favor, but what we have yet to learn can quickly become our curse.

"We don't deviate. We stay on course—"

"I know, Killian. We all do." Basher steps closer. "We've done this a few times, you know?"

I nod, bracing my hands on my desk. My body hums with unease. "I have a feeling the winds are going to change and take us in that direction, which is more off course than we can spare right now." I look at her. My instinct is always right, and she knows it. "If we aren't careful, it will send us right toward the sandbanks and we won't know it until it's too late."

"Agreed," Basher says, and I hate that it sounds like she's

placating me. "We stay west." She stares at me with a concern I've never seen before. "Kill, this isn't just about Surg or going home this time, is it?" I watch as Basher's concern shifts to understanding and her eyes widen. "It's about Brynn," she realizes aloud. "What is it about her that troubles you so much? Well, other than she doesn't like you very much, and you're used to *everyone* liking you," she teases. A small curve of a smile twitches Basher's lips. "Wait, do you think she's going to kill you? I thought we agreed she's just hotheaded and angry. It's entertaining, really—"

I almost laugh as I consider little Skadi killing me after my haunting past with the goddess herself. A goddess I believe has saved me more than once.

"I'm not worried she'll kill me," I confess, though it would be poetic. "She reminds me of someone, is all."

"Well, *whatever* it is about her, you'd better get it sorted. Because once we pass the isles, the storms will only worsen, and we need you to focus."

"I know that, Basher," I grind out, and when she braces her hands on her hips, I force myself to meet her gaze.

She cocks her head. "Do you?"

16
BRYNN

When I'm finally finished with the net Killian's crew has been waiting for and I've helped Bo finish his rope, I go back to Phillip's bedside to find Doc has taken all tinctures, gauze, and salves, leaving me nothing to clean his wounds with.

I squeeze my eyes shut, fingernails digging into my thighs as my hands ball into fists. Straightening, I walk back over to Bo. "Doc wouldn't have taken all the supplies she brought down for Phillip back for no reason, right?"

Bo shrugs. "Unless the captain told her to."

I grit my teeth. "That's what I thought. Is he punishing me?"

Bo's brow furrows. "For what?"

I wave his question away, realizing he wasn't there last night when I'd upset Killian and sent him stalking away. Having already come down here angry once today, it doesn't seem a far stretch to assume Killian might still be heated with me about that. But to doom an ailing man out of spite? I just *pray* he is not as horrible as that.

Glancing at a fitfully sleeping Phillip, I shake my head.

"I'm going up to see the captain," I tell Bo, and head straight for Killian's cabin.

The wind ravages my hair once I'm above deck, and I stalk through the crew securing the ship. The rain pelts my face, but cold as it is, I hardly notice as I head for Killian's cabin, my footsteps only faltering as the ship sways with the waves.

I knock on Killian's door, glaring through the window at him and Basher as they glance up from their conversation at his desk. Neither of them looks surprised to see me.

Killian frowns as I push the door open. "Why did you do it?" I ask. "Are you trying to teach me a lesson? To put me in my place?"

"Is that possible?" he mutters, and runs his hand over his face with a deep sigh.

My glare sharpens on him.

Killian nods for Basher to leave us.

Basher's expression is one of amusement, and her gaze skims quickly over me as she walks out the door, the wood protesting as it shuts behind her.

"I assume this is about Phillip," Killian says, his attention no longer on me but on the rolled map on his desk. A compass and paperweights are placed along the edges.

"Of course it is. You took away all the comfort he has left."

Killian leans over his desk, marking something on his map. "You can think me as heartless as you'd like, but there is a ship full of people, and we're just shy of two weeks left of the journey. We need to ration our provisions, should something happen."

"But he's dying—"

"Yes, he is." Killian's expression mimics callous, cold stone; he's so different from the man I talked to last night. "There is no hope for him, Brynn." My name is both surprising and sharp on his tongue. "I will not continue to waste what limited resources we have. Surely you see the sense in that."

I do, though I don't like it, and I grip the back of the chair in front of me tighter. "And that's the *only* reason?"

"What other reason would there be?" His question is measured and edged once more with something I can't quite discern.

"I thought—" I stop myself, realizing how idiotic and self-centered I sound.

Straightening, he crosses his arms over his chest and looks at me. "You thought what?"

I bite the inside of my cheek. "I upset you last night."

"So you thought I would punish you?" He stalks around his desk toward me. "Everything I do is for this ship and the safety of the people aboard it. It's not about you, no matter what your ego likes to think." He jabs a finger in the air at me, and the look in his eyes is scathing, a necessary reminder that he's not only drunken Captain Blackburn, he is more than that. He's powerful, indomitable, and uncomfortably imposing. Killian is the Reaper. "The sooner you grasp that, the easier this will be for all of us, because your ignorance and foolhardiness continues to put everyone aboard this ship in danger. Get that through your head."

My chest heaves as he looms in front of me, but I'm not sure if it's with shock and fury or humiliation.

"Do I make myself clear?" Killian's voice is low and filled with authority, something I only seem to grasp when he's thoroughly vexed with me. "I said, do—"

"Yes," I bite out.

His shoulders stiffen. The swirling ire in his eyes is as tumultuous as the sea itself, and as his jaw clenches and his chest heaves with mine, the air changes. It hums and shifts.

Killian takes a step back, his severity melting away a little.

"Your friend was given nightshade," he says, deflating before my eyes. "He is in no more pain. That is all I can offer him now."

That . . . gives me pause, and my shoulders slump a little. Killian did not leave Phillip to suffer in his final breaths, and part of me knows I shouldn't be surprised. Killian is many things, but he is not heartless. Tug, Basher, and the passengers huddled below deck are proof.

"You could have led with that," I tell him.

He rubs his brow with sudden exhaustion.

I'm not sure how long we stare at one another, a battle of wills and silent tit for tat, until finally, the ship rocks, sending his candlesticks sliding on his desk, and he blinks. "Now, go. Get below deck," he says, not unkindly. His eyes linger on my lips for the breadth of a moment. "The storm is worsening. You should not be up here—"

The horn sounds before Killian can finish, and I see the swell in the distance through the window, rising as if the sea is opening its mouth to swallow us again.

"Go!" he demands. "Secure yourself with the others, and don't come up for anything."

I nod and rush for the door, flinging it open with Killian hot on my heels.

The crew is shouting through the rain, and water sloshes onto the deck. They're only halfway finished switching the sails, but even I know by now it's too late for that.

The ocean roars as I race toward my side of the ship. I can hardly see a foot in front of me as the wind howls through my ears, tearing at my hair as rain pelts my face.

I hear a snap, shouts immediately following, and as the ship lurches forward, I lose my footing. I don't know what happens, but the force of a falling tree collides into me, my head yanks back, and the wind is knocked from my chest.

Insurmountable cold and pain follows, then wave after wave, the ocean swallows me deeper and deeper.

17
BRYNN

Frigid salt water sears over my flesh like steel blades as the dark depths consume me. My lungs burn with the need to expand. To breathe. Any attempt to reach the top escapes through my fingertips as I grasp for purchase in the biting cold. But I can't feel my fingers or my legs.

A vicious swell forces me deeper into darkness—further away from life on the surface and closer to death. I feel Ran, goddess of the sea, running her finger down my cheek as if she's welcoming me home.

With another violent tumble, my limbs flail, my head cracks against an unyielding surface, my flesh scrapes against jagged rock, and then the panic subsides.

The quietness descends.

The need to breathe feels less important as my fears, whatever they had been, float away like tiny bubbles to a safe place —a silent place.

The pain is forgotten; the terror is no more.

All I want to do is sleep.

. . .

. . .

. . .

Only vaguely do I feel something powerful and excruciatingly strong squeezing my fingers, too frozen to move.

Then my mind fades into a murky blackness.

18
BRYNN

Birds caw and clamor.
A rumble ebbs and echoes.
Grit press into my palms and cheek, but the world is no longer churning.

My face stings and my skin feels like stretched leather as I force myself to roll onto my back.

Everything aches, and I groan, blinking up into the impossibly bright gray that hangs above. I blink again, fingertips digging into the earth beneath me. Land—I'm on land. Then I remember . . .

Waves.
The biting cold.
The fear.
The darkness.

I jolt up as the storm crashes over me again—memories of the frigid, pummeling waves, of the surge and pull as I drowned. I was drowning.

Staring at my hands covered in black sand, I try and fail to make sense of it. Surely, I should be dead. I felt the kiss of Ran's welcome and her beckoning me to the bottom of the sea.

But . . . I peer around. *Here I am.*

There is no anchored ship. There is no one and nothing but me and the ocean stretching as far as the eye can see.

I was drowning and now I'm not. I am safe, I tell myself. *I'm alive.*

Wind whips around me in a sudden swirl, and I gasp, my eyes fluttering closed. Despite the cold in my bones, an indescribable warmth curls through me, and I lift my face to the wind. To Njord. To this sudden life, pumping through my veins.

Just as quickly as it comes, the wind tames to a slight breeze, and chills rake over my skin. My matted hair and the wet clothes plastered to my body become impossible to ignore as the dire realization that I have no idea where I am sinks in.

An island? A dangerous land that stretches between Norseland and New London? In a sudden panic, I glance around and behind me.

Rugged cliffs kiss the sky, green and glowing in the muted daylight. Water falls in narrow streams, turning this way and that down the mountains, like grains etched in wood. Birds nest on ridges and flap their wings before they take flight, soaring on the wind.

I've never seen anything like it here. So much life. So much beauty. But in such an otherworldly place, it's as equally terrifying, and my heart lodges in my throat.

Another wave tumbles against the shore, and the surf rises, water soaking my legs and the black sands beneath me. It's not rocky like at home, but malleable, and I dig into the ground I thought I'd never feel again.

Collecting myself, I lick my cracked lips and climb stiffly to my feet. Dried salt tightens my skin, and my body feels as battered as when I woke on the *Berkano*. Ivar's fists were nothing compared to the pounding of the ocean's violent waves, though. The suffocating weight of the sea tossing and pulling at me, filling my lungs until I couldn't breathe.

I shiver again, peering down at my tunic. It clings to the corset beneath my vest, and my leather pants are cold against my skin. It's only then I realize I don't have my cloak to warm me.

Staring at my blue fingernails, I remember the searing pain and vice-like grip on them as I was falling down—down—down. Then . . . nothing. I don't know when I washed ashore, but I've been wet for too long, and I must find shelter and warmth.

I peer down the shoreline. The beauty of the waterfalls cascading over the cliffs are lost on me this time because nature can be as brutal as it is beautiful, and without a fire, I might not survive a day in this place.

My nerves fray with alarm as I try to convince myself being the sole person in a place like this can't be any harder than living in a snow-covered Norseland full of enemies. At least here, there is food nestled in the cliffs and fresh water falling from the mountains. Still, I've never been alone, and I can feel my growing unease rolling in with each crashing wave.

Unless I'm not alone at all. I have no idea what or who inhabits this place, and the cold tendrils of uncertainty weasel their way in once more.

Something in the water catches my attention, bobbing in the distance, and the gravity of my situation subsides, just a little. Ignoring the way my body aches with each jerk and movement, I hurry into the surf.

As the object washes closer, I reach for it, only to find it's a slat of wood, too soggy to burn. The sand sifts beneath my boots as I wrestle with the waves to pull it ashore, praying the wood will dry quickly so it will be of use later.

"Need some help with that?"

Shrieking, I spin around, and wince as my side hinges and

my lungs constrict. The wood falls back into the surf as I take in a bedraggled Killian striding toward me. He grabs the edge of what I can see now is part of a large crate, and lugs it ashore with little effort.

"You're here," I rasp, and realize my heart is beating with as much elation as it is with complete and utter shock.

"Unfortunately," he grumbles.

"But—" I remember something hitting me on the ship. Something falling, and I shake my head. "What happened?"

Killian pulls the wood farther inland so the rising tide doesn't take it out again.

"Why are you here?" I continue, my mind in chaos. "And—how the hell did I get thrown overboard?"

"One of the booms snapped," he says, wiping his hands on his clothes, a little dryer than mine.

"It did *what*?"

"I told you we needed new bracings. There was a reason all of those extra ropes were important." He pulls a piece of seagrass off my shoulder and tosses it aside. Sand glistens in his close-clipped beard, and if he has dark circles under blue, bloodshot eyes, I can only imagine what I must look like.

"Wait," I rasp as his words sink in. "Are you saying this is my fault? Because I didn't get some of the ropes completed fast enough?"

Killian finally looks at me, his gaze sharp and filled with annoyance. "It's a contributing factor."

"Had I known," I start, and almost immediately wave the words away. "This is unbelievable."

Killian grabs my hand and turns it over in his palm, shocking me once again. Somehow, he's warmer than I am. I don't know what he's staring at. My nails, blue from the cold, or is it the sand crusted to them? I yank my hand away.

His eyebrow arches and he looks at me. "I'll tell you what's unbelievable," he finally says. "You seem to be at the forefront of every mishap we've had since leaving Norseland."

I gape in disbelief. "You can't possibly blame all of this on me. How did you even get here? You weren't anywhere near me."

Killian averts his gaze, and for a moment I don't understand. "Wait—you saved me," I realize, and a strange warmth trickles over me. "*You*, who told me it's madness to help someone, that it's one of your only rules—"

"I know my own rules," he gripes, brushing past me. "And I already regret it."

I peer out at the ocean, dumbfounded. Grateful. Humbled because the man I've been so angry at could have let me drown, but he didn't. He risked his life to save mine.

"Thank—" When I look at Killian, he's walking inland toward a break between the cliffs.

I'm not sure where Killian is going, but he heads farther away from me with each determined stride, and it feels imperative that we stay together. Whether he expects me to follow, I don't know, but I do.

"Do you know where we are?" I ask, coming up behind him. "Is this an island?"

"Yes, one of many in the Isles of the Lost Winds," he says, so offhandedly, I'm not sure I should be comforted by his lack of concern or annoyed. "We'll sleep there tonight," he says as he continues past what looks like a shallow cave. But it sounds more like he's talking to himself. "Stay here," he mutters, pointing to it.

My eyes widen as I look inside. "Stay here? Why?" It's a rocky alcove providing just enough shelter to keep us directly out of the wind. "We need to find food and water—"

"What do you think I'm doing?" he calls over his shoulder, and I continue after him.

"Well, I'll help you," I say, but it's mostly under my breath because Killian is walking faster than I can keep up. My body is not happy with me, but until I know we have what we need to survive this place, I can't simply sit back and wait.

We pass between the two cliffs that open into a narrow valley. Tiny waterfalls carve their way down the rock faces on both sides, joining into a stream. It snakes its way through the canyon, easy enough to walk along as it flows out to sea. The cliffs, on the other hand, with their black, sharp stones, are as menacing as they are stunning.

My boots crunch through water-worn rock as I keep a steady pace behind him. "How do you know where to go?" I hate that I sound like a child tagging along, but I'm not about to let Killian, the only soul I know in this place, out of my sight.

"We need to get warm," he says over his shoulder.

"And you have a plan for this?" I confirm.

He takes a few more hurried steps. "Of course."

"Do you mind telling me what it is?"

"Start a fire."

Rolling my eyes, I move faster in spite of my body trembling with cold and stiffening up. I don't see any trees or shrubbery, but I say nothing and continue behind him in silence.

But as the minutes continue to pass, I can't keep quiet. "Killian, will you at least tell me where we are going?" I ask, walking around broken hunks of volcanic rock. We have an entire valley of them outside of Northhelm, and it's then I realize the black beaches and rugged cliffs are part of a volcano, which is terrifying in its own right.

Another waterfall cascades from above, misting my face as we pass, and my steps quicken once more.

"While you were sleeping," Killian starts, as if I was simply resting my eyes for a quick nap. "I explored the island a little. It's the one I thought it was, which means there's a stash of supplies in the side of that mountain." He points a hundred steps ahead.

"Wait," I say, stopping behind him. "You've been here before?"

"Isn't it obvious?" He peers around as if assessing the land anew. "It's been a while, though. We just have to stay alive until the ship finds us."

My chest swells with hope. "You think they will be able to?"

"Eventually. The question is how long it will take them to locate the right island. There are a dozen in this cluster." Killian isn't thrilled to be here. That much is obvious, and while I don't blame him in the slightest, I am immensely grateful he is. I'm patient and can wait. It's the uncertainty we'll ever be found part that worries me most.

"I think there are shrub fields over those cliffs," he finally offers. "We have to get warm and build a fire before the sun goes down, or we'll freeze to death." I swallow thickly, detecting the slight concern in his voice. His strides are quick, wide, and sure, which gives me a slight peace of mind, but still, I struggle to keep up with him. My toes are numb in my wet boots, and my body feels on fire.

Finally, Killian stops at a cliff that looks just like the rest, and peers up at a bush that grows out of the side of it. "It's here," he says to himself. "Just high enough the water won't reach it when it floods."

I glance wide-eyed ahead, imagining the ravine full of rushing water. It makes me feel sick to my stomach all over again. I don't want to think about so much water. Ever.

"Do you need help?" I ask, glancing up at the bush again. It's higher than I'm comfortable with, but if food and supplies are up there, I will do whatever he needs.

Killian hops over a large rock and begins to scale the cliff.

"Killian—"

"Stay there," he commands. A few pebbles fall as the side of the cliff crumbles a little.

I'm in no shape to climb, nor do I want him to regret saving me more than he already has, so I do as Killian says, squinting up at him instead.

Though his hand and foot placements seem sure, he does slip a few times, causing my breath to catch and my heart to stop. But Killian keeps climbing as if he's done it a dozen times before. When I think of the masts and rigging of the *Berkano* that reach high into the sky, I imagine he's used to heights.

A few minutes pass, and I settle into suspended apprehension as the wind picks up. It licks over me, and a bone-racking shiver quickly follows. It's one thing to be cold and moving around, but standing here, the daylight fading and the wind whipping through my hair is worrisome. I'm not sure I've ever been as cold as this. There may not be snow here, but it feels as if Skadi and Njord hover around, winter and wind dancing as one.

I know Killian can feel the bitter cold as much as I do, but he acts wholly unaffected as he moves with determination. A wash of gratitude nearly knocks me down; I don't want to be indebted to this man, but I am. His presence alone offers unexpected comfort.

I swallow the stirring emotions away, knowing neither of us would know what to do with them. So, I happily leave that conundrum for later.

"Watch yourself," Killian calls, and drops a large sack onto the ground. It thuds against the rocks, and I hurry over to it. "Can you lift it?"

Wrenching it up, I heave the sack over my shoulder in answer, and breathe through the pain lancing my rib with a grimace.

Killian grunts as his boots hit the ground, landing on his feet. His eyes level on me, waiting.

The sack is heavy, and my fingers are so cold, they barely work, but I nod, single-minded.

"Good. Head back to the beach. I'll be right behind you."

I frown.

"I need to dig up the other chest and you're slower than me." He points toward the beach. "Go." It's another command, and I don't have the energy to argue with him. Besides, though I hate to admit it, I know Killian is right, so I head back the way we came.

The sack is made of an old sail, and though it's hefty, its contents are malleable, like there might be clothes or a tent inside. I'd be perfectly content with either.

By the time I reach the alcove on the beach, I glance around the nook. It's an outcropping, protected by surrounding rocks and the overhanging cliff.

With a grunt, Killian stalks in behind me and sets a medium trunk, dusted in dirt, on the ground. His eyes meet mine before shifting down my body. "Take off your clothes," he says, and unties the sack I hauled in.

I know he's trying to help me, even if his delivery is lacking, so I begin to remove my damp clothes, my tunic coming off first.

As the sack unfurls, I see a few fur blankets, and a different type of chill pebbles my skin, this one in anticipation.

Killian tosses one of the blankets in my direction, and suddenly, I can't get out of my clothes fast enough. My boots come off next, then I wiggle out of my pants that cling to my legs. The corset, however, is a different feat entirely.

"I—" I pause, waiting for Killian to finish smashing the lock on the trunk open with a rock. "I need your help," I say. "Please."

Killian glances up. His eyes find my Skadi markings first, as if they're a beacon to him, one I don't quite understand yet, then he does a double-take, realizing I'm mostly naked. Standing, he wipes his dusty hands on his pants and motions for me to turn around.

Giddy with the promise of warmth, I do so without hesitation. But as I stand there, waiting, Killian doesn't move.

Pulling my hair over my shoulder and out of his way, I glance back at him. "What's—"

Killian stares at my back. "Who did this to you?" he says, so low it sounds like a growl, and his eyes follow the trail of burn marks that mar my body from my back down to my thighs. Lessons I've learned and prices I've paid for keeping Estrid and me alive.

"They're from a long time ago," I tell him. Though, depending on which scars he's referring to, that might not be true.

Another gust of wind shudders over us, and when I shiver this time, Killian unties the corset stays without another word. His fingertips are deft and gentle, but the instant he is done, he shoves a blanket at me and stomps back over to the trunk, riffling through everything more aggressively than necessary.

Knowing the mangled crew Killian runs with, I can't imagine my back is the worst he's ever seen. That it seems to anger him this much surprises me.

I let him be, though, and wrap the blanket around my shoulders, relieved by the instant warmth. "Oh my gods, I love you," I breathe, utterly content.

Killian's head snaps to me.

"The blanket," I explain, rolling my eyes. "Don't worry, I still loathe *you*."

He smiles to himself and hands me another blanket. "I'll be back," he says, nodding toward the back of the outcropping that looks deeper and more promising. "It's warmer over there. It should be dry, too. I'll be back soon to start a fire." Killian lugs the trunk deeper into the shelter, and I pull the sack along with me as I follow.

"What about you?" I ask as he nestles the chest between two rocks.

Killian takes a knife out of it and sheaths it in his belt, then a dinged-up canteen, and he slings the empty sack onto his back. "I'll gather firewood."

"But you're freezing—"

"And we'll be dead without warmth," he counters, and his bitter tone makes my hackles raise, as usual.

"There are plenty of furs here, Killian. Get warm first. Or at least change out of your wet—"

"I said I'm fine." His eyes lock on mine, but they shift away just as quickly before Killian stalks off, leaving me in a cocoon of warmth, alone.

19
KILLIAN

Having set foot on twelve of the islands, I mentally sort through the layouts I've charted over the years, evoking the details of this one. When I reach the top of the cliff and see shrubs and flower fields, I recall the island more clearly.

Purple lupin scatters the tundra-like landscape, their blossoms bending in the wind as it tunnels over the valley, relentless. And with the ocean spanning to the north and the mountains rising into the clouds to the southeast, I remember instantly: what this island boasts in size and resources, it lacks in accessible beaches, and it's submerged in near-constant cloud cover—both of which will make it more difficult for the *Berkano* to find us. The fewer beaches we have to watch while we wait for their approach is the only blessing.

I crouch, opening the old sail to fill with tinder and branches to burn.

With the sun setting and still so much to do before the temperature drops further, I move swiftly, hacking at the shrubs and tossing them into the sack. I can barely feel my hands, numb with cold. But I know that slowing down will only make it worse, so I move faster.

I hack at the brittle branches of a tealeaf willow, the closest to a tree there is on the island, and toss them into the sack. It would be faster if Brynn were helping me, but I don't need the added distraction of her presence; she's been the cause of too much already.

You're a foolish bastard, Killian. I'm not sure if it's my father's voice, my brother's, or if it's mine, chiding me for putting myself in this position. But the truth remains: I'm on an island because I jumped in to save her, when I would not have done that for anyone else.

Laughing, I run my fingers through my hair, willing the gods to divulge their grand plan for me. Brynn would wish me dead—she hates and distrusts me—and yet, the image of her has given me solace since I was eleven years old, and I wanted more time with her. I *want* to put these demons to rest, and somehow, she feels like the answer.

With a low, desperate groan, I shake my head and continue hacking shrubs into pieces.

Basher was right. I need to get my head on straight.

When the sack is full, and the sun is glowing crimson on the horizon, I follow a well-worn animal path down the side of the cliff to the bottom. I can barely feel my hands anymore and the cold is nearly unbearable, but I stand at the beach, staring at a flatter part of the cliff face.

Absently, I finger the red sulfur stone in my pocket I'd pulled from the trunk, kept for this very purpose. I must leave a mark for Basher to find us, but the question is, which one?

20

BRYNN

I don't know how long I wait for Killian to return, but I keep myself busy. After draping my damp clothes over some rocks, hoping they will dry by tomorrow, I lay a pelt out to sort the contents of the sack that he dumped into a heap.

Two more fur blankets for Killian to use, tied tightly with a tether.

Two bottles of alcohol, one wrapped in a pair of men's pants and one in an extra shirt.

And a pair of well-worn boots.

Setting the booze aside, I roll the clothes and tuck them away, not wanting to overstep by wearing what isn't mine.

The setting sun turns the sky from crimson to inky blue, and the wind worsens as night sets in. Wrapping myself tighter with the blankets to stay warm, I sort through the trunk Killian pulled from the cliff.

A mending kit—bandages and a canister of sticky salve that smells like hawthorn.

A coiled rope.

Another knife, smaller than the one Killian took with him.

A pistol and ammunition.

And flint to start a fire.

My unease lessens a little at the sight of that, as if the promise of warmth is somehow closer, and I make a round pit of stones in the sand for a fire when Killian returns. I'm glad we have sand to sleep on, instead of snow or the stone that lines the wall behind me.

Collecting the crumbled rocks strewn about our little shelter, I toss them aside, out from under my bare feet, and when I'm finished, I sit with nothing else to do but wait.

Without the fur blankets, I would certainly freeze by the end of the night. And that Killian is out there, wet in the wind and cold to the bone, makes it impossible to appreciate my own warmth, and I grumble at him for that.

Finally, rocks clack and crumble, and I hear Killian approaching before I see his outline in the night. I hurry over to help him lug the firewood inside.

"It's fine," he says, strain in his voice as he brushes past me. But I feel the wind on him, the cold wafting off his skin, and hear the tremble in his voice. Killian drops the sack full of the branches and wild grasses on the ground, and removes the full canteen from around his neck.

I take it more greedily than I mean to, pulling the plug and gulping one swig after another, reveling as the water coats my tongue and rushes down my parched throat.

Killian sets to making the fire in the stone circle, and I wave for him to move away. "I can do it," I say, crouching beside him. "Take off your wet clothes and get warm."

"I'm fine," he says, moving the fire starter out of my reach. But he's not fine, he's shaking.

"Killian," I command this time, reaching for his hands. They are as cold as ice, and my eyes widen with alarm. I clasp his fingers in mine to warm them. "I can do it," I say more gently. "You should get warm—"

"You're wasting time," he grits out, yanking his fingers from mine, and I nearly fall backward.

"What the hell is wrong with you?"

"Enough," he growls, jolting to his feet.

I jolt to mine as well. "What's your problem, Killian?" It's a desperate whisper when all I want to do is scream.

I can barely see his eyes in the darkness, but I can feel them boring into me. "You." His resentment, borne from something I am oblivious to, rakes over me, and whatever gratitude and concern I have for him hardens to stone.

"Then why the *fuck* did you jump into the water after me?" My chest heaves against his, and I want to smack the shit out of him. But instead, I take a step back. "Do you want to freeze to death? Because you're being foolish. Whatever you think of me, I *am* capable of making a damn fire. I've lived in the snow my entire life. Or do you think me a complete idiot?" When he doesn't respond, I continue. "Take off your fucking clothes, Killian, and wrap this around you," I demand. I toss a blanket at his face.

He growls, but I ignore it.

"And stop treating me like a wilting flower and a burden, because I am neither."

I don't know if it's my tone, my words, or something else entirely, but Killian huffs with what sounds like a laugh.

I focus on the fire, striking the steel over the tinder and the sticks piled on top of it.

Killian tugs off his boots, and I strike a few more times, until finally, the flame catches, and I lean forward to blow the embers hotter. Through a veil of the building blaze, I watch as Killian reaches behind his head and pulls his damp shirt off. His pants come off next, landing with a soggy thud on the ground.

As the flames burn brighter, I see every inch of Killian's well-honed, tattooed body—from flexing thighs to corded stomach—as he bends down to collect the blanket from the ground.

Before he can catch me ogling him, I lean down and breathe more life into the flames, reveling in their heat against my face.

Killian is a jackass, I tell myself, refusing to feel anything other than annoyance toward him.

He's a drunk. An arrogant—

"What's wrong?" he asks, a lilt of concern in his voice.

My eyes pop open. "What?"

"How bad is the pain? You're grimacing."

An arrogant ass who's only nice when he wants to be. I finish the thought and wave his concern away. Straightening, I tell myself the flush on my cheeks is from the fire, not his observing gaze. "I'm fine," I say, and clasp the blanket tighter around my shoulders.

Killian crouches on the other side of the fire as I busy myself, putting more fuel on it. The blanket covers all but part of his tattooed shoulder as he lifts his hand to the flames.

Something is wrong with me, because I study his scruffy face and pensive expression for far too long before I look away again, and my blood stirs, warming me from the inside out.

Suddenly, Basher's face flares to mind, and I can't help but imagine he would prefer to be stuck on foreign shores with her.

I clear my throat. "Assuming that was fresh water falling over the cliff," I start, needing to fill the silence. "We might be able to find fish."

"There aren't any in this estuary," Killian says with certainty. "But there's crab, and while you're resting tomorrow, I'll set fox traps."

I glare at him, and Killian must feel my stare because his eyes meet mine.

"You were nearly dead a week ago," he reminds me. "And

based on that dried blood on your neck and the new bruises on your body, you took a good beating in that storm. It's not up for debate." His captain voice is as annoying as it is commanding, but he's not the captain or the Reaper right now. He's just . . . Killian.

"Brynn."

My eyes dart immediately to him. He rarely uses my name.

He folds his arms over his knees, his flickering blue gaze fixed on me. "Whatever you're thinking, don't. We don't know how long we have to wait for the *Berkano* to find us. We can't take any unnecessary risks. All right?"

I swallow. "All right," I breathe, reluctant. He *is* right. Our resources here are too finite to risk my getting hurt more, but the same could go for him.

"It's agreed, then." He seems momentarily pleased, and I turn back to the fire. The tightness in my neck has worsened, and I reach back to feel a laceration thick with dried blood, then the lump on the back of my head.

"Will you tell me how bad it is?" I ask, meeting Killian's gaze again. I can only hope it turns into nothing more than a swollen cut and the pounding headache I've had since waking.

He nods, and I rise to my feet, walking around the fire to sit beside him. We sit shoulder to shoulder, both of us wrapped in blankets as he lifts my knotted hair away to assess the wound. His hands are warmer now, and his fingertips brush feather-soft against my neck, making my eyes flutter closed.

"It's red," he says quietly. "Probably from the salt, but it doesn't look deep." He lets my hair fall around my shoulders again. "How is your knife wound?"

I run my hand over my bare skin, shielded by the blanket, and prod the cut just a little. "Tender," I admit. "But it hasn't reopened."

"And your ribs?"

My brow furrows. "How did you know about my rib?"

"It's the only reason Basher keeps a corset, I can assure you." There's a softness in his voice when he says her name, and after hearing such affection when he spoke of Tug, it's easier to see Killian and his crew as a family.

"You two are together," I say, trying to recall if I'd seen Basher and Tug interacting, and if she was very motherly. I can barely picture Basher being nurturing, though, and the thought flits away.

Killian's brow twitches slightly, and he looks into the fire. "No," he says, holding his hands to the flames once more.

I frown at him. Killian doesn't seem certain, or perhaps he wishes they were. Either way, I leave it alone, and reach for another blanket to cover us. An added layer of warmth I know we'll need later tonight.

"So," I start, welcoming a change in the subject. "What makes you think your crew will find us?" I rest my chin on my knees and stare into the flames, allowing myself to breathe with relief for the first time since I woke on the beach.

"Because I know them," he says simply.

"I can't imagine what it would be like to have so many people loyal to you," I muse. "A brotherhood of sorts you can always count on." I smile to myself. "I bet you have never felt alone because of it."

"People with fulfilled lives don't keep to the sea," Killian says in an unguarded moment, and I study the way his mouth sets, his thoughts deepening. "We are all searching for something—peace, perhaps. The restlessness is what we all share, and for many, like Basher, there is no home or reason to do anything else."

I watch the firelight dancing in Killian's eyes, blues and grays and a little gold flickering in them as he loses himself. He's gone for several heartbeats. Drawn out moments that take him somewhere far away from this beach.

When he blinks himself back to present, exhaustion

instantly settles into his features. But it's me Killian looks at. "You should sleep," he says, his eyes scanning my face. "Stay close to the fire to keep warm. I'll keep it going."

"Killian, you need sleep too—"

The plea in his eyes gives me pause, and I do as he says. Whatever haunts him has followed him off the ship, and I am too tired to argue.

"Fine," I breathe, and spread the last blanket on the ground beside the fire. The sand is surprisingly hard against my aching body, but at least I'm no longer swaying with the rhythm of the sea.

I watch Killian's outline against the dancing flames until my eyes are too heavy to keep open.

Remotely, I feel the weight of another blanket on me, and reveling in the warmth, I drift to sleep.

21

BRYNN

At first, I feel the heat of him behind me. Then I feel trembling and shaking. It's only when I peel my eyes open I realize the fire embers are low, the alcove is cold, and at some point, Killian came to sleep beside me. And he isn't the one shaking with cold, it's me. Instead, Killian is dreaming.

A low sound rumbles through him, followed by a whimper.

Peering back, I watch his form in the darkness and hold my breath. When Killian moans this time, I consider waking him but hesitate. I don't know why. Maybe because I would not want to know if Killian had listened to me, troubled in my sleep, the way I am listening to him. Or perhaps a sliver of me worries if Killian wakes, he will move or leave the cave, and I am not ready for that either.

Instead, I unfurl myself, leaving him covered in the extra furs as I wrap mine tighter around me and tend to the dying fire. I poke and prod at it, bringing it back to life, all the while wondering what Killian dreams about.

It doesn't sound terrifying, not like a nightmare. But then there's a hitch in his breathing, and he jolts himself awake.

Killian sighs behind me, and though I can feel his gaze, he says nothing.

"I grew cold," I tell him, my voice raspy from sleep. A gust of wind whistles through the alcove to punctuate the frigid temperature.

"There's another place we might try tomorrow," he rasps. Killian reaches for my shirt, draped on the nearby stones. "Someplace dryer," he adds as he puts it back, and I assume our clothes are still damp despite the fire. "Only, we won't be able to see the beach."

He doesn't seem to like the idea of that, and I don't blame him, but I leave that conversation for later.

For now, I let the heat of the flames press against my face, and warm chills trickle over me. "I've been cold all of my life," I think aloud. "Living in the snow—it comes with the territory. And yet, the dampness here is so different from the sharpness of constant winter. I'm not sure which is worse."

"You will have to get used to it," Killian says, rubbing his hands over his face. "New London is a soggy, misty place. Perhaps not as cold as this, but it can be just as unpleasant."

I could shove the questions that burn to be asked away like all the others, but it's just Killian and me on this island, with far too many unknowns piling up to let them all go unanswered. "If you've been dreading New London," I say, "why are you returning?"

Killian looks at me, firelight making his stormy eyes gleam. "Who says I'm dreading it?"

Scoffing, I tilt my head and stare at him.

The slightest hint of amusement tugs at his lips. "Because it is my duty to my family to return," he says, his brow furrowing slightly.

"Your family?" I nearly splutter as I realize I'd never considered he was taking us to his actual home.

He lies back, peering at the low rock hanging above him.

"So, your family keeps the woefuls—"

"Workers," he clips.

"*Workers,*" I amend, rolling my eyes. "You aren't selling them—or, us, I guess—to someone else."

"I told you, you would be protected. What did you think I meant?"

I shrug, my head shaking. "I've never been shipped off to be a worker for someone. I have no idea what to expect."

"You would if you weren't so busy being too angry at the world to listen—"

"Angry? Of course I'm *angry,*" I practically seethe. "You wanted to cloak Norseland in fear of the Reaper," I say with a heaving chest. "It worked, Killian. That fear, along with other atrocities in your name, have taken my *entire* family. So, forgive me if I'm *angry.*"

When Killian glances at me this time, he has the decency to look shamefaced.

"Is that what haunts you?" I ask.

"Nothing haunts me—"

"Ugh. No more games." It's an angry plea. An exasperated wish. "When you're not drunk, you're brooding and just as unpleasant as I am."

"Well, you aren't the most pleasurable woman to be around," he says curtly.

I huff, shaking my head again. "I suppose you're right," I whisper, too tired for bickering tonight, and pick at a curling piece of hide on the blanket. "I did see you at the Iron Horse, quite enjoying yourself. I haven't seen you laugh and smile like that since I've been on the ship." As the flames crackle and catch in the wind, my thoughts darken. And the longer the silence stretches between us, the more I think of Estrid.

"I am taking you to my brother," Killian offers, his voice somber in the quiet.

The heaviness in his tone makes my heartbeat falter a little with alarm, and resting my cheek on my knee, I look at him. I think his profile might as well be carved of stone until he blinks.

"You will work on his estate, in the forges and in the fields, like all the people from Norseland who came before you—slaves in the eyes of New London's council, yes—but you will receive protection in exchange. You will not be cold or hungry. My brother will not mistreat you." He's quiet a moment, and when I glance at him, he's staring at me. "You will not have to worry about being assaulted in the streets," he murmurs.

"Only if I go to your family's estate," I add, because Killian warned me how dangerous New London is, especially for women.

He nods. "The Blackburns instill as much fear in New London as the Reaper's reputation in Norseland, but the government will do all they can to ensure *they* remain the absolute power. Without our estate, we are nothing there. That's why it's imperative that we continue to produce, to provide what the Council requires so that my grandfather's life's work remains as he intended. The estate keeps the people we bring into the country safe from the Council of Four." He looks at me, eyes fierce. "Briarwood is a refuge, no matter what you think. And living on the estate affords you a life you won't find anywhere else."

I don't argue with him because in truth, I am curious. And life in Briarwood sounds easier than any life I've had in Northhelm since my parents' death. And yet . . .

I look away from Killian, the thought of being beholden to someone else making my insides knot. Especially a family who took mine from me in the twisted games of the Fates. Would I still have my parents if not for Killian's charade? Would my brother and parents—would Estrid—still be alive if it weren't for the sway the Reaper holds, and the fear his power and reputation spreads like plagues and shadows?

"Why Norseland?" I whisper, feeling a tightness in my chest. I stare into the fire flames, fighting the urge to reach out and touch them, to feel the physical burn instead of what writhes in my heart. "Of all the places you've gone, why is it Norseland the Reaper haunts?"

I don't think Killian hears me over the wind, until finally, he answers. "Because it is where my family is from."

My gaze shoots to Killian, only to find him staring at what little he can see of my arm tattoos. "Despite what you think you know, long before the Reaper, men burned villages in the name of Queen Sigrid. Some queens have been worse than others, but her legacy remains the same—rule with brutality and fear. My grandfather fled Norseland after his village was attacked by the queen's warriors, and he shipwrecked on New London's shores."

"He made it across the North Sea?"

"Yes. He was the first in my family to do so."

I recall the map painted on the wall in his navigation room. "He found a way across, which is why you can sail it while so many others cannot."

Killian nearly scoffs. "Others are imbeciles who reference maps from before the Great Turning. It's not only lands that have changed, but much of the sea as well. My grandfather charted these waters before he found himself in the Black Country, and the seafarers of my family have continued to chart it every voyage since."

It takes me a moment to comprehend what Killian is saying. "The legend of the Reaper."

He meets my gaze.

"So, your grandfather came back—*you* keep coming back—for the woeful thralls in Northhelm, to take them to Briarwood." I shake my head. "For *generations*?" I can't help the acid in my tone.

"Yes," he says defensively. "Exactly."

How many workers could his family possibly need? I keep telling myself it could very well be a far better life in Briarwood than in Northhelm, and yet, a man who sails the expanse of the ocean, who knows every nook and cranny no one else does, offers no other alternative than to work for his family.

"It is better than any other life they might have here or in New London," he says, reading my mind. "How is it you still cannot see that?"

His words are like a buzzing wasp in my ear. Grating. Dangerous. "How is it that you cannot see that is no option? Not really."

Killian sits up, his furs falling from around his shoulders as he points toward the sea. "Every single person on that ship had an option, Brynn. They had a choice. Why do you think a few from Von's forge did not join the others? That was *their* choice."

"No—"

"Yes," he bites out.

"No, I mean, that's not what I was referring to."

He drops his arm into his lap, huffing with exasperation. "Then what?" he grinds out. "Please explain. Because no matter my intentions, you take offense to my every word."

I chew the inside of my cheek. I've done a terrible job expressing myself to Killian—or too well of a job, maybe—and it has gotten me nowhere.

"I understand what you are saying," I start, my voice as calm as I can manage as I choose my words carefully. Though I would love nothing better than to pull at my hair, I clear my throat. "I understand that you are offering them a fuller life than they'd have in Northhelm, or any other city in Norseland. But . . ." I bite my cheek, hesitating. "Why must the choice be indentured servitude to you or to someone else at all? You make it sound like there are only two options—what you offer, and the life we already come from."

"That's the reality, whether you like it or not."

"Says the man who sails around the world, drinking his way between ports." I grip the furs between my fingers, wishing momentarily the *Berkano* never returns so that I don't have to accept the fate I woke up to aboard it. "Can you honestly tell me there is no better place, no better option any of us have, than going to your family's estate to be a slave, even if we are only slaves on paper? You've been everywhere, Killian. You can take us to any other part of the world to build our own homes and farm our own lands. It doesn't have to be for *your* family in New London. Does it?"

Killian stares daggers at me, but I know he sees my point, so I relent. His family *needs* us, and while it's a desirable outcome for people like me to have shelter and protection, the truth remains: he could offer us a different path, if he chose to.

"You can judge me all you want, because I know you blame me for every horrible thing that's ever happened to you," he says coolly. There's not so much anger in his voice as there is detachment. "But your friend Bo is on that ship because he wanted an inkling of something better, which is what my grandfather intended—a mutually beneficial situation for everyone. So, that's what I do. Sail back and forth, just like Norik and my father did before me." He lies back down, arms crossed under his head.

As defensive as Killian is, there is discontent in his heart, and I want to know why. I *want* to understand him.

"I'm done talking about this," he clips out, reading my thoughts again. "You can do whatever you want when the *Berkano* returns—stay here, alone with your freedom, if you wish it so badly—but I have a duty to my family, and I will not let you taint the legacy of good they have done simply because you choose suffering out of stubbornness and principle."

Or perhaps I crave the ability to choose at all, since I've never gotten to before. Even in Northhelm, every choice was borne of desperation, just as Bo's choice to come aboard the *Berkano* was made out of survival. It's still a choice, one I see clearly, but if given the option of this wild place with no restraints to toil in, or Killian's estate in New London, which would each of us choose?

I prod the fire's embers. They break apart, floating into the air—sparks in the glowing darkness. We are hidden here, and not just from the brunt of the elements.

My head snaps up. "Killian—"

"No more talk," he grumbles, but I ignore him.

"What if the *Berkano* comes and doesn't know we're here? They can't see us."

He huffs out a breath, his back to me. "The red stones," he says quietly, and my eyes dart to the drawstring bag peeking out of the open trunk. "I drew on the cliffside before returning. My crew will be able to see it in the daylight."

"A signal fire would be too difficult to keep burning through the night," I realize. "But what about the smoke during the day? They will find us more quickly if we build a fire—"

"As will others," Killian says, shaking his head. "No fires or smoke."

My hand grips my prodding stick tighter. "You said no one sails these seas. None that survive, anyway."

"Not typically, no. But men are men, and there are many corners of the world that know no better. And it would be ignorant to think we are the only ones capable of surviving the isles' storms, even if Norseland rarely attempts it." Killian sounds too grave to be merely speculating.

"Who else have you seen in these waters?" I whisper, uncertain I want to know the answer. If the Reaper and his men fear them, I would be foolish not to as well.

"Real slave traders and true pirates." He peers over his shoulder at me. "My crew knows I will not build a fire. Basher will look for the red markings. Even if it takes longer to find us."

Knowing I must trust Killian and his judgement, I nod, but that he would sound so grave about other men unnerves me. "If slave traders or pirates came," I say, unable to ignore the thought, "wouldn't they fear you—the infamous Reaper? Surely they've all heard of you."

"Perhaps. But who am I, alone on an island with only a woman at my side?" He meets my alarm with a cocky grin, lightening the mood a little. "That's how they would see it, anyway. They don't know how scrappy you are, little Skadi."

His ease tampers my alarm only slightly, and I wrap my blanket tighter around me to stave off the sudden chill. I'm not certain it's entirely from the cold, but I shiver all the shame.

"Come." Killian rolls over, facing me. "Try to get some sleep. We need rest and warmth."

Whatever tension I felt between us earlier is dissolved, for now, and Killian's protective tone has me scooting back over to him.

Wrapped in the extra furs, we fall into a steady rhythm of breaths and heartbeats. And with the heat of the fire against my face, and Killian at my back, I melt into his warmth. *It's inconvenient to find comfort in my enemy*, I think. But after today, it doesn't feel right to call him that.

It's the last thought I remember before I fall asleep.

22

BRYNN

I wake many times throughout the night, and when I finally give up trying to sleep, the sky is barely an inky gray. Killian snores softly at my side, wrapped in his cocoon of furs and blankets, dead to the world.

Despite my exhaustion, I'm still too unsettled to sleep. Because of Killian. Because of where we are and what my life has become. And I can't seem to escape the sensation I'm still moving at times, undulating with the swell of waves on the ship I'd finally grown accustomed to.

My stomach knots with unease, but it rumbles with hunger too, and I decide to find sustenance. Locating a food source will give me temporary peace of mind until Killian can set his traps later.

After stoking the fire once more, I dress in my mostly dry clothes and set off to explore. My body hurts; there's no escaping it. But lying still is worse than walking, so I embrace the tug and strain of my healing muscles and battered body as I make my way into the morning, the empty canteen slung around me to fill.

The sea practically roars as I step out into the gray morning, the waves crashing against the rugged shoreline. White-winged gliders caw as they sail in and out of the dense fog that shrouds the island.

I walk the coastline, scanning it for anything promising that might've drifted in overnight, but it's all jagged rocks and sandbanks. The wood Killian and I pulled ashore yesterday is still out of the water's reach, and bits of seaweed are balled up all over the sand. Knowing most seaweed is edible, I make a note to come back to it after I've explored a little more.

When I'm far enough away, so much so that the alcove is almost out of sight, I see the red X on the towering rock face. The facade is less rugged here, the best place for Killian to leave his mark. It must have taken him an hour to trace the giant X over and over until it was so deeply red and bright, the *Berkano* might see it.

Peering over my shoulder, out at sea, I imagine his ship, somewhere close on the horizon, searching for us. They will never see the X in all of this mist, no matter how garish it is.

Refusing to think too much about it, I continue down the beach. I've never seen one like it before. The black sands are otherworldly. The green and yellows sprouting from the cliff faces are breathtaking. The salt, however, is hard to ignore, crusted on my clothes and drying out my skin. I taste it when I lick my lips and feel it in every crevice of my body.

I head for one of the waterfalls to wash my face and fill the canteen, scoping out a potential path up the mountainside as I go. Killian might know about this island, but I have yet to see much of it, and sight unseen, it makes me anxious.

When I finally reach the waterfall, the spray is icy against my face, but I embrace the feel of it against my skin and the promise it brings. It spills over the cliff in a steady stream, breaking and splashing against crumbled rocks at the base, before it flows out to sea. It's inviting and my body hums with eagerness.

The canteen falls from my fingers to the ground, and I crouch to sample the water. It's not briny, but perfectly fresh, and I can't slurp it down fast enough. It awakens my insides, rejuvenating me in a way I hadn't anticipated, and when I've had enough, I uncap the canteen, filling it to the brim.

A rock crab skitters into a little crevice, and I grin wickedly. "You can hide," I tell it. "But I will find you." And I'm content, having just found us some breakfast.

The spray of the fresh water misting in the air taunts me, however. Being ice cold against my tongue, I know what it would feel like against my skin. Yet the promise to wash the sand and salt away is almost too tempting to ignore.

Decided, I cap the canteen and set it aside, peeling off my clothes before I can change my mind. It's not as if I had someone to heat my bathwater in Northhelm. Cold water is all I've ever known, and I won't shy away from it now.

Tossing all of my clothes to the side, minus the corset I wasn't able to put on, my body tenses, already braced as I hold my breath to step under the glacial spray.

"If you wanted to bathe," Killian says, and I spin around with a shriek. "You could've told me." I hate his grin as he eyes me up and down.

"Curse you, Killian! Stop sneaking up on me like that."

He reaches down for my shirt and holds it out to me. "Come. I will take you someplace much better than this."

Unwrapping my arms from around me, I snatch it from him, glaring.

"Don't be cross with me," he says with a chuckle. "You were the one too busy muttering to yourself to hear me approaching." Killian's smirk grows wider.

I grumble at him, shivering as I slip back into my clothes. "I wanted to get the salt off me. And find breakfast, which I did," I tell him, nodding toward the black-legged crabs dispersing as my shadow descends over them. Feet damp from the spray, I struggle to tug on my boots.

Killian reaches for me, gripping my arm as I falter.

Our gazes meet, his grin widens, and I glower at him until I'm finally finished.

"Well, which is it?" he says. "Do you want breakfast, or to be clean?"

"Bathe," I say quickly, because suddenly I salivate for it. "I want to bathe."

He chuckles. "You won't be disappointed."

23
BRYNN

I follow Killian along an animal path in the rocks that gives way to wild grass and low dunes. A narrow river runs between them, feeding into the falls behind us.

"Where does all the water come from?" I ask, unable to take my eyes from the alien landscape. Bursts of steam rise in the distance with no trees to impede the view. Even the mountains tucked into the lifting mist seem nothing more than primordial remains, reaching toward the heavens with their rocky peaks.

"Those mountains," Killian says over his shoulder. "These islands see rain more than they see the sun. It's why we call them the Isles of the Lost Winds. It's as if all the storms gather here, blotting out the daylight. So when the skies clear, everything bursts and blooms. Water is one thing you never need fear you'll run short of."

I can imagine it, though I note the fog is thinning, and daylight, muted as it is, peeks through. The dewy groundcover sparkles, as does the soil I crouch down to sift between my fingers. "It's so strange," I quietly muse. "Like black rocks crushed to sand."

Killian's shadow spreads over the earth, and I glance up to find him looming over me. His brown, sun-kissed hair is mussed and curling behind his ears. He has an open expression I find comfort in. Not like the mask he wears as the captain. And not the cocky drunk always grinning. The face staring down at me now is a Killian I haven't seen yet.

"It's ash from the volcano," he explains. "This whole place is made of it, I imagine. One monstrous volcano that has formed all of this isle—or, so we think. There are two larger than this one, but some are the size of my ship."

I smile, uncertain why that amuses me, but it does. "They just sprang to life then," I realize, eyeing a shrub of round, purple berries. "Some of the islands must be barren compared to this." Stomach rumbling, I kneel beside the berry bush, staring at the shape and color of its fruit before I begin picking.

Killian watches me battle its thistles. "You pick them as if you know those berries aren't poisonous," he says, finally crouching beside me. His warmth and male scent are impossible to ignore, so I move to the bush next to it, picking until my hands are full.

"Well, are they?" I transfer some of the berries into his hands.

"Are they what?"

"Poisonous?"

Killian eyes me carefully. "No," he says with a smirk, and plops one into his mouth. "They are crowberries. But it's careless to assume they aren't, nonetheless."

This time, I'm the one who smirks. "Perhaps. But darker berries are generally safe, are they not? It's the red and white ones we should be wary of."

His expression narrows with mischief. "And who told you that?"

I shrug. "Experience."

Killian's quiet as I plop a berry into my mouth.

"You're staring," I tell him.

"I know."

"Well, stop—"

"How many times have you gone hungry?"

My hand stills, and I glance at him. "Why do you ask?"

This time, Killian shrugs.

I chew the inside of my cheek. "Enough times to know I never wish it to happen again." I pick a few more berries, ignoring his gaze.

"Is that why you tied yourself to a man like Von Magnusson?"

I snort. "Why wouldn't I?"

"Because his vile temper was known throughout the city."

"Yes, well, show me a man with even a sliver of authority in Northhelm who isn't a brute—"

"But you chose the most notorious of them all. That's why we picked his workers to begin with." Killian plops another berry into his mouth. "You don't strike me as someone who would easily accept anyone's authority, let alone someone as cruel as him."

"Hence some of my scars," I joke, but in truth, I know it isn't funny, and Killian's frown only confirms it. "Look," I say, sucking the blood from a thorn prick on my finger. "When each day is spent simply trying to exist, there are scant options if you want a roof over your head and a warm place to sleep. My sister and I—" Emotions lodge in my throat, and I have to clear them away. "She was special to him. It ensured our food, shelter, and protection. Besides, I think you understand the way Northhelm works enough to grasp the danger we'd have been in had she resisted him."

"If he offered you both protection, why did Basher find you in the alleyway, at another man's mercy?" His question prods at me, poking at truths I don't want to think about.

"What's it matter?" I bite out, and rise to my feet. "It's over and done. They're all dead." I hate the wobble in my throat, but there's no holding it back. "We wouldn't have even been out there that night if we hadn't been running from the Reaper." I've told Killian this before, but I see the regret in his eyes this time, glassy and glaring. "I don't say it to be cruel, but it's the truth. And if talk of your life is off-limits now, so is my past. I don't want to think about it."

"Fair enough," he says after a moment, and though I've all but lost my appetite, I don't like the abrupt silence in place of his questions either.

I pop a berry into my mouth, Killian's eyes tracking the movement. The berries are tart but not unpleasant, and his gaze lingers on me as our uncomfortable silence stretches. A blush threatens my cheeks, but I arch an indignant brow instead. He's making me squirm on purpose. "Well? Say something if you're going to."

Another smirk lifts his cheek, and Killian tosses a few berries into his mouth. "Come on then," he says, and continues toward the mountains.

As the ground slopes and we hike downhill, I feel slightly weak and lightheaded but chalk it up to utter exhaustion. The hunger is gone, sated by what few berries I've had and the knots permanently settled inside me.

Killian tosses his last handful of berries into his mouth as we pass openings in the earth that give off the bouts of the steam I'd seen in the distance. They smell unpleasant, but the air warms instantly around us.

"Stay clear of them," Killian warns. "I might be impulsive, but if you fall into one of *those,* even I won't save you."

I roll my eyes and trail behind him. "Where are you taking me, exactly?" We give the steam holes a greater berth, though I don't take my eyes off them. They're fascinating, really. And I can't help but wonder how deep the holes go.

"Be patient," Killian says over his shoulder. "You'll see."

The grassy dunes get farther behind us as we reach the rockier foothills of a mountain, and each of Killian's footsteps become more certain. "It should be just down here."

"Tell me," I hedge, "How many times have you been to this island? Because you seem to know it very well."

"I have a knack for remembering things."

"Right, well, it seems you couldn't have planned us washing ashore here any better, what with you having a stash of goods in the cliffs, and all."

"Yes, well, I make it my mission to be good at just about everything."

My hand flies to my chest in mock surprise. "Wow. Such modesty."

Killian chuckles, but after a few steps, he gives me a strange, sideways look. "When you look for trouble, you have to endure the consequences." He says it with such gravity that it sounds more like a confession or warning, which only piques my interest.

"Trouble?" I eye him up and down this time. At first, I think it's a jibe toward me, but I hesitate. "Have you shipwrecked here before, Captain?"

He shakes his head. "But I did run away once, back home. I was lost in the woods for days."

"It sounds like an adventure," I tease, but Killian is too quiet to have found any humor in it.

"It taught me a lot," he finally says. "And I've had to live with the consequences ever since." My gaze shifts between him and the uneven rocks we descend.

What consequences? I desperately want to ask him, when finally, he stops at the mouth of a cave and forces a smile. "Here we are."

24
BRYNN

"Just down in here," Killian says, nudging me along. "Careful on the rocks."

We follow the path illuminated by daylight as it filters in through the fissures in the side of the mountain. When I see the underwater pool glowing back at me, I grip his arm. "Good gods," I breathe, gaping at the blue lagoon etched in stone. The faintest bit of steam rises and dances just above the surface like rainbow jewels glittering in the sunrise. The warmth, the beauty—I feel lightheaded all over again, and Killian peers back at me with a grin.

"It's a bit of a walk, but worth it, huh?"

"Um, yeah," I splutter.

I barely take my eyes off the glowing pool as I follow. "This is mesmerizing, Killian." It's only a whisper, barely heard over the draft whirling by.

A real smile quirks his lips, and fleetingly, I realize I've seen that grin more in the past few hours than in all the days I've known him combined. I don't know what's changed since last night, but I welcome Killian's smiles. I'm even beginning to look forward to them.

"Well?" he says when I stop beside him. "Are you getting in?"

Even if the warmth floats in the air, promising utter ecstasy, I can't help the ripple of unease that gives me pause. "Is it deep?" I lean forward to peer inside. The rocks are shadowed at the bottom, obscuring its depth.

"Yes, it's deep." His voice is soft and closer than I expect. "But there are plenty of ledges to sit on. You don't have to dive to the bottom." I know it's silly that I should be leery of a small pool of water after having been tossed ashore by the ocean, but I can't help the way my palms sweat at the thought.

Killian brought me ashore, though. And it's only then I stop to think how difficult that had to have been for him.

"Um." I turn to face him.

Killian tears his gaze from the water. His eyes glow like the cave pool, and he cocks his head, his smile waning a little. "What?" A frown darkens his features. "You will be safe, I assure you." He mistakes my contemplation for fear.

"I haven't thanked you," I confess, and somehow, last night, with only blankets separating Killian's body from mine, I didn't feel nearly as vulnerable as I do now, standing here with him, the truth of what he risked sinking in.

"For?"

"Saving me." My shoulders slump. I'm not sure why they feel so heavy. "Whatever your reason, you jeopardized your life for me, despite your rules. I know I would be dead right now, if not for you."

He blinks, stares at me a moment longer, then purses his lips. "You're welcome," he finally says, but he seems uncertain once again.

I hate that I don't understand him. And more so that I desperately want to. Biting my bottom lip, I nod, feeling as if there is more to say, but for now, it's all I can seem to manage.

"Well," he says, looking me up and down. "I brought you all the way down here to bathe. So, get in." A smile tugs at his scruffy cheek. "You could use a good soak."

I shove his shoulder, unable to help a grin of my own.

Killian nods toward the cave entrance. "I have to piss. Be right back." He sidles past me and climbs up the rocks and out into the daylight.

Swallowing my apprehension, I stare at the pool as I tug off my clothes. A couple of blisters scream on the bottoms of my feet as I pull off my boots, but they are easy to ignore as I dip my toe into the water. Groaning, I close my eyes and bask in anticipation.

The stones are smooth, and the water sloshes around my shins as I step inside. It's euphoric, and lowering myself to sit, I sigh with absolute pleasure. "Oh gods, let this be the afterlife. I would stay here forever." My body is consumed by heat, setting the coldest parts of me on fire, and as I splash the water over my arms, my eyes flutter shut.

No more chill in my bones. No more salt on my skin.

The heat soaks into every pore and soothes every aching muscle. The tension in my shoulders and arms melts until it's as if I'm boneless and could float away. I've never felt something so decadent and luxurious. And every second that passes convinces me I've never truly lived until this moment of utter contentment.

I splash water on my face and gently scrub what's left of the sea off my skin. When I'm content with that, I run my hands through my hair, only for them to catch on knots from days of neglect. Picking through the tangles to rid myself of the worst of them, I eye the bottom of the pool. The water is glorious and covers most of my body, settling just below the swell of my breasts. But it's not enough, and I yearn to submerge myself.

A few pebbles clack and roll into the cave as Killian approaches. "How is it?"

"Hmm. Perfection."

Killian chuckles, and I peer over my shoulder as he pulls his shirt off. His tattoos vary in vibrancy and significance, stretching over his muscular arms, wrapping onto his back and chest. All of them are important. All of them fascinating.

The wayfinder—pointing toward Killian's many paths in life.

The tree of life—rooted in worlds both seen and unseen.

An intricate Web of Wyrd—connecting past, present, and future fates.

But it is Njord's runes, scrolled down Killian's spine, that take my breath away, and I stare down at my own markings.

Running my fingers over Skadi's name on my forearm, I understand Killian's interest in them. Not only is she the figurehead of his ship, she is the begrudging wife of Killian's patron of the sea, of sailors who bring wealth to the just and deserving—she is the wife of Njord. It's always been said Njord blesses the Reaper's journeys, however, his connection to the gods clearly runs deeper than that.

I glance at Killian's body again, studying the markings that seem overwhelmingly apt. The muscular curve of his backside flexes, his thighs and arm muscles taut as he tugs off his pants. I have seen naked men, but there is something about Killian that is breathtaking, and reminds me he is a man, not a monster. But I would have to be blind to forget that.

Unnerved, I look away as he tosses his boots and clothes aside with mine. My heart is beating so quickly, and frazzled, I tug at my tangled hair.

"Let me help," he says, stepping into the pool.

"No, it's fine—"

"Stop it, I insist." As Killian sinks beside me, his throat moves with a hum of contentment, and when my eyes linger too long, I decide noticing *anything* about him is forbidden. Splashing water on my face again, I exhale deeply.

After a brief moment of reverie, Killian moves closer, his thigh brushes mine as he pivots to face me, motioning for me to turn my head.

"I know hair detangling is not on your list of *captainly* duties, so . . . Thank you," I say quietly. It's another kindness from him I hadn't expected.

His fingers are deft, and though he tugs a little, he is gentle, far more than I usually am. "I've tended to my share of knots and braids over the years," he explains.

I lick the water from my lips. "I imagine so." Remembering the women surrounding him at the tavern, I peer down at my wrinkling fingers. "Does Basher know?"

"Likely," Killian says. "Basher knows everything about me. But what, exactly, should she know this time?"

"About the women at the tavern—"

His chuckle cuts me off. "I've told you, Basher and I are not together."

"Are you sure? You seemed uncertain before," I say wryly.

When his fingers pause in my hair, I peer over my shoulder at him.

Killian looks saddened. "Basher still mourns the loss of her husband," he says. "The queen's men killed him—nearly killed her as well, but she survived and was taken as a thrall instead." He looks at me, waiting for me to understand. "We share a bond, but we are not together."

Basher's protectiveness of Killian makes sense, then. "She said you saved her life."

"Basher gives me too much credit. Besides," he continues. "I was referring to my niece before." There's a mischievous glint in his eyes. "She has a red, wild mane that will never be tamed."

"That's . . . surprising," I admit.

Killian runs his fingers through the loosening knot. It's slow and careful, almost reverent. "Paige's hair is not quite as wild as yours, though." When he's finished, he tugs playfully on the ends.

I smile to myself, wondering what his niece is like. I can tell he misses her; there's sadness in his voice. But talk of family is off-limits, so I don't bother asking. "How did you find this place?" I say instead. My voice is only a whisper in the cave.

"Basher and I were exploring once—there are a couple of them, actually. But this is the only one cool enough to swim in."

I smile. "It was well worth the trek." I don't realize my eyes are closed until I register the light brush of Killian's fingertip tracing one of my scars, and flinching, my eyes fly open again.

"Apologies," he says as I pull away from him. "That was—I shouldn't have done that." The water swishes around us, and I tuck a strand of hair behind my ear.

"It's okay," I breathe. "It was just surprising, is all."

Killian's eyes latch onto my arm markings again.

"I finally figured it out," I say, a little breathless.

His gaze lifts to me. "What's that?"

"What they mean to you. Well, at least I understand why you might find my tattoos so amusing."

His brow crumples slightly. "Amusing?"

"Skadi is carved into your ship, and her husband etched into your flesh, the way *she* is etched into mine." I shrug. "It's oddly coincidental."

Killian looks at my markings again, only this time he reaches out, taking my arm in his hand. "It is not only that," he whispers.

The pad of his thumb brushes the runes, and a breath escapes my lips. As my eyes flutter closed, I lose myself to the sensations of his touch.

"When I was lost in the woods, there was a rainstorm." His voice is silk and smoke. "I'd cried myself to sleep in a shelter of boulders by the creek. The storm was so violent and the wind so loud, I didn't realize the creek was flooding until it was nearly too late."

"Flooding?" I whisper.

Killian's expression darkens, and he lets go of my arm. He looks almost regretful as he leans back against the stones and peers into the water. "A woman took my hand. A woman with those same exact runes down her arm."

My eyes widen. "Skadi?" While it is not unheard of that the gods visit us in dreams and apparitions, that it would be her sends chills over my skin.

Killian's eyes glaze over, and his voice grows distant. "She helped me to my feet. And when I woke, she was gone. I was still nestled in the boulders, but I was in the rising water."

"She saved you," I breathe, the hair on the back of my arms and neck standing on end.

"Of course, it was all a dream or a trick of my mind," he says easily, but I can tell he doesn't believe that. Every time he looks at my arm proves as much. "She is the very symbol of my family—sewn into every tapestry and mentioned in every story." Killian smiles to himself as his eyes meet mine again. "It would make sense that she was with me that night. But still, I have never forgotten it . . . Nor will I."

"I wouldn't either," I whisper. "I—" Suddenly, the world tilts, and for a moment, I think I'm falling. I reach for something to steady myself.

"Brynn—"

I clutch Killian's shoulder as the world swirls once more before settling back into balance.

"What is it?" I feel Killian's hands on my arms.

"I'm just dizzy—I'm okay." I exhale a steadying breath. "I'm okay," I repeat.

Killian takes my chin gently between his fingers as I blink the world—and him—back into focus. The concern on his face makes me smile because it seems so out of place. "I'm fine, Killian." Gripping the stones, I try to stand.

"Careful—"

I nearly stumble, uncertain why laughter bubbles out of me.

The water sloshes, Killian grumbles, and he grabs hold of my arms to sit me on the edge of the pool.

It's then I remember the berries and meet his gaze. "Are you sure the berries aren't poisonous?"

"Yes. I ate three times as many as you, and I'm fine." He smooths the wet strings of my hair away from my temples and cheeks, scrutinizing every inch of my face. "You are pale when you should be flushed from the heat," he says. "And I know you are not dehydrated. The heat must be getting to—"

My stomach growls, and Killian's brow furrows deeper. "When was the last time you ate something?"

"The berries, of course."

"Aside from the five berries you ate before giving them all to me."

"I—um," I rack my brain, trying to remember. "On the ship. Tug brought us potato stew and—"

"Potato stew was three days ago," he practically growls, then his eyes narrow on me before flicking over my body. "Did you eat it?"

I glare at him, not liking the accusatory tone in his voice. "Of course I did."

Killian groans. "Your body needs food, Brynn." He sounds more worried than irritated.

"I haven't had much of an appetite. Besides, I've gone longer without it than this. I'll be fine," I promise him.

"That doesn't mean you should," he snaps. "You've been stabbed and beaten and thrown overboard—"

"There's been a lot going on, you know? My stomach's been in knots for days. It hasn't been much of a priority." I can't help my annoyance. "I'm not a child, Killian."

He stares at me, skeptical, and I feel my chin tremble as I realize how weak my body really is and how hollow my stomach feels. "I wasn't hungry," I say more meekly.

His eyes soften, and he tucks my hair behind my ear. "The heat is making it worse," he says. "Come on, little Skadi." Killian takes my hand and cradles my arm in his as he helps me to my feet.

"I can walk by myself."

"Yes, I know," he says derisively. "But I won't let you until we get out of this cave. So, deal with it." His stare is more of a challenge, and I roll my eyes. Satisfied with his victory, he helps me sit on a rock to dress.

"Really," I tell him, "I'm fine. It passed. I feel better now that I'm not in the water."

Killian hands me my shirt. He's looking at me differently, studying my body in a way I don't like, like he's seeing me for the first time. Judging me, not appreciating.

"Stop," I tell him.

His eyes meet mine as he tugs on his pants. "Stop what?"

"*Assessing* me."

"You're naked," he says with a roguish grin, and he pulls on one of his boots. "I like looking at naked women."

"That's not what you're doing, and you know it."

His grin widens. "You know nothing, little Skadi."

I scoop my hair out from the collar of my shirt. "I hate this," I tell him.

"I know. And I don't care." He drops my boots beside me and hands me my pants next. "We'll save trapping and shelter searching for tomorrow. Today, I cook you a crab feast."

I watch as he shrugs his shirt on, covering up his body that's charted with his life's story, like one of his maps.

"Do you know how to cook?" I ask.

"I can do everything, remember?" Killian winks, and he's so cocky, I snort a laugh.

25
BRYNN

From inside our little alcove, I watch the sky deepen its orange hue as the sun sets somewhere behind the clouds. I'm bathed, my belly's sated, and I'm wrapped happily in furs, unable to do much other than bask in the moment.

"So," Killian starts, plopping down beside me with a bottle in hand. "How was your feast?"

I grin, unable to help myself. "You mean the crab I boiled?"

"I brought them to you." He cuts the wax seal off the glass with his knife as if he's done it a thousand times before.

"Yes, you did. Thank you. And it was delicious." He pulls the cork from the bottle with a pop. "How was yours?"

"Honestly, I couldn't have cooked it better myself."

"Well," I huff. "That's a given."

Before Killian takes the first sip, he offers me the bottle. "Whiskey, from home."

"No, thanks," I murmur, shaking my head.

He takes a drink as my stomach rumbles, and his eyebrows pop up. "Still hungry, little Skadi?"

"Not in the slightest," I promise him, and rub my belly. "I

guess my body doesn't know what to do with so much food. It's been a while since I was actually full." I'm not sure why, but my cheeks flush as I admit that.

"How long have you had to live like that?" Killian asks gently, and my cheeks burn brighter as I look away.

I want nothing more than to change the subject, because he already knows too much about me—he has already *seen* too much. But maybe that's why I tell him. Or maybe because even the painful memories of Estrid are better than none at all.

"After our farm was burned," I say, clearing my throat, "my sister and I were unable to tend to what bit of land was left. Our home was gone. So was our family. Looking back, I don't know if we left because the memories were too painful, or if it was because we were afraid the Reaper's men would return, but . . . we went to the city to search for help, shelter, food—anything." I sift a handful of sand between my fingers. "It was worse there, though."

I don't tell Killian that we learned to survive amid the livestock and other street urchins, but just barely. That we'd resorted to scouring the sewers for anything that moved, and after a while, I couldn't keep doing it, and stupid as I was, I nearly lost my life for stealing meat and bread scraps from a trapper.

Closing my eyes, I feel the cool, sharp blade of his skinning knife pressed to my throat as if the edge still slices my skin. *"What will you give me in return for your sister's life?"* I can still hear the sickening purr in the man's voice as he eyed Estrid, and the sudden understanding that dawned on her face. She was only thirteen the day she realized she'd grown into her beauty, that men liked her blonde hair, big blue eyes, and cherubic face.

"I was too impulsive one day," I start again, picking at the well-worn fur beneath my fingers. "We got into a bind, and that was the day we discovered other ways to get what we needed to survive." I stare into the fire, part of me missing the swing of the forge hammer and the burn of my muscles always coiled with self-loathing and resentment. "We hadn't feasted often, but we never starved either."

The fire flames crack in the draft, and I feel the weight of Killian's gaze on my face, but refuse to look at him. I can't. I don't want to see his sympathy or judgement, or anything in between.

"Here," he says, offering me the whiskey again. "It's far better than that rubbish you northerners call schnapps."

I huff a small laugh and take the bottle, swallowing a mouthful before I hand it back to him. My eyes water as the whiskey burns going down, and Killian grins, pleased.

"See. It's good stuff." Bringing the bottle to his lips, he takes a gulp and closes his eyes with a gratified sigh.

"*Us* northerners," I correct, licking the tinge of smoky-sweet from my lips. "Your family is from Norseland. You said so yourself."

Killian shrugs. "Only on my father's side." He leans his head back on the stones behind us, and his eyes close. Watching him this close, I notice his dark beard is golden in some areas when the firelight touches it. And it's already more unruly than it was two days ago. But it's his long lashes pressed against sun-kissed cheeks that hold my attention the most.

He sighs, far less content than he should be right now, with his booze, warmth, and a full belly, and I know it has something to do with her.

"Will you tell me?" I ask, and nestle deeper into my furs.

"Tell you what?" he asks softly, his eyes still closed.

I swallow thickly. "About your mother." I feel the little girl inside me clinging to the hope that he will, though I don't know why.

Killian's eyes open, shifting to me. "I thought we weren't

talking about our families." I can hear the edge of his walls armoring up again. I know I'm too close to what haunts him, but I can't let it go. Not this time.

"I just talked about mine," I offer as payment.

"So it's tit for tat then?" Tilting his head, Killian sighs in exaggerated defeat.

"You said your mother is not from the north," I start, trying to coax him into it. "I'm curious, is all."

He takes another swig of his drink. "No," he says, and stares at the rocky overhang above. "She wasn't. But funny enough, she was a little like you." He doesn't sound very amused, he sounds sad, and I know she's no longer in this world.

"Like me how?"

He smirks. "She had very pert opinions and a tenacity that drew my father to her—that's why he purchased her, I think."

Shock gives me pause. "She was one of his workers?"

Killian shakes his head. "No, she wasn't a worker. My mother was a breeder."

I gape at him.

"It is the way things are usually done in New London—wealthy men who need heirs purchase and trade for women of good breeding. They need sons to carry on their family legacy and continue producing materials for the Council to rebuild their once great city." Killian looks at me, weighing my expression, which I try to curb, though I doubt I'm very good at it.

"My father was a serious man, like my brother," he continues. "But unlike Greyson, my father followed every rule and agreement expected between our family and the Council. That is why he purchased a wife instead of falling in love with someone first." The pain in Killian's voice is raw and reedy, but I don't know if it's for his mother and father, for his brother, or for himself.

"Don't fret, little Skadi. It was not a terrible, loveless

marriage, as I'm sure you're thinking. My father was a good man, and my mother every bit his match."

And yet, it occurs to me that Killian was not a happy child. "Why did you run away?"

He traces a fissure in the rock wall with his fingertip. "I said my brother takes after my father, and it's true. I've always been more like my grandfather, though less idealistic. I never felt at home in Briarwood." He drops his hand into his lap, staring into oblivion. "I ran away because I was tired of Greyson receiving all of my father's attention. I wanted my parents to worry about me for once. Instead, I put into motion every regret I've had since."

I hold my breath, praying Killian will continue, because despite his reluctance, I think deep down he wants to. Like maybe, here on this island, he might be able to leave some of his troubles behind.

"While I was trying to teach my family a lesson, the gods decided to teach me one instead." His voice thickens with pain. "My mother fell ill while she and my father were searching for me. She died some weeks later. They said it was her lungs. That it was likely something she'd been struggling with for quite some time, but never told my father about. And her worry, her searching for me—I'd only made it worse."

My eyes burn in the weight of Killian's guilt; it's heavy and suffocating in the air. "I'm sorry," I whisper, but when Killian looks at me with a false smile that radiates disgust, my stomach drops again.

"Before my parents found me, I'd stumbled upon a village in the woods. I hadn't realized they knew my family, or that they'd gotten word to my parents. I was too busy falling in love with the girl who would eventually become my best friend . . . and my brother's wife." Killian huffs a laugh. "I lost my mother, drove my brother and father closer together, and the love of my life chose my brother instead—the twisted repercussion of that single, foolhardy decision."

His expression darkens. "I resented everyone else for what had happened, up until the day Rebecca died in childbirth." Killian looks at me with self-loathing. "The worst part? That day, the day my brother's life was crumbling around him, the first thing that came to mind was . . . *good*."

26
KILLIAN

Brynn stares at me with horror. Her eyes shimmer with disbelief, and I know what I've just done. Laid myself bare for her to judge—and not the Reaper this time, but me, Killian Blackburn. The man I'm far more ashamed of, ten times over.

"Killian—"

"I loved Rebecca," I say in a rush, unable to stomach what Brynn might say next. "I would never wish her harm, and yet, as my brother's world fell apart, a small part of me felt sated. So, if you hate me for any reason, little Skadi, hate me for that."

"It seems you hate yourself enough already," she says, her voice barely a rasp.

When I look at her, those light blue, expressive eyes are round with sadness, and I take three desperate pulls from the bottle, averting my gaze. The whiskey burns going down but I revel in it. It means the weightlessness is closer. "That's how horrible a brother and son I am. How selfish I've always been."

Having spent the better part of my life seeking danger and trouble—testing my fate when I've felt listless, resentful, and without purpose—only made seeing Brynn's scars for the first time more gutting.

"Imagine it," I say with a humorless laugh. "Someone like me, with means, position, and freedom, squandering my life away while so many others are born into a life like yours. All because I couldn't have *everything* that I wanted."

When Brynn doesn't say anything, I'm glad, but as the moment drags on and I can only hear my heart beating in my ears, I can't stand it any longer, and I glance at her. She looks as if she wants to say something, and I can only imagine how scathing it will be. But she remains quiet. She doesn't utter a single word.

"You asked me why I don't wish to go home, little Skadi," I say, staring into the fire. "It's because I am my worst self when I am there, and it is better for my brother that I am away. And . . . perhaps better for my sanity as well." I smile again and lift the whiskey before taking another drink.

"I know my opinion means little," Brynn whispers, so low I barely hear her over the slosh of the bottle, but I hold my breath. "But you ran away when you were a child. You could not have known the consequences of your actions." She smooths her hand over the blanket, as if she's comforting herself. "If I were to blame myself for all the things I should've done differently in this life, I would have been swallowed by regret." She looks at me. "I would have jumped off that ship without a thought, because the last thing I told my brother before he died was that I hated him. All because he ruined our family outing for the day, and I had to do chores instead." Her voice thins with pain and longing. "Whatever your past, and whatever your regrets, Killian, you are a good man. And you know I don't say that lightly." The words warm my chest, and my expression, whatever it is, makes her cheeks flush as well.

"You see selfishness, and yes, perhaps you have been at times. But what child hasn't? I'm certain your mother would not blame you for what happened to her. And you are not the only brother to have ever felt resentment and acted on it. You are not the only person to want what you can't have, or wish things were different."

Exhaling the tightness in my chest, I watch Brynn so closely, I see the tears in her lashes before they fall. I don't know if her tears are for me or her, or a sad mix of both, but she wipes them from her cheeks before they can get very far.

"You saved me when you didn't have to, Killian. And whatever my qualms with you are, what you do for the people on your ship inspires and gives them hope. It's an opportunity that will change their lives forever. So," she says, swallowing thickly. She takes a deep breath. "Whatever your regrets, know that what you do matters, that it's not selfish in the slightest—in fact, it's dangerous and you put your life at risk every single time. If nothing else, you can be proud of that."

Without the ire in her voice, without the judgement darkening her eyes, I don't know what to do with such words. I haven't felt this raw in so long, nor so free. I don't know how to react. All I can do is feel, and what I feel is a gravitational pull to Brynn I've had since the first night I saw her on the ship. The pull I've been both fighting and trying to understand every moment since.

"The truth is," she says, gaze lost in the fire. She tucks a strand of hair behind her ear. "Even if my head tells me that you could do so much more for those people—for us—the fact that you do anything at all makes you a far better man than any I've ever met."

I don't know how long I stare at her, but I can't bring myself to look away. I have a thousand questions yet all I can do is study her profile. The way her sloped nose moves when she purses her lips, and the way her hands tremble ever so slightly as she wipes another silent tear from her cheek.

Uncertain how to fill the silence, but knowing I can't stand it a second longer, I lightly toss the whiskey cork at her shoulder. That seems to stir her back to me.

"Careful, Brynn," I say, smiling as her glistening eyes meet mine. "Your kindness is showing."

Just like that, her mouth curves in a smile, and the tension between us dissolves a little.

Brynn snatches the whiskey from my hand and takes a swig. She makes the most adorably contorted face and hands the bottle back to me.

"Don't worry," she says, gasping. She wipes away the whiskey remnants with the back of her hand. "I still resent you."

I chuckle and lean back, nestling into place again. "Good. I wouldn't know what to do with you otherwise."

27
BRYNN

After a night of sound sleep, thanks to whiskey and a full belly, I feel rested, stronger, and more centered as Killian and I start our walk through the sparse, rocky landscape. Our conversation last night was unnerving in so many ways, and yet, I've never felt closer to him. Like, finally, I understand him a little. And though I half expected him to wake up angry and regretful that he'd shared so much with me, his edges seem smoother, his smile more genuine, and I revel in it.

Fox dens and rabbit holes in the hilly mountainside are our mission, and we scope out our surroundings for better shelter and our next meal. With our tasks in order for the day, it's easier to focus on something other than the change between us and what it means.

"We could sleep in the hot cave, if nothing else," I think aloud, and adjust the small sack flung over my shoulder. A whiff of the crab bits we've brought for bait catches my nose, but the scent is whisked away by the wind almost as quickly.

"I'm sure we'll find something," Killian says thoughtfully.

"The island is nearly the size of Northhelm. There should be plenty of nooks and crannies to camp."

"Where did you stay last time you were here?"

Killian crouches down to study animal tracks in the damp earth. "Tents," he mutters, distracted. "On the beach."

We continue onward, and I should probably learn from Killian's tracking, but my attention flits this way and that, soaking in the new and strange surroundings. "How long ago?"

Killian looks back at me. "Always so many questions."

I grunt a laugh. "If the situation was reversed, you would have just as many."

His scruffy smile quirks up in the corner. "Four or five years ago, we stopped here to make some repairs to the ship. It was just the crew, and we had some time to explore the island."

"And you thought to hide supplies then?"

Killian nods. "Well, Norik thought of it. Keep an eye out for a cave," he says, crouching a few paces ahead. He presses his fingers against the animal tracks again and peers around.

"I thought we were hunting fox, not bears," I jest.

"A cave for us to sleep in," he clarifies, nodding toward a cluster of rocks. "I've already found the fox den. I'll set a snare over there and add the bait. Crab this far inland will be an irresistible treat for them." He mutters the last part to himself and motions for the sack I've been carrying. "Why don't you set a trap by the creek bed," he says, glancing in that direction. "The path there is well worn."

My eyebrows shoot up. "I would be happy to once I learn how to make a trap."

Killian tilts his head, the rope he's pulled from the bag frozen in his hand. "Do you mean to tell me you have never had to trap your food?"

"Trap? No."

"Hmm." Killian collects palm-sized rocks from the ground, so I do the same.

"You know, I might've lived on the streets before, but I was never a complete animal, living in the wild."

Killian peers over at me, his expression unreadable as I drop a few rocks on the ground beside him. "My mistake," he deadpans, but the look in his eyes is skeptical. "I guess I would have thought Brynn the Brave could do anything she put her mind to. Sounds like you might actually need me around, then." There's a playfulness in his voice, and though he's teasing me, I can't bring myself to smile.

"I'm not brave," I say, because impulsiveness isn't the same as bravery. "And I think *need* is a tricky way to put it, don't you?"

Killian chuckles to himself and points to the shrubbery behind me. "Break a few branches off, would you? I'll use them to hold the snare up and hide it at the same time. And make sure the branches have berries on them, should our furry friend need extra incentive."

Leaving Killian to tie and knot his noose, I walk toward the bushes heavy with crowberries, closer to the rocks. I've barely broken off a branch when the hair on my arms stands on end.

"Do. Not. Move," a male voice rumbles quietly behind me.

I freeze. Hold my breath.

Straining to listen above the breeze, I hear the taut creak of a bowstring as an arrow is readied.

My eyes train on Killian's back as he constructs his trap, completely unaware, and I will myself to stay calm.

"Do not scream," the man warns, closer to my ear this time.

Little does he know, I am not the screaming type. Rock, stick, his own arrow—I would use anything I could get my hands on to maim him before I would ever scream. "Untrain that arrow from my back, or you will be sorry," I grit out.

A cool knife blade glints in the corner of my eye and

presses against my throat. A soft chuckle follows, brushing my cheek. "You were saying?" another voice says.

I squeeze my eyes shut, counting the space between each of their breaths to gauge whether the men's bravado is false, or if the man with his hand at my throat twitches with any uncertainty. But all I hear is a deep inhale, and the blade is steady. I detect no stench of desperation. Only, the two men—the bowman and the man with the knife—are so close I can feel their warmth behind me. Their calm, measured breathing means they are thoughtful and relinquished the element of surprise knowingly when they spoke to me. They want something; it's the only reason I am not dead, yet.

The wind tugs at my tangled, loose hair, and I swallow thickly, my heart racing as I realize how foolish we've been not to have searched the island for others.

"What do you want?" I bite out as coolly as I can.

"To know if there are others with you on the island."

"There aren't," I confess, assuming he'd be swifter to kill us if he thought they were greatly outnumbered.

The man with the bow steps into my periphery, his dark hair catching the breeze as he trains his arrow on Killian's back.

"Assuming that's true," the man behind me continues. "I think it's best to determine the sort of danger you and your friend pose."

"Says the man with the knife to my throat and an arrow to our backs, while we remain unarmed," I seethe.

He chuckles at my ear, and I imagine he's watching Killian as closely as I am. "That you are unarmed means nothing," he muses. "I bet you wish nothing more than to—"

"I'm still waiting on those twigs!" Killian calls back, oblivious as ever. With the wind rushing through the valley, there is no way he can hear a word we're saying.

"If you let me have that dagger," I taunt, "I will show you

how dangerous I am." I know I should play a terrified and helpless woman, but my indignation won't allow it.

"Call to your friend," he commands. "Now."

I lick my lips, nervous what Killian might do, but I have no choice. "Kill—" I say, clearing my throat. "Killian!"

"What's the matter little Skad—" Half turned, his body tenses, a flash of fear darkens his eyes, and then everything about him hardens.

Ever so slowly, Killian rises to his feet, the shift in his countenance not only visible but also palpable as he changes from cocky-grinned Killian to a man not to be reckoned with. A man with a sudden wildness in his eyes that frightens even me. "What do you want?" He sounds deceptively calm.

"To know if you are friend or foe," the bowman says to my right. "What are you doing on this island?"

Killian's attention shifts from the bowman to me, his gaze communicating something I don't quite understand but don't have time to ponder, before he looks past me at the man holding the knife to my throat. Were it not for the bowman's arrow, I might've tried to outmaneuver him already, but if I tried, either Killian or I would surely be shot through.

"We fell overboard during a storm," Killian explains. "And she is unarmed, so you can let her go."

"I don't think so," the man behind me says through another chuckle. "I have a feeling this one's bite is worse than her bark."

Killian's eyes narrow slightly. "You are intelligent men, then," he says, glancing between them. "You would've killed us already if you were going to." He nods to the bowman. "Put your weapons down and let's get on with it."

It's strange to watch Killian like this. Me, a bystander as the wheels in his mind turn and severity edges his voice. I hadn't realized I'd come to understand him, but I see the way his chest rises with equal measure, how his finger twitches at his side, and his mouth forms a tight line as he considers the men and the danger they pose.

"You are not stranded here," Killian muses aloud. "You live on this island." Once again, his gaze shifts between them.

"Aye, and you are strangers," the bowman replies.

Killian dips his chin. "We came ashore two days ago."

"And how is that, exactly?" the man behind me inquires. "Because no one sails these waters but the Reaper and his men." His apprehensive tone fills with acidic hate. "Unless you are one of them?"

I wince as the knife presses more sharply into my throat.

Killian stiffens, but before he can demand anything, I confess, "I woke on a ship." All I can think as the words spew from my mouth is that it's better to keep them focused on me while Killian figures out what to do.

His eyes level on me, though his expression gives nothing away.

"The sail broke during the storm, and I was tossed overboard."

"A thrall ship?" The bowman shakes his head. "Lies. You do not look like slaves." He glares at Killian. "He does *not* look like a captive."

"And what would you know about thrall ships and captives?" I seethe, glaring at the bowman from the corner of my eye. It's practically a snarl, and the knife at my neck pierces my flesh. "Think whatever you want, but I am not a liar." All I can see is dark, braided-back hair that's come loose around his boyish face. He must exchange a look with the man behind me because his stance shifts slightly.

"Prove it," the bowman demands. He's clearly familiar with how woefuls live to ask such a thing. Chieftains don't force their workers to mar themselves with brands, so much as woefuls begrudgingly accept them to showcase loyalty—to pledge service in exchange for protection.

"Do as he says," the man behind me requests. "Just to ensure you're not telling us tall tales." His tone seems slightly apologetic.

The bowman motions for Killian to move closer to me, so he can train the arrow in one general direction.

Killian does as commanded, and when he is closer, the man with the knife steps slowly away and into view. I think he and Killian exchange a look of warning before I am entirely out of the man's grasp and can glare at both him and the bowman as they stand in front of us, waiting expectantly.

Both men have thick beards, lines around their eyes, and weathered skin from the elements. But the bowman is younger and leaner than the red-haired man that was at my back.

"Well then," the bowman says impatiently. He looks more than willing to let loose his arrow. "Prove to us you are no threat."

I grin impishly. "I never claimed I am not a threat." His eyes narrow with annoyance as I turn, unfastening my vest. "I said I woke on a ship." The words fall easily from my lips because they are true.

I meet Killian's shadowed gaze as I hand him my furs, and I wonder what plays behind his eyes. It almost looks like regret. Or is it concern? Maybe he thinks I will tell them who he is. Maybe he fears I will do something rash and get us into trouble. It wouldn't be the first time, I'll give him that.

"I have no distinguishable markings," I forewarn, and pull my shirt up in the back, stopping when I know enough of my skin is exposed for them to see some of the old scars and new bruising disappearing into my waistline.

Chills spread over my body, and I can feel my puckered flesh tightening as the cool wind licks over me.

"That's enough," Killian tells them, and meeting his gaze, I lower my shirt and slowly turn around.

They stare at me. I have no proof of who or what I am,

because I am whatever I've had to be over the years. But I've convinced them of enough, for now. "Until a week ago," I say, loud enough for them to hear over the howling dunes, "I worked for Von Magnusson."

"I know of Von Magnusson," the redhead says. "He does not let his laborers wander far. If you are here, what has become of him?"

"First, tell me of the Reaper," I say as Killian hands my vest back to me. His eyes lock on mine, but I look away. "It was not fear I heard in your voice when you spoke his name."

The man with the red beard and hard, green eyes sheaths his knife in his belt. "No, not fear. *Never* fear," he says. His clothes are lined with gray and white fur, his boots made of hide, and his stature is straight and sure. He was someone who once commanded a room when he entered it. "Loathing," he explains. "He took everything from me. My family's means of—"

"Your means?" I say, realizing the Reaper would only come to him if he was a chieftain or the like. "You mean your workers?" I grit out. "You are a slave master—"

"No," he says brusquely. "But my father was a chieftain and brick mason for the queen. And for all my fighting to change that—to stand up against her—look what it got me." He opens his arms, gesturing to the island. "This is my life now. I am the lord of nothing."

"Am I to feel sorry for you?" I clip, glancing around at his absolute freedom. A man like him could never appreciate something like that. Not like I would.

He glares at me. "I don't ask for your pity, I only offer you truth. We are here because we fled from the queen—because once the Reaper was finished, I had no wife, no home, no father, and no lands. He burned all I had to ashes, and I knew the queen would come to claim all I had left to give her." With a furtive look at his companion, he finally takes a breath.

But all I can think is, *burned?* I look at Killian, feeling sick to my stomach as I consider how similar it is to my story.

"Were you there?" Killian asks, his voice holding a hint of desperate curiosity I hadn't expected. "Did you see the Reaper with your own eyes?"

"I didn't have to," the man grits out. "I found one of his banners, tattered in the debris. And who are you to ask questions?" he retorts. "You do not look like a thrall."

"That's because I'm not," Killian says coolly. "I am Killian Blackburn. I was sailing for my estate in New London." That Killian is telling the truth, or at least half of it, surprises me, but then, he can't very well tell the men the whole of it, and I wait with bated breath as they consider such a tale.

The younger man scoffs. "You are an Englishman from the Black Country—sailing these waters?" He shakes his head. "I don't believe that either."

"Well, take the truth or leave it," Killian says with utter indifference. "But when I don't return to port on my ship, my brother will come looking for me. Perhaps all of New London will."

I frown, wondering if that is an embellishment or truth.

"For now, we are biding our time, waiting for the ship to return. We mean you no harm. But if something happens to me, I can promise you will have an army of Englishmen on your beach in the months to come." The threats etching his tone aren't subtle, and the two strangers standing in front of us clearly believe him, because the red-haired man looks entirely intrigued while the other looks a lot more troubled.

"Well, Killian Blackburn," the redhead says. "I am Leif, and that is Hans, my brother by marriage." He meets his brother's gaze, and reluctantly, Hans lowers his arrow. "Perhaps," Leif says, looking at me, "we can put whatever grudges we have aside, and share a meal and the fire tonight. I long to hear about life away from this place. And it appears you could use some looking after."

"How do we know this isn't a trick?" I ask. "That there aren't more of you, or that you won't try to rape and kill me?"

Leif grins. "I doubt your companion would allow that to happen," he says. "Besides, I don't think my sister would either."

My eyes widen. I wasn't expecting a woman on the island.

"Nor would you, I should think," he adds.

I watch him closely, my head tilting as his countenance shifts before me, from trepidatious to intrigued. "And Killian? A moment ago you would have put an arrow through him."

"God would not want me to let fear rule my judgement, risking the death of an innocent man."

"Your god," I say with a chuckle. "Since when?" All I can think of is the rot and ruin throughout Northhelm, and the poor innocents who pay the price because of my gods and his.

"You cannot judge us all the same," Leif says. "Just as I cannot judge you, two strangers who have given me no reason to distrust you—yet."

Killian and I glance at one another as Leif and Hans exchange a similar look of uncertainty. Whatever Leif believes, he is placing a lot of faith in us to welcome Killian and me into his home, among his family.

"Thralls and masters, stuck together on this island," Leif mutters, turning for his discarded belongings. "What are the odds of such a thing?" The cross around his neck glints in the muted daylight, and I laugh out loud. Christians and pagans. Njord and Skadi. Killian and me.

Suddenly, I'm the focus of all their attention, and reeling my laughter back in, I shrug. "I'm beginning to think the gods have a sense of humor," I explain, waving their confusion away.

Leif seems amused as well, and his green eyes twinkle.

"Come. We will take you to our homestead on the eastern side of the island. It's a ways over these hills." Leif waves us over, and the men collect their empty fishnets, discarded by the rocks.

I lean into Killian. "Are we trusting this?"

Killian doesn't take his eyes off of Leif and Hans as we follow slowly behind them. "For now, I think we have to."

"Do you know anything about him? About what happened to his lands?" I ask, praying the answer is no.

Killian shakes his head, and suddenly, as if something dawns on him, he meets my gaze. Only a few inches away, his eyes search my face. "It wasn't long ago I would have thought you wanted me dead," he says. "You could have told them the truth, but you didn't. Why?"

Because I was wrong about you. Though the thought is fleeting, my cheeks heat. "A life for a life," I whisper, even if that is not the only reason. "You saved me from drowning. Now I have repaid my debt."

A knowing grin curves his lips. "My life is in your hands, then?" he muses as we fall into step behind our new acquaintances. "How utterly terrifying."

28
BRYNN

Past the rolling dunes, the land opens to a rugged plain of wild, bending grasses and more whipping winds. The gray horizon meets the darkening sea off in the distance, and nestled at the bottom of a cresting hill, protected from the brunt of the wind, are two stone cottages with grass-covered roofs.

Animal pelts hang on lines that stretch between two outbuildings, and on the other side are rows of drying fish, their silver scales glinting as they catch the breeze. Smoke rises from one of the cottage chimneys, a garden of greenery grows in crudely cut barrel rounds, and a woman with strawberry-blonde hair coiled atop her head freezes. She clutches the laundry she's hanging, her fear and shock in seeing us obvious.

Leif's sister, I realize. She murmurs something to a small boy as we approach. He can't be more than six or seven, and the instant he sees us, he runs into the house.

"Tora," Leif says as we stop a dozen paces away. "We have company for dinner."

She looks as distrusting as she does displeased, glancing between her brother and husband.

Leif stares at her, his expression giving little away, but Hans's eyes narrow on us in warning.

"I'm Brynn," I say, before the thick silence can linger too long. "He is Killian." I try to find the softness in my voice so as not to frighten her too terribly. I can only imagine how worried she is about her son's safety with two strangers standing outside of her home, on a remote island in the middle of the sea. She likely thought she'd never lay eyes on strangers again.

"You must have a good reason for bringing them here, brother," Tora says, barely dipping her head to me in greeting.

"They have news of Norseland," he says, and that seems to have enough merit of its own. "They fell overboard during the storm."

Her eyes flash in disbelief, and she scans me up and down.

"It's true," I offer. "Well, more like I was thrown overboard." I grip my side as the memory of the crossbeam against my body ripens.

"And you?" Her attention shifts to Killian. "Did you happen to fall overboard as well?"

He shakes his head. "No, I'm just the fool who jumped in after her."

"I can't swim," I add. "We woke on shore two days ago."

Tora's expression softens a little. "You're lucky you were so close to this place, then."

"Yes," Leif says. "And she has wounds that could use attention. I thought perhaps you might take a look." It's not a question, and Tora looks at her brother, then at her husband. He leans in and whispers something in her ear before kissing her cheek reassuringly. It's clear he doesn't trust us, but I can't hold that against him. I wouldn't trust them either, had I not been forced to.

"Come inside," Tora says, wiping her hands on her apron. "We'll leave them to—" She glances at the three men and waves her hands, exasperated. "Do whatever they do," she grumbles, and turns to go inside.

Making my way toward the larger cottage, I spare a look in Killian's direction. Our eyes meet.

Be careful.

This should be interesting.

I'm right here if you need me.

A single glance conveys it all, and the relief it gives me is mirrored in Killian's pensive gaze. I'm not sure if he and I became reluctant allies when he saved me, or if it happened yesterday when he took care of me because he cared. Regardless, it feels strange to part from him, if for no other reason than I only trust two things at the moment—Killian and my instincts.

I step inside the cottage, brushing my fingers over the moss dusting the stones as I go.

"Close the door behind you," Tora says. "Wood is precious here, and I don't want the heat to get out."

The door creaks as I shut it behind me. Warmth accosts me in the best possible way, and my eyes flit closed of their own accord. Having been in the wind for two days with little reprieve, my skin is windburned and my lips chapped. Like the hot pool, I would stay in the warmth of this place and never leave, if it were possible.

Opening my eyes, I find the young boy watching me with a wide, curious gaze, though his mother's bores into me, her expression more wary than intrigued.

"Don't worry," I tell her, walking toward the long table in the center of the room. "I only pose a threat to handsy men who forget their manners."

The corner of her mouth lifts slightly, and she gestures to the bench in front of me. "Have a seat. I'll get you something warm to drink."

As Tora flits about the stone hearth with a barely-crackling fire, I peer around the comfortable space, feeling an acute sense of longing—a nostalgia I've missed in the years since my childhood.

I want this. A home. A warm place to lay my head each night. The freedom to fish and farm and struggle for my own means of survival, not someone else's.

I swallow the sudden emotion that swells in my throat, blaming the unexpected itch of envy on my exhaustion and receding adrenaline from a day of startling and life-threatening discoveries.

Licking my lips, I stare out the crack in the shuttered window with a perfect view of the sea. The outline of another island materializes through the light mist in the distance.

"Over here." Tora speaks cautiously, and only then do I notice I'm standing in their sleeping area, next to the boy's bed nestled beside theirs.

I glance at the down pillows and fur blanket, imagining life here, and shake my head. "Apologies," I whisper, knowing I've overstepped. "You have a nice home."

"We have worked very hard to find a comfortable life here." Tora's words serve as another unnecessary warning. "Tank," she clips, calling her son over. "Sit here and play with your sea stones." The boy listens without a word.

"He's quiet for a child," I say as I sit down on the bench across from her and her son.

"He doesn't like strangers," she says, her brusqueness turning to sadness in her voice. "Not after what happened in Norseland."

I eye the little boy with red hair and freckles, like his mother and uncle. His green eyes shift to me, and the moment he sees me looking at him, he averts his gaze.

"I am not much for strangers either," I tell him. "So I understand."

His mother sets a hollowed horn cup on the table filled

with a steaming drink. "It's a tea made from the grasses that grow here. It's bitter, but it will help you recover more quickly." The woman's eyes shift over me as she unclips a basket of herbs hanging from a rope above us. "You look exhausted," she says. "And like you could use a little meat on your bones."

I glance down at myself. Do I look so bad? Or is it that she is not used to the harsh life in Norseland anymore?

"And I have a salve for your burned skin."

I lift my hand to my face, gently pressing my fingers against my cheek. "Sunburn?"

She nods. "The sun, wind, and seawater are a deadly combination," she offers. "Your cheeks are only pink, but still, you can put this on." She hands me a seashell with a strange goop in it. "Put it on your lips and any wounds you have as well."

I take the shell, bringing it to my nose to sniff. It's astringent, and I pull it away.

"It's licorice root. It will help with whatever ails you."

Tank stares at me, but I pretend I don't notice as I thank his mother. "I appreciate it." Carefully, I remove my vest and glance at the kid, minding myself as I try to pull my arm out of my sleeve so he doesn't get an eyeful of my battered body.

"Tank," Tora says over her shoulder. "Fetch me some water for supper." Reaching on tiptoes, she gathers dried seaweed from one basket and potatoes from another.

"Yes, Mother," he whispers, and he takes the empty pail by the door and disappears outside.

With him gone, I pull my arm from my sleeve and study the knife wound. "Believe it or not, it's a little better than it was," I mutter.

Chills ripple over my skin as I spread the salve over it with my cool fingers.

Tora huffs with amusement, and when I look at her, she shakes her head.

"I'm amusing to you?" I try to guess how much older she is than me—ten years, maybe. But the years lived, and the life experienced in those years, are very different.

"Not amusing at all. But my brother bringing you here makes sense now."

"And why is that?"

Tora looks up from tearing the leaves off a withered plant into a pile on the table. "How did you fall overboard again?" she asks, instead of answering my question. There's an elegance about her, or rather, what used to be a highbred lady of Norseland. Now, her fingers are calloused like mine, and there's a weariness around her eyes I doubt was there before.

"It was a series of terrifying, unfortunate mishaps. The bracings on the sails broke during the storm, and I was knocked overboard."

"And the man?"

"Killian?"

Tora nods. "He really jumped in to save you during a squall?" She lifts her eyebrow, and whether it's her motherly instincts or simply that she is distrusting, her skepticism is evident.

Scratching the side of my face, I huff out a disbelieving breath of my own. "Yes, crazy as it seems. I'm still not sure exactly why he did it."

Tora crouches down for an earthen bowl beneath the table. "Isn't it obvious?"

I laugh, though it sounds almost bitter. "It's not what you think," I promise her. "We are not quite . . . friends. At least, we weren't before we were forced to be."

She glances at me through her blonde lashes and sprinkles some crushed spices into the bowl. She mixes in some of the herbs as well. "And the knife wound on your arm?"

I pause, frowning at it, glossy in the firelight. The crisp winter air and Ivar's hot breath on my face assail me again, full force. I see Estrid's eyes flash at me, glistening in the moonlit snow.

"My sister and I were attacked." My voice is hollow, even to my own ears, and my thoughts drift as the fire across the room becomes a haze of soft flickering light. I can't feel the warmth of it anymore, only the harsh wind of Northhelm. "It feels like a lifetime ago, and yet—" A tear trickles down my cheek, surprising me, and I quickly wipe it away.

Tora stares at me from across the table. "She is gone, then?" she whispers, and I hear her own longing in the words.

I nod, exhaling as I pull my shirt down again. "It's only me now."

"Surely not only you," Tora says, and glances out the window at Killian, following Leif toward an outbuilding. "I can't imagine your friend out there would risk his life for just anyone."

I frown, staring at him. Watching him. A part of me knows that's true. But why me? Because of Skadi?

"No," I whisper. "Perhaps not." As he disappears inside the shed, another question surfaces. *Does he feel a strange, undeniable pull to me too?*

29
KILLIAN

"We should take the dried fish off the line before the evening mist sets in," Leif says, glancing at his brother.

Hans rests his bow and arrow against the wall of the shed, reluctant as ever. I'm not certain his eyes have left me since we arrived.

"Killian can help me finish with the nets."

Hans doesn't argue, but he doesn't have to say a word, I know he distrusts me. But it's Leif who is in charge, that much is clear. It's been bred into him, just like all New London landowners and Norseland chieftains.

With a final cautionary glare in my direction, Hans steps out into the darkening afternoon. Beyond him, the boy dunks a pail into a barrel on the side of the house, filling it with water. Hans stops to check in with him, ruffling his hair before moving on. As the boy goes about his chores, I see how comfortable this life is for him, and wonder how long they've been on the island.

The amount of moss clinging to everything would suggest

eons, but the time it would take to secure enough supplies and build this place is no small feat.

"You have been here a couple years," I say, knowing it couldn't have been much longer than that. These were empty hills when last I was on the island.

"About. Yes," Leif says, and he tosses me a net. "Untangle what you can, and we'll hang it from the hook." I peer around the interior of the stone outhouse, surprised by how well it's built, with mud and rock and dry grasses.

"So, tell me, new friend," Leif says, his voice careful. "Your ship was a thrall ship bound for New London?"

I look at him, uncertain how to answer that. The Reaper would say yes, and I would say no. The pull between Norseman and Englishman might succeed in tearing me in two one of these days. Even if I feel like neither most of the time. I belong to the sea instead. Or maybe I'm a captive of it. Either way, I'm not sure which answer would suit my circumstances best.

"Okay," Leif says in my silence. "We'll start with an easier question."

I look at him.

"The girl, Brynn—she means something to you?"

I smirk. "That is the easier question?"

Leif flashes me an attentive, sidelong look and shrugs.

"I do not consider them thralls," I tell him instead. "I was in Northhelm to find workers for my estate."

"And you would sail all the way to Northhelm to find workers? Are there none in New London?"

"It is not as simple as that."

"Nothing is," Leif agrees. "Will you at least tell me how you are able to navigate the unsailable seas between both countries? I've never known anyone to do it . . . save for the Reaper." His gaze lingers, and I can't tell if he's still questioning any ties I might have to the Reaper, or if he thinks I'm lying about being an Englishman entirely. I doubt I sound very much like a Norseman or an Englishman, having spent life between both worlds. So I imagine it might be difficult to tell.

"How did you find this island?" I ask him instead.

Leif hangs the empty net from the hook. While the one I straighten is made of seaweed twine, his is an actual rope he must've brought with him, or found in the ship graveyard I know lies just beyond these cliffs.

"By accident." He peers out the doorway, and I know that look in a man's eyes, the hollow one that's dark with regret. "We fled the north, uncertain what we would find, but knowing there had to be more. Praying we'd find someplace . . . but we were willing to die trying, because death was inevitable either way."

"You fled from the queen, but you said the Reaper burned your home and took all you had."

"And he did," Leif says curtly, and his eyes narrow as he looks at me. "In burning down my family's brickhouse, and taking or killing all of my workers, the Reaper left me with nothing but hate and a broken heart. You think the queen cares *why* she isn't getting her bricks and mortar? Why her watchtowers and depositories aren't going up?" He shakes his head. "You have spent too much time away, Englishman."

The more I learn about Norseland, the more I realize he and Brynn are right.

"Between the Reaper and Queen Sigrid, Norseland grows worse by the day. I'm surprised it's not completely burned to ash," he says, looking at me. "I bet it wasn't hard to find workers to sail with you to New London."

I shake my head. It never has been. The truth is, the queen hasn't corresponded with the Reaper in years, hasn't summoned us when we are in port. In fact, she's done more than turn a blind eye in recent years. Our last two exchanges have not been among emissaries, but us leaving our goods in unmanned and unwatched depositories. Strange as that is, I never thought much about any of it, because I didn't care.

"Killian?" Leif watches me closely. "Have you known the wrath of the queen as well? Or perhaps the Reaper? You look . . . haunted, just as I feel most days."

Inhaling a deep breath, I lean my shoulder against the doorway, shaking my head as I watch Tank struggle with a sloshing pail of water. "I think I've just realized how ignorant I am," I admit. "Lost in oblivion for the past decade."

Leif comes to stand beside me, peering out at his kingdom, sowed with his own hands. "I can understand the feeling," he says. "When I'd returned from business in the east to find everything was gone, I—" Leif shrugs. "I became nothing. A shell. I joined Hans and Tora on their journey because there was nothing else for me in Norseland. I figured if I was going to die there, I might as well die at sea or somewhere else with the only family I had left.

"Then one day, it was as if I woke, standing right about here, staring out at this valley, and something inside of me stirred again. The loss of my wife still aches every single day, but to see that a place like this exists for Tank, a life free from puppet masters, helped me find my faith again. My only fear now is that one day others will find this place and everything will change." He stares at me for a good long moment, then looks away. "And my only regret," he adds more solemnly, "is that my wife is not here to see it."

It's clear he still mourns her, and yet, Leif has helped his family find refuge here. He's given them a second chance at life, the same chance I know Brynn desperately yearns for.

"I admire what you've done," I confess. "It is what my grandfather did years ago. He fled Norseland, and like you, he ended up on foreign shores, and now my family is one of the most powerful in all of New London."

"It is safer than they say, then? Better than Norseland?"

I shake my head. "New London is different," I admit. "Better in some ways, but at its core, it's much the same."

Leif hums in understanding. "Then we made the right decision staying here." He steps out into the cold wind. "We've always wondered if we should keep sailing. Explore what else might be out there, but we didn't want to push our luck." Strands of his red hair catch the breeze, escaped from his braids, and we head to a small smokehouse.

"You'll have to tell me more about New London," he says. "I've always wondered about it. It's all but myth and legend to most of us."

As Leif continues on, my mind wanders to thoughts of Skadi. To the dream woman that's haunted me all my life and that I've felt with every cool kiss of the breeze. I think of Brynn, waking on my ship, about us on this island, and the future she fights against.

But as I watch Leif, a third path is clear. The right path. A freer path than what I can offer Brynn. And I know how all of this must end.

30
BRYNN

Tora refills my tea as the door opens and the three men walk in, Tank coming in behind them, lugging his water pail at his side. In an instant, the cottage feels small, and the atmosphere in the room changes with the scent of men, their imposing forms, and so much movement.

There's a strange look in Killian's eyes when I meet his gaze. A look that's different from any I've seen in them before. A regret and maybe even frustration I don't understand, and I wonder what was said outside, and if I should be worried.

Leif's eyes skirt over me before he hands his sister a small, skinned animal that smells like woodsmoke. Hans pays no attention to me as he ruffles his son's strawberry-colored hair and kisses the top of his head. It's a fatherly gesture I hadn't expected, given that Hans's severity remains predictably in place. He's hardly warmed to us yet.

"If you're to be inside," Tora says. "Take your muddy boots off. And Tank," she commands, though not unkindly, "fill the pot, please."

I help Tank pour half of the water pail into the pot clasped on a hook above the fire.

"Hans," Tora continues, bustling about, "bring in some haddock for seaweed stew while Brynn and I make some seed cakes to bake over the fire. We better get a move on if we're to feed everyone before midnight."

The men scatter about, Hans stepping outside for the fish while Leif pours each of us a cup of green water. "It's the closest we have to ale," he explains, offering me a fresh cup. "And it's better than that tea you're drinking there," he teases.

"She's to finish the tea first," Tora chides, nodding to my mug. "Don't come in here, mussing things up now."

I try not to smile at the exchange, and chug the cooling tea down as Leif smiles beneath his mustache. Once we each have a cup of green ale, Killian and I take a drink. It's herbaceous and briny, and I assume it's made from seaweed.

"Leif, finish hanging the clothes on the line for me, and find something clean in your trunk for your new friend to wear. I'll tend to Brynn. I won't have them smelling up my house."

"As you say, Sister." As Leif jumps to task, I decide I thoroughly admire this woman.

"Brynn," Tora continues, eyeing me up and down. "I'll find something for you to wear." She nods for me to follow her.

As she rustles through a chest by her bed, I stand to follow and lean into Killian. "What's wrong?" I ask, peering up into his eyes. Their steely blue is edged with shadows as his gaze shifts over my face. "Killian?" I say, straightening. "Should I be worried?"

He averts his gaze. "No, it's nothing."

I frown. That can't possibly be true. "You—"

"Brynn," Tora says, beckoning me. She holds up a pair of hide pants and a shirt. "These will have to do."

With a final glance at Killian, who is purposely not looking at me, I go to her. "Thank you, Tora," I say, distracted—worried despite Killian's halfhearted reassurance.

Tora nods toward a wash bin. "You can scrub down over there, if you wish." She looks between Killian and me, her eyebrow lifting curiously, then she wipes her hand on her skirt and walks away.

"You can help me as soon as you're finished," she calls over her shoulder. And taking the hint, I go to wash up, wondering what, exactly, changed in the past hour.

For the first time, I'm not indifferent or angered or curious about the thoughts that plague Killian—I'm worried.

31
BRYNN

We empty five jugs of ale between all of us, Killian and Leif drinking the majority. At first, I thought drinking was necessary to breach the awkwardness, but Leif and his sister, even skeptical Hans, seem to revel in having company. And quickly, talk among us becomes easy.

Belly brimming with hot stew and my mind a tad hazy, I observe our hosts, trying to imagine them feasting in a grand hall in the finest wolf furs and silver adornments. I have a dozen questions about Leif's life before, about Han and Tora's life together. But this moment of temporary bliss and comfort is something I need far more than answers, so I let the questions lie.

Instead, my eyes shift to the modest wooden cross hanging on the other side of the room above their bed.

A week ago, I was living amid religious unrest with thugs, Christian and pagan alike, roaming the streets. A week ago, I was sleeping on a hay pallet in a workhouse, the Reaper haunting my dreams. Now here we all sit, the Reaper and I drinking seaweed ale in the warmth of a family's home on an island in the middle of nowhere.

I chuckle to myself, at a loss what to think, though I feel it all acutely—the heaviness, warm and comforting as it is, clinging to me. When I look at Killian, I find he is already staring at me, watching me as the table chatters, talking over one another. His eyes are glassy, his smirk ever-present, but it's not the same. It doesn't reach his eyes.

Taking a slow glug of his ale, Killian finally looks away.

Leif, jovial as ever, bangs on the table, boisterous from too much drink. "You should have seen us the first year," he says. "Uncertain how we would make it work, but we knew that we must." He shakes his head. "We hadn't thought our longboat would even make it this far. But alas, when we saw the mountains through the fog, I knew it was a beacon. That God had smiled down on us, and this was our new beginning. Even if it took Tora's urging to get me this far."

Despite their physical differences, Killian and Leif are the same in so many ways. The longer I sit here watching them, the more I see it. Two men who have had the weight of the world on their shoulders, who would be friends in another life, if Killian wasn't the Reaper, the man Leif has sworn to hate.

"You are quiet," Tora says beside me.

"Am I?" I glance at her. Even *her* eyes shimmer with a sated look of bliss. "Perhaps the men are boisterous enough for the rest of us tonight."

She smiles, if a bit sadly. "I have not seen my brother smile nor laugh like this since before we left Norseland."

I find that hard to imagine. "Where did you live?"

"Near Talon Bay."

"That's east of Northhelm?"

Tora nods. "Our grandfather was one of the queen's confidants, and so the title of chieftain was passed down to our father."

"Was he a good man?" I ask, forgetting myself for a moment. Perhaps if I hadn't had any ale, I would not ask her such a question. But I do, and I wait for her reply. "Your father," I mean.

"He was," she says sadly. "He was not as revolutionary as Leif, but he was a good man."

I turn to face her better on the bench. "Revolutionary?"

"When I moved into the village, to Hans's family farm, and we had Tank, Leif became somewhat of a rebel. It was a point of contention I often heard about, from both my father and my brother."

"What did Leif do?"

"Besides fall in love with one of my father's slaves and take her for his wife?" Tora laughs sadly. "He spoke out against the queen." She shakes her head. "Never trusted her. Or rather, he'd always been wary of her. Leif knew my father was only a means to an end, that our father was working himself to the bone, working his laborers to the bone, for a queen who was more of a whisper than a presence. Her men came around to check on my father's production twice a year, to ensure the store houses and depositories were being built to their satisfaction, but that was all. When my father and brother offered her men hospitality during their stay, they stole from him, raped his servants—did horrible things. And Leif was done keeping his mouth shut. He was convinced the queen wasn't real anymore. Her thugs were all anyone ever saw."

I nod, knowing it's true. I've never seen the queen. Then again, she would never come to a dirty city like Northhelm, even if it's the capital.

"So, Leif began to question what was happening in Winterwood. And the more he voiced his questions, the angrier my father grew, because he did not want unfavorable attention."

"And then they came," I breathe, realizing the guilt Leif must have felt.

"Our father sent Leif on a fool's errand somewhere, and when he returned, the village remained, but our father's estate was burned to nothing. It's easy to imagine why," she whispered.

So many times in my life, I told myself to keep my mouth shut about something, only I couldn't. So many times, I've wondered if even one of those moments might've changed the course of my and Estrid's lives. I feel guilty enough in my actions over the past weeks, let alone years, and my throat thickens as I imagine Leif's regret.

"Koraline—Leif's wife—was like you in many ways. She was outspoken and brutally honest."

My attention flicks to Leif with sudden fascination. A future chieftain by birthright who loved a slave girl. "I admit, my mouth has gotten me into trouble more than a few times."

"Yes, well, it's what he loved about her. She kept him honest in a world that would have shaped him to be a monster if he'd given in. In the end, though, what happened to her nearly did turn him into one. If he hadn't come with us," she says, her voice watery with grief, "I don't know what would have happened to my brother."

When I look at Leif again, he is laughing at Hans's drunken slurs. This time, I see Leif in a new light. A softer light. I feel sick for him that he lost his love. That he lost his father and his means of surviving in Norseland all because he spoke out against the queen.

Leif catches my staring and lifts his mug to me and takes a drink. Though I don't think much more will fit in my stomach, I take a sip because he is our host, and it would be rude not to. His eyes linger on me a little longer, but I'm too busy watching Killian, who looks discomforted as he glances between us.

I'm not sure why, but I avert my gaze. "How long have you and Hans been together?"

Tora smiles, cheek against fist as she rests her elbow on the table. "We were betrothed when I was twelve," she says wistfully.

"And lord, how I hated him." We both laugh as she rolls her eyes, unable to suppress a growing smile. Her teeth are a bit crooked, her nose a tiny bit sharp, but her eyes are endless pools of blue, and her smile lights up the whole room when she allows it to. Yes, I see why Hans stares so longingly at her, even now, after all these years.

"He's such a hardheaded ass sometimes, but I find I can't live without him." She chucks a piece of stale bread at him, and he jolts in his seat.

"Aye, what was that for?" Hans's gaze skips between us.

Tora only smiles broadly and chucks another one at him. With a goofy grin I haven't seen on Hans, he catches the bread and tears a chunk from it like a wild beast. Tora rolls her eyes at him and looks away. "Do you see what I mean?"

I laugh, but the weight of her attention settles on me next. "What about you, Brynn of Northhelm?"

"What about me?"

She glances at Killian. "You and the Englishman?"

Huffing a laugh, I drink the last of my ale and lick my lips. "Me and the Englishman," I parrot. "He is the most infuriating, complicated man I've ever met. If we can get off this island in one piece, I will be glad for it."

Tora snorts dubiously. "Well then, what about before? Was there no one back in Northhelm?"

"No," I say, shaking my head. Fleetingly, I think of Bo and pray he is doing all right, that he's looking after Phillip. "No one that means to me what Hans means to you." I watch her husband, utterly entertained as he makes faces at Tank. Hans is goofy when he's drunk, and I like that about him.

"Then it sounds like, despite having woken up on a stranger's ship, there was little to leave behind." There's something maternal in Tora's tone, and I look at her. "Perhaps God thought it was time you found happiness, Brynn of Northhelm."

My brow lifts, and as I search her face, I'm not sure what I see. An offer of friendship? Reassurance?

"If your god wanted me to have a new life, why would he take the only thing that made it worth living?" I can't help the ache in my voice or the threat of tears in the backs of my eyes.

"That is part of your journey—of all of our journeys. Perhaps only as you are now can you think beyond what you were. What you thought you must be."

Tora's words are claws against my skin, and she must see how they rankle me.

She rests her hand on mine. "I don't say any of that lightly." She glances at her brother, and considering the turn his life has taken, her honesty rings true.

Tora shakes her head sadly. "Even though I would impale the Reaper if given the chance," she says quietly, her tone hard and filled with hatred, "he has, in a way, done us a kindness. Here, on this island, we live a far better life than we ever had in Norseland. No real fear. No one to tell us how to live. My only real regret . . . is that Koraline is not here with us."

I frown, Tora's words striking an unexpected cord. "You said Leif was a revolutionary, so much so that even your father worried he would draw unwanted attention."

Tora nods. "Leif was not the only man in Talon Bay without a stomach for cruelty. He was simply the most vocal."

I rub my temple, my mind half numb from drink and my thoughts racing. "If the Reaper only takes from the worst of the worst, he would not have gone after your family." I shake my head, considering my own village burned in the Reaper's name, and try to make sense of it all. "Why are the majority of the attacks on peaceful villages and decent families?" I glance at Killian as a pattern begins to form.

"You claim to know the Reaper's intentions?"

My attention snaps to Tora, and her expression steals my

breath. Her eyes narrow as she glances between Killian and me.

I inhale a deep breath, shaking my head. "We have heard rumors, is all." It's my first true lie since meeting them. "The Reaper burned my village as well. I'm simply trying to make sense of it." Lifting my empty mug, I groan. "The ale is not making it easy."

Tora doesn't seem to hear me as she stares at Killian for far too long.

"Tora?" I hedge, nudging her attention back to me.

Finally, she tears her gaze from him. "I think presuming anything about the Reaper is dangerous, at least in this house." She eyes me closely. "We should speak no more of it."

My heart pounds with uneasiness, and I nod. "Of course. My apologies."

Tora downs what's left in her cup, watching me over the brim. She could say something now, press me for information or demand more answers from Killian in front of everyone, but she doesn't. Thankfully, Tora lets the conversation go, and I turn to the guys, praying for less incriminating conversation.

"—family's important in the Black Country," Leif asks. "I have no doubt you're telling the truth, but how is it a villager from Norseland became one of the most important men in New London?"

Killian smirks, but it's not with humor, and I wonder what he will say next. "I'm not certain *important* is the correct word," he admits.

"Then what is? You claim an English army would come for you." Hans presses. Though it's not so much doubt and distrust in his words as curiosity.

Curious myself, I wait for whatever Killian will say next. Will it be a truth or a lie?

He turns his mug around in his hand before finally speaking. "We have clout," he explains. "Because, in short, my grandfather woke the sleeping city seventy-five years ago, and my family has been helping them rebuild it ever since."

We all gape at him. I might even bite my tongue in surprise. The very city he has warned me of isn't simply where he lives, but one his family helped create? The sudden racing of my heart and the crease between my brows has me looking away from him. I'm not sure why that surprises me, or why it's hurtful to hear. It changes nothing he's told me. *Does it?*

"You are English royalty, then?" Hans asks with a chuckle, pouring himself more ale before filling his brother's mug next.

Killian grins. "You could call it that," he says, and his eyes meet mine. "Whether I wish to be or not."

Somehow, the burden on Killian's shoulders feels heavier now, even to me. I don't ask any more questions right now, worried I'll give too much away, but my mind reels with such knowledge.

"Was it really shrouded in black like the stories say?" Hans asks, filling Tora's mug next.

Killian shrugs. "Perhaps once, but it is lush and green and a beautiful country, though it quakes nearly as often as the sun rises and sets."

"So it is a dangerous beauty," Leif muses.

"Aren't they all?" Killian quips with a smirk, and I roll my eyes.

"It's still a wonder what you were doing in Norseland, then," Tora says cautiously, and everyone's laughter dies away. "Collecting workers, or so you say, but why come all the way from New London to do that?"

She knows. Tora knows Killian is the Reaper—my gut knots, confirming it's true. Or at least she more than suspects it. Still, she doesn't call him out, and I pray it stays that way. That our new friends will remain that, for a little while longer, at least.

"Honestly?" Killian says, resting his elbows on the table.

"It is a conversation for another time, when I have not had so much ale, but the larger our estate becomes, the more workers we need. Workers that are not traced by the Council."

Leif looks at me, and I can tell he's uncertain if I knew this. I did, parts of it anyway, but the reminder that I am nothing more than a worker in his grand plan still stings.

I take a sip from Tora's mug since mine is empty. "Lucky me to wake on such a ship," I mutter, and lick the ale from my lips.

"Aye," Leif counters. "Perhaps you *are* lucky. You're no longer in Northhelm. You're here with us—free to do as you please without suffering the consequences, and I would dare Killian to say otherwise." Leif eyes him carefully, waiting for a protest, but Killian says nothing.

When Leif looks at me again, he rests his hand on mine, his eyes soft and reassuring. "You can stay here with us, Brynn. If you want to."

I smile, if a little weakly, glancing from Leif to Hans and then at Tora. Their expressions are indiscernible—not surprised or welcoming, nor put out by the idea.

I'm about to tell him it's not possible that I stay here, but realize that's not true. I belong to no one, and I have no reason to sail to New London, not anymore. In fact, Killian all but threatened to leave me here during our argument on our first night here. The difference is if I stayed now, I wouldn't be alone.

"Something to think about," Leif says, stirring my thoughts. He shrugs as if he didn't just offer me everything I've ever dreamed of.

Killian stares into his mug, turning it around and around on the table. I'm not sure why I want him to look at me, but I need to see what thoughts play in his eyes. He doesn't, though, no matter how much I will him to. In fact, the silence between breaths seems to stretch unbearably long and is painfully uncomfortable.

"I need to take a piss," he finally says, and Killian rises from the table. In four strides, he disappears out into the night.

The others say nothing about it, and Leif and Hans fall back into chatter about stocking for winter, but I feel Tora's eyes on me. Her focus is fire-hot against my face, and whatever she sees, it's far too close to the truth. I just pray that, whatever it is, she likes us enough to keep her musing to herself, just a little while longer.

32
BRYNN

I stare up at the rafters, night shadows seeping into the cottage through cracks and crevices. The wind and distant waves are a calming melody outside, and I'm painfully aware of how exhausted I am, and that I could be sleeping right now—that I *should* be. Who knows when I'll get another night in a warm, dry room on Leif's comfortable feather mattress.

But I can't sleep. All I can think about is dinner tonight. About the queen and her quarrels with Leif. About the northerners who are targeted by raiders, acting out in the Reaper's name.

And about Leif's offer—that I could stay and live here if I wanted. There's a protectiveness in Leif's eyes when he looks at me, an urging, though I don't think it's borne of intrigue or loneliness. But compassion.

Either way, I know remaining here is the best possible choice I could make for myself. That, like Leif and Hans and Tora, I could easily call this place home.

When Killian takes a deep breath, I turn my head to stare at his back. Why would the queen risk censure from the masses by allowing innocents to die in the name of the Reaper, knowing it is not he who burns her workhouses and kills her chieftains and her people? Because she has to know it's not him, doesn't she? The Reaper is only in Norseland once or twice a year. It's impossible for him to make such waves throughout the country.

"Killian?" I whisper, certain he's still awake. His breathing hasn't changed since we lay down, even in his drunken state. When he doesn't answer, I roll onto my side and try again. "Killian?"

"Hmm," he grunts.

"I need to talk to you about something."

His shoulders rise and fall, but he says nothing.

"Killian—"

"If you want to stay, Brynn," he says flatly, "stay." In spite of his clipped tone, he doesn't sound angry so much as weary. "You'll be happier here on this island than in New London, tethered to my family."

I blink at his back. "Okay, but that's not—"

"I know what I said before." There's an edge to his voice this time, an exasperation, even if we've barely spoken tonight. "But in your mind, you'll always be a slave to someone if you don't stay here. You'll end up resenting my brother and me. So, stay and save us all the headache."

I find I'm speechless, shocked by his unsolicited, brutal honesty, though I'm not sure why. Killian's been hot and cold since I met him.

"You think I would resent you if I went to Briarwood?"

He huffs a feigned laugh. "Don't you already?"

I open my mouth to say *no* but stop myself. I do. Or rather, I did. "That's not what I wanted to talk to you about," I say instead.

"Well then," he gripes with annoyance. "What is it, Brynn? I'm tired."

His brusqueness makes me bristle, and any concern I have for Killian's reputation as the Reaper flits away on the draft that whirs through the cottage, and I glare at his back. "Absolutely nothing," I grind out, and turn to face the wall instead.

Knowing Killian, he did have his crew commandeer Leif's workers at one point, but he was just too drunk to remember.

Determined to get some sleep, I settle deeper under the blankets and wonder when the ship will come, so I can be rid of the Reaper, once and for all.

33
BRYNN

Despite my efforts, I barely slept. Killian snored all night, which might not have been as annoying had I not been so angry with him. By the time the muted morning peeks through the shuttered window, I decide a cloudy sunrise is far more enticing than lying next to Killian.

With a huff, I climb off the mattress, not caring if I wake him. Killian doesn't stir in the slightest, and that he can sleep like a babe despite the past few days only annoys me more.

Still in the clothes Tora lent me, I'm already dressed, but imagining cold water on my face and some licorice root to chew on, I leave my hair in the braids running down my back, steal Killian's long sleeves, and spare him a final glance before I head out the door.

The cool air enlivens my groggy senses, and I close my eyes to the crisp morning. Fleetingly, I imagine what it would be like to wake up every day to the coastal breeze, and wonder if Killian isn't right: I should stay here. I'd regret it if I didn't.

You might regret it if you do. I don't know where that thought comes from, but the implications of it make me uncomfortable, and I latch the cottage door behind me.

The homestead is quiet. As far as I can tell, no one is awake. Even the house seems still, save for a faint tendril of smoke still rising from the chimney. Spotting a water barrel on the side of the house, I walk toward it, inhaling the fresh air. When did breeze become so calming?

A splash of cold water on my face wakes up every nerve in my body, and with a shiver, I dab my face dry on my long sleeve. With nothing more than the gray clouds of dawn and the distant cry of seabirds, I head up the hill to watch the horizon, snagging a licorice sprig from Tora's garden along the way. Unpleasant as the taste is, the tang of it against my tongue is oddly fresh, and I tear another piece between my teeth.

When I reach the top of the hill, I pause. It seems I am not the only one awake. Leif sits with his knees bent against his chest, and his loose, red hair catches the wind. His profile makes me smile. Eyes closed and face to the wind, he appears the very picture of everything I wish to be someday: content.

"Am I interrupting?"

His eyes pop open and crinkle in the corners. Leif doesn't even look at me as he smiles. "Not if you promise to speak softly."

With a chuckle, I walk over and plop down a few inches away. The earth is damp, but I ignore it easily enough. "Headache from too much ale?" I ask as he shuts his eyes again.

"Headache. Bodyache. Even my cheeks hurt. I forgot what it was like to laugh so much."

"I know what you mean," I muse. "Who knew being stranded on an island would be the most at ease I've been in as long as I can remember?"

Leif peels one eye open in my direction, though he has a faraway look about him. "It took me so long to find peace in this place after my wife died," he confesses. "Now, I can't imagine ever leaving."

"After all you'd been through, you didn't welcome the change in scenery?"

Leif bends a blade of grass between his fingers. "It was hard to let go of home. Of the past." *Of my wife* goes unsaid, and Leif clears his throat. "When you live a restless life, it's hard to accept the silence." His gaze drifts to mine and shifts over my face. I don't know what he sees when he looks at me, but there's recognition in Leif's expression. A look of empathy in his eyes. His features are a bit weathered and coarse, but he's handsome and his countenance is kind.

"Tora told me your wife was a servant," I confess, uncertain how raw her absence still is.

Leif runs his palm over the wild grass. "Did she, now," he grumbles.

I peer out at the horizon, where the ocean meets the gray. "Imagine how different life would be if there were more men like you—honorable and compassionate, and fighting against the rule we've all been born into."

"I think there are," he muses, and the longer he looks at me, the more I discern his meaning.

"Killian is lost," I tell him.

Leif's cheek twitches as he loses himself in thought. "We're all a little lost, I think."

"True," I say on a sigh, and shake my head, mentally exhausted. "But whatever Killian is searching for, I'm not sure I'll be around when he finally finds it."

"No? I thought there might be a connection between you two." Leif's green gaze isn't probing so much as curious.

"I don't know what I think about Killian," I admit. I consider how much has happened in such a short time—waking in the bowels of his ship only to find I'm now stranded on an island with a ghost I half expected wasn't real. "I thought I hated him, but that seems so long ago now." I shrug.

"Regardless, I don't think he and I will ever find common ground."

"You have not known each other long," Leif muses. "Give him time."

I snort a laugh. "Trust me, the weeks feel like years."

He grins slightly and peers back out at the birds sailing above the whitecaps. The way they ride the wind, barely flapping their wings at all, looks effortless, and I admire how free they must feel as they swoop and dive, coming up to ride the breeze again.

"Were you serious?" I ask, stirring the companionable silence. "Last night—was your offer for me to stay a drunken one?" I give him a slanted look. "It would be okay if it was. You barely know me."

Leif watches me a moment.

"Or," I continue, tucking a strand of hair behind my ear, "now that you know of New London, do you think you will go there as well?"

Leif leans back on his palms and nods to the ocean. "It's something I've been thinking about," he admits. "We've known from the beginning it's only a matter of time before more people found this place. So, leaving now while we have the chance, instead of waiting for when it might be too late, would be wise. And," Leif continues, "there's Tank to think about."

I nod with understanding.

"We wanted to give him a new life, a chance to have a *full* life, and with only the three of us, he will never find that here. But," Leif says, heaving out a breath, "if what Killian says is true, and New London is a dangerous place much like Norseland in many ways, what is the right decision?"

I shake my head, wondering what sort of protection Killian can give them. Or would Leif, Tora, Tank, and Hans be taken as workers, like me?

"I would choose the island," I think aloud. "But then, I am not a boy in need of friends, and I don't care much about a companion for the future. I simply want to . . . live," I say easily. "I want to choose what I eat at mealtime and which chores need tending to." I close my eyes, imagining waking up each morning similar to this.

The sky darkens as thicker clouds roll by, the waves continue to crest below, and eventually, Leif sighs a deep breath.

"It is too early for such conversations, but know this," he says, our gazes meeting. "Whatever happens, this place can be yours as much as it is ours."

Leif's sincerity is a gift I hadn't expected, and a lightness sweeps over me with the wind. "I admit, the idea gives me a sense of peace I have never felt before." Closing my eyes, I lift my face to the wind again. "Even my bones can feel it—yearn for it."

"Good," Leif says with a stretch. "Then at least one of us has an easy decision to make." He climbs to his feet with a groan. "Though I would love nothing more than to spend the morning with you, new friend—" He nods toward the churning clouds on the horizon. "We only have a few hours before that storm arrives, and there is much to do before we're stuck indoors for a time."

I nod. "Then I will help you."

"I'd never say no to that." Leif offers me his hand, and using my good arm, he helps pull me to my feet. He takes a step away and pauses. "Rest assured, Brynn," he says with more solemnity as he stares toward the cottages. "If you decide to stay, there are no strings. No expectations." His eyes meet mine. "I just wanted you to know that."

I purse my lips, uncertain how to answer—uncertain I can as emotion balls in my throat. I'd considered that might be a price I would have to pay, even if it was only in the very back of my mind. Perhaps because he is a man with no companion on this island. Or because most men would only offer such a kindness for a lofty price.

"That is—" I start, and lick my lips. "Unexpected."

"So is your friendship. And that is all I have room for in my heart, even still."

I nod in understanding, gratitude bringing a thankful smile to my lips.

As the wind picks up, Leif waves me toward the cottage. "Come on, then," he says. "The day is starting without us."

34
BRYNN

Along the jagged cliffs, below the hills Leif and his family call home, the island feels far more ominous. The waves crash against the rocky shoreline, the wooden carcasses of ships creaking as the sea beckons them back out into the open waters, only, the rocks refuse to let go.

It's a swirling deluge of tide and current, feasting on the remains of what must be dozens of rotting ships. Most of them look like Killian's—behemoths from another era and world; what's left of people having fled the dying lands during the Great Turning.

The seals, basking on the distant rocks, quiet only when the cruel wind rushes over us. And the gulls caw, uneasy as we disturb their nesting grounds. It's not eggs we're after, however, but scraps of wood. To dry for smoking, for the fire, and whatever might be required when the snow sets in.

As another violent wave crashes the rocks, spraying me with sea-foam, I can't help the disquiet that leadens in my stomach. On the horizon, the ocean is deceptively calm. But here, against these cliffs, it would break my bones and pull me under before I could even call for help.

Killian wasn't exaggerating when he said most men couldn't sail these waters. The more I learn about this place, the more in awe I am that we arrived here at all. Because if it's not sandbanks exposed by low tides, it's the storms sailors must be wary of. If not the storms, it's the mountainous rocks reaching up from the depths. I can see them out there, peeking through the whitecaps as if they are standing guard, barely visible and waiting for their next victim.

The thwack and thump of axes above deck breaks the ocean's hold over me, and I scan the exposed belly of the ship. I search under debris and seaweed for usable items, picking through crabs and shells, and pilfering old crates and trunks crusted shut with barnacles and rust.

As the boat creaks in its precarious angle, I can't help but stare with an erratic heartbeat at the angry waves just below my feet. It's no wonder Leif doesn't do this often and why Tank and Tora stay on the safety of the rocky shore. Had I not been so stubborn when Killian told me to stay aground, I wouldn't be second-guessing my determination to help quite so much.

With a steadying breath, I swing the butt of a hammer at the lock on a rusted trunk, nearly losing my balance. I brace myself on the splintered wood with a curse.

Killian leans over, peering through the busted boards at me, frowning. "I didn't save your life in those waters for you to die on a ship," he chides. "Be careful."

Leif's chuckle reaches my ears as his axe hits wood again.

"Worry about yourself," I grumble with a final glance at Killian's perturbed expression.

Refocusing on my task, I crouch to sort through coins. A woman is etched on the face of them, and since they mean nothing to me, nor to our cause, I move on to the next chest. There are nets to be repurposed, and I find a few candlesticks that might be useful, some soggy books I chuck to the side, and a string of pearls Tora might appreciate.

A child's peal of laughter carries up from where Tora and Tank collect shells and seaweed on the shoreline in the distance, and the day darkens as the storm clouds move in. The grayer the sky becomes, the more difficult it is to see in the shadows of the rotting ship carcass, so I make haste.

Once I've filled one of the usable nets with what can be salvaged, I find better footing and brace myself to climb to the deck with the others. The wood is slick with moss and weak with rot from so much moisture in the air. I'm almost to the top deck when a gust of wind rushes the ship. Loose strands of hair lash at my eyes, stinging them as I try to see.

Before I can process that I'm slipping, Killian reaches out to grab my shoulder, steadying me. There's a momentary flash of fear in his eyes before his expression hardens again.

"I'm heading up," I say, more to reassure him he doesn't have to worry about me anymore, because I don't like his hard edges that have formed since yesterday. I thought we'd been making progress, and yet, he's more prickly than ever.

Taking a deep breath, I secure the net of goods around my back and shoulders, climb over the stern, and onto the safety of the cliff. I'll need both of my hands to make it up the narrow path to the top.

I might have reckless tendencies at times, but unless it's flight or fight, I try not to be stupid. Maybe it's the fact that I've now been assaulted by the sea, but that—hacking away at the ships—seems a bit mad.

I would do it again though, to help them. *And I likely will.* The desire to stay is hard to ignore the more I talk with these people. The more comfortable I am around them, the more I dread the unknown that awaits me in Briarwood. The question looms, however, that if they were to leave with Killian, would I stay here alone?

"We're right behind you," Hans calls as the men finish tying down the wood to haul up. Although he and Leif have done this before and move with practiced steps, I would bet this is one of their least favorite tasks on the island. And one of the reasons Leif wants to explore the others so badly.

While this place is the size of Norseland's largest city, it is an island all the same, with as much mountainous rock and gravel as it has rolling green hills. Save for the crab, seaweed, and fish, its resources are limited. There is water and shelter. But wood is scarce, and the animals are small and could easily be overexploited if Leif isn't careful.

I make a mental note to ask Killian what the other islands have to offer and if some of them might be better suited for life out here.

It's a rocky climb, but there's plenty to grip onto along the cliff for purchase. Hans and Killian push in the back, and Leif pulls the pallet by a rope tied around his upper body, offsetting some of the weight.

The men huff and grunt behind me, and I keep moving, anxious to reach the top. The wind is roaring up here without the mountain face to shield us, and lifting the rope over my head, I discard the net sack of goods with a clatter and hurry over to help Leif with the bulk of the sled's weight as he breaches the top.

But I'm too late. Rocks move beneath the sled, tumbling and plummeting over the edge into the waves below. Everything shifts just as Leif registers the wood is about to topple over too, him going with it.

"No—" I reach for his arm to yank him my way, my bad arm burning with pain, but I clutch onto him as hard as I can, using all of my body weight to pull him back.

Hans and Killian shout in panic as the sled continues to slide off course. Its pull is too strong, and I get yanked with Leif, falling to my knees as the sled slips back down the mountain.

Leif curses. Tora shrieks below. Hans shouts, grimacing as

he tries to control the sled, and Killian jumps over it, nearly clipping his foot on the corner as he lunges for Leif, skidding back down the path.

Killian grabs hold of the edge of the platform, his muscles flexing as he clutches onto it and heaves, allowing Leif to regain his footing. Killian's face is a mask of calm determination. His eyes crisp and clear.

Uncertain what else to do, I slide down to grab hold of the other side.

Leif, Killian, and I pull as Hans pushes the back, his feet slipping out from under him in the loose soil, until finally, most of the wood is safely atop the cliff, and we are all alive—shaken and barely able to catch our breath, but alive.

Leif untwines the rope from around his torso and tosses it aside, collapsing beside Killian. Hans falls down beside them, and I clutch my knees as I watch, my fingers quickly finding the grasses and damp earth to grab hold of for reassurance. Then, all of us gasp for lungfuls of air.

A hundred heartbeats pass between us, as do more breaths.

I don't realize how sweaty I am and how close that really was until my mind finally begins to settle and I spot a seabird on one of the rocks, staring curiously at us. What a sight that must've been, and I can't help the sudden swell of relief and gratitude that all four of us are still here.

Leif sits up, wiping his brow with the back of his arm.

"Well, Killian," he says with a barely restrained chuckle. "I think you just saved my life." I hear Leif's relief and see it in his eyes. He reaches out his hand, awaiting Killian to take it.

I tuck an escaped strand of hair behind my ear to no avail, and notice a beat of hesitation in Killian's eyes before he finally takes Leif's hand and accepts his gratitude with a nod. "It's nothing you wouldn't do for me," he says. But when Killian's eyes meet mine, I see the regret shadowing them, a certainty that if Leif knew who Killian was, that wouldn't be true.

Leif stands with a groan, then hauls Hans up as well. He reaches for Killian's hand again next, and both men's arms shake with fatigue as Killian climbs to his feet.

"And you," Leif says, coming over to stand in front of me. I peer up at him, squinting at his shadowed face against the gray afternoon. "You nearly went over the cliff with me."

"But I didn't," I say as he helps me to my feet.

"You bought us some time. Thank you for that."

I'm about to shrug it off when Hans gestures to the sled. "You got this?" he asks. "Tora is freaking out, on her way up here right now—"

Leif waves him away. "Go. We can take it from here." As Hans hurries down the hill, Leif looks at us, heaving another sigh. "Well, I think that's enough excitement for one day. Shall we return?"

35
BRYNN

We're not back at the homestead an hour, and the wood is nearly unloaded into the drying house. The clouds have all but broken above us, and the sky and sea are an ominous hue as the wind thrashes the world into a frenzy.

When Tora calls us into the house for food and warmth, Leif and Hans lean the last of the planks in staggered rows against the walls.

"I'll take the ropes back to the toolshed," I tell the guys as they groan and crack their backs from such a taxing day. A hot mug of tea by the fire sounds like the greatest of luxuries right now, and I can't put everything away fast enough.

I roll the last of the rope when Killian strides purposefully by, heading away from the homestead. Peering up at the baleful clouds, I shut the door to the toolshed. Leif and Hans look at me with a strange expression before they walk toward the house.

"He insisted," Leif says over his shoulder.

"Insisted what?" They don't hear me over the wind and

walk into the house. Shaking my head in utter confusion, I hurry after Killian, jogging a few steps before I've caught up with him. "Where are you going?"

"I need to check the markings on the rocks to ensure they're still there," he says. "You should go inside with the others."

"What—" I peer up at the impending storm. "*Now?*"

"Yes, I should have done it first thing this morning."

"Killian, the rain—"

"I can't chance my ship not finding me, Brynn. You might have the luxury of staying here, but I don't." His tone is one of anger and frustration, not so much of concern, so I know he's only telling me half the truth.

"What's this really about?" I ask, trying to keep pace with his long strides.

"I told you." Each of his steps are determined, eating up the landscape as we make our way toward the ravine.

"Yeah, the mark on the cliff." I glare at him. "But I don't believe you."

"That's not my problem."

"Actually, it is. What if something happens to you out here?"

"What if it does?"

"Stop it," I say, grabbing his arm. "What the hell is your problem? You've been in a foul mood since we met Leif. Are you feeling guilty because of what happened to him and his family?"

"No," he says curtly.

We follow the hills past the cave with the hot pool, toward the other side of the island. "I know it wasn't you, if that's what you're worried about."

"It's not," he says, his pace quickening as he blinks into the wind.

I step over a stone, realizing we're nearly to the gorge already, so it appears I am going with him. "Then what the hell is it?"

Killian stops and glances behind us, realizing how far we've walked. With a sigh, he rubs his brow. "You should turn back," he says, wiping the raindrops from his face. "Go—before the storm gets too bad. I can hole up in the cave until it passes."

I shake my head. "No."

"Dammit, Brynn—"

I continue into the ravine ahead of him, and begrudgingly, Killian follows.

"Stubborn brat," he grumbles behind me.

"And you're not?" I scowl at him. "I don't know what crawled up your ass and died, but I think you should tell Leif the truth about who you are."

"What?" Killian looks at me like I've lost my mind. "No. What good would that do?" Killian moves more quickly as the rain turns from a drip to a shower. "I don't want to risk someone getting hurt."

"But if you tell Leif who you are, that you didn't do what he thinks you did, he will forgive you."

"You've known him for what, two days?" Killian shakes his head. "We've lied to him so many times now. How can you be certain?"

"We haven't lied at all, not really," I point out. "Besides, it's just a feeling I have."

"Yeah, well, they'll want to blame someone, just as you did, and that someone will be me."

"Unless it's the queen, using your reputation against you to rid herself of possible rebellion."

That gives Killian pause, and he looks at me, really looks at me for the first time since we started walking. He doesn't say anything as his gaze shifts from me to the path. We hurry forward. "What makes you think that?"

"Because my village and Leif's brick factory have something in common," I tell him, all of it clicking into place.

"We can talk about it later," he says, but I shake my head. Killian will find a reason to disappear again, or he will be too drunk to listen, or Leif will be around.

"Think about it," I press on, the talking helping to keep my mind off the cold seeping into my bones. "My village had no love for the queen, or Chieftain Klaus, who my father and many families toiled on their farms for. The Reaper showed up and put an end to all of it. Same with Leif and his father. The more people hate and fear you, the less they'll hate the queen."

Killian shakes his head. "The worse I look, the worse she looks. And if you can't convince me, there's no way you'll convince Leif."

I stop as it dawns on me. I barely feel the chill anymore as the rain drips down my face. "Not if she plans to kill you and your crew, Killian. Once you've served your purpose." Licking my lips, I brush wet strands of hair from my face, barely able to see through the pelting rain as I hurry to keep up with him. My clothes are drenched, again, and I wrap my arms around myself as if it might stave off the storm.

"I told you to stay behind!" Killian shouts, eyeing me up and down, and a part of me wishes I would have. But to know Killian was out here alone would not have sat right with me.

We continue in silence. Streams of water trickle down the sides of the mountains as we pass and puddle around our feet. "We have to hurry," Killian calls over the wind. "It's going to flood."

Our pace quickens to a jog, my blistered feet slowing me down as Killian pushes faster ahead. A flash of movement catches my eye, and blinking through the rain and my wet lashes, I see rocks rolling down the side of the canyon wall. Tumbling faster and faster, and heading toward Killian.

"Killian!" I scream, but he can't hear me. Without thinking, I grab a rock at my feet and lob it at him, nearly stumbling. It hits him in the back, and Killian spins around. He glares at me as I spring forward, and the moment he registers the rolling rock coming for him, his eyes widen. I yank him out of the way as the granite boulders rolling down the mountain crack and crash into each other.

Wet, rocky earth cuts into my palms and seeps into my pants as I gape at the hunks scattered on the valley floor.

Killian looks at me, both of us heaving and barely able to see through the rain. It drips from his eyelashes and beard, the ends of his loose mane matted to the side of his face. But Killian's eyes are so crisp and clear, I can't look away from them as they shift over my face. I'm not sure if he's dubious or shocked, or a little of both, but he simply stares at me before his gaze shifts to my mouth.

I climb to my feet as my teeth begin to chatter. "What would you do without me?" I offer Killian my hand to help him up and my bunched sleeve exposes my runes. Killian stares at my hand before he pushes himself up to his feet.

"You should have stayed with Leif."

"Wait, what?" I say, dropping my arm. "That's what you have to say? I just saved your life."

"Consider us even, then." He sidesteps the broken boulders, eyes shifting to the cliffs, ensuring there are no more rockslides, and he jogs the rest of the way through the canyon.

"You've got to be kidding me!" I shout, beyond sick of him. I stay a few paces behind, needing space so I can decide what I'm going to do when I finally get to the shelter that we'll be stuck in together.

By the time I reach it, Killian's already striking a fire to what remains of the wood from our crab dinner the other night. Water drips from him, sending puffs of steam into the air as it drops into burgeoning flames.

"I need you to tell me what's wrong, Killian. We were getting along fine. Now you're back to being a dick, and I'm getting tired of it."

He glares up at me but says nothing.

"No comment," I mutter. "I figured."

There's another stretch of silence while Killian simply stares at the fire. Unlike him, I don't want to stew in discomfort or freeze to death, so I pull my wet jacket off and drape it on the rocks by the fire to dry. My clothes are at Tora's, so other than the wet ones I borrowed from her, I am at the mercy of the fire and blankets again.

All I can think is we almost died on the cliff today, and yet, here we are, at odds with one another again. "Right back where we started," I grumble.

"I told you to stay behind," Killian gripes, his eyes drifting to me as I pull my boots off. "I wish you had," he says more softly.

I don't know if I was supposed to hear the words, but they sting regardless. "Fuck you, Killian." I take a step closer, my wet clothes hanging on me, forgotten. "You act like I'm an affliction—"

"That's because you are."

I point to the ravine. "I just saved you, you ass. And I've done everything I can to keep Tora's growing assumptions of who you really are in check, so that Hans and Leif don't shoot an arrow through your chest."

Killian's jaw clenches, and his eyes sharpen on me like gleaming daggers. "I didn't ask you to do any of that."

I throw my arms up, my side twinging a little. "You didn't have to, Killian. That's what friends do."

"We are not friends," he says coldly.

I shake my head, as incredulous as I am gutted, even if I

shouldn't be surprised. I shouldn't care. I should hate him. And maybe I still do. "You're right." I bite my cheek, tasting blood. "We're clearly not."

"You're the one who wanted to kill *me*, remember?"

"I'm beginning to remember why." The words are snide, but it's all I can do not to step closer and punch him in his arrogant face.

Killian glares at me. I scowl back. Whatever it is between us feels like poison, and I feel sick to my stomach.

With a groan of frustration, Killian rubs his hand over his face and tugs his fingers through his wet hair as he rises to his feet. "I can't do this with you," he says. "I'm too tired."

"Fine." I turn away from him, truly uncomfortable around him for the first time. "You win," I say, hating the break in my voice. I've never felt more unwanted or more like a burden in my entire life. At least Von saw my worth, even if it was only to use me to his benefit. "Those three strangers treat me better than you," I whisper, and I grab my wet jacket off the rock.

"What are you doing?"

"Leaving you alone, like you wanted." I reach for my wet boots.

"You can't go back out there, Brynn. That ravine is going to flood."

"Don't act like you care." Jacket and boots in hand, I move to leave before the tears come because they are far too close to the surface. The last thing I need is for Killian to know he made me cry.

"Brynn, stop—" He grabs my good arm.

"Let go," I seethe, and my stomach somersaults as I meet his imploring gaze. It hurts to look at, makes my eyes burn, and I don't understand it—any of it.

"Please," he says, and all his frustration melts away.

I try to tug my arm away, but he grips onto it tighter. "Killian, let go of me," I fume. Whatever I'm feeling is unwanted and dangerous.

He shakes his head. He's so close I have to look up at him, and each inhale is a heated mixture of wind and damp earth, sending warm chills over my cool skin. I can't breathe or think straight, and I hate that my insides swirl with desire. I want this man. There's no denying it anymore, and I hate even more that I want someone who infuriates me to the point of tears.

I glare at him, but Killian stares at my mouth, unblinking. "You—"

His lips crash against mine, warm and slick from the rain, and my words are forgotten. I freeze for the skip of a heartbeat, then every nerve in my body comes alive.

The moment his mouth parts and his tongue sweeps mine, an involuntary moan escapes me, and I drop my jacket and boots, kissing him back. It's a frenzy of wanton anger. Days of tension and frustration igniting a firestorm I've tried to smother, and I bite his bottom lip, tasting a tinge of blood.

Killian growls, low and deep in his chest, and presses me into the stone wall. It's a minor discomfort when all I can think about is the heat of his body and making my cold fingers move as fast as I want them to. Over him. Tangling in his hair. Raking down his back.

He lifts my jaw, eyes meeting mine in a reckless, suspended moment. The intoxication. The passion. The infuriating pull between us is laid bare, and when his teeth graze the column of my neck, a riptide of pleasure escapes with a ragged breath, and my body clings to his.

I want him.

To feel him.

To be anywhere but in my head and drowning in my heart.

His hands skim down the slope of my back and grab the swell of my hips as he presses into me.

"What the fuck is wrong with you?" I gasp for breath as his

hand roams under my shirt, up my stomach, brushing the underside of my breasts. And with another moan, I grind against him.

"You," he growls.

I fumble with his belt, desperate to free him from his pants. To seep into his warmth. To feel everything he's been holding back. "The feeling is mutual."

Killian unclasps the rest of my vest as I tug his trousers open. He grabs the loose collar of my shirt and yanks it down to expose my breasts. Palming one, his mouth descends on the other, his tongue hot against my nipple. I arch into him, feeling the pinch of his teeth, and grip his hard and thick length in response.

Hissing, Killian lifts his head. "Dammit, Brynn."

"I'm sorry," I rasp, anything but apologetic. I bite his bottom lip. "Are we playing nice again?"

He lifts a brow, a devilish smirk curving his mouth.

Gripping my thigh, Killian lifts my leg, pressing me firmly against the wall as he palms himself with the other. I've never seen his eyes so wild or his movements unrestrained, and in the breadth of a moment, he's inside me. This man who infuriates me. Who utterly consumes and unravels me. I'm full of him, moaning in pleasure-pain, and cursing his existence as he sinks deeper into me.

I'm on the verge of indescribable bliss when Killian pulls out, teasing my entrance.

"I hate you," I rasp. Gripping onto his wild mane, I wrap my legs around his hips for better purchase.

His fingers press into my thighs with bruising pressure. "No more lies, little Skadi." His mouth covers mine, his hips grinding into me as he thrusts inside me again. "I can't bear it."

I cry out as my body yields to his, greedily seeking all he's held back from me. Every angry word and muttered resentment.

He swears against my skin, my name escaping his lips as my nails score his arms and down his back, urging him closer. To thrust harder. Faster.

The rest is a delicious frenzy of curses and clawing, of quiet confessions and angry promises, and Killian and I lose ourselves as wind crashes with wave, Njord and Skadi swirling in a chaotic storm around us.

36
BRYNN

Wrapped in each other's arms and fur blankets, Killian and I sleep through the night so soundly, I don't wake until muted daylight filters in and the fire is all but embers. My body aches, but it's the welcome kind this time.

Feeling rested for the first time since I can remember, I almost smile. Then I realize last night, whatever that was between us, has likely left things even more uncertain than before. And as much as I want to lie in Killian's arms and feel a semblance of belonging and true protection, I'm afraid to see the look on his face when he wakes. The regret I'm almost certain will follow. And even more unnerving, how much that would crush me.

I tell myself it's only because I don't want to be added to Killian's long list of regrets. But I know it's far more terrifying than that. Whatever inexplicable connection exists between us, last night only made the tether stronger and more difficult to ignore, and if Killian pushes me away again, it will hurt all the more.

Peeling Killian's arm off, I climb out from beside him. As usual, he snores like the dead, not disturbed in the slightest. My clothes are actually dry this time, and I dress quickly, deciding to head to the X on the rocks. I might as well make myself useful while I stew and wait for whatever comes next. Killian was so worried about it last night, I figure it's the least I can do after distracting him.

I pilfer the red chalk from the trunk, grab the canteen, and leave Killian to sleep. When I step out into the daylight, I'm happy to find that a little blue breaks through the cloud cover, filling me with a hopeful sort of excitement that we might have a reprieve from the wind and gloom.

Walking the length of the black, sandy beach, I note the briny scent in the air from the seaweed that washed ashore in the storm. I decide to fill the old sail sack later, to take back to Tora, and continue toward the red marking on the rock. Killian was right to worry about it. It's barely visible after the storm.

Dropping the canteen into the sand, I climb up onto the rocks and begin scraping them with blood-red stone. Powder covers my hands, and a hint of sulfur meets my nose. Straining, I reach the top corner of the X, and make a few determined strikes on the rocks as I imagine Killian doing this same thing with far more ease than I am.

Images of him—of us—flash to mind, and desire stirs in me again. Followed by mortification that I might've done something stupid. Then, more unease follows, which I hate most of all. It's fragility—a foreign and unexpected, emotionally weak sensation I've never felt toward anyone other than Estrid. Because Killian was right last night, I don't have friends. I don't have family. I am alone in this life now, save for him, and even that will change in the days to come, a reality that makes my heart ache.

Even if it's not love between us, it's not exactly hate

anymore either. And yet, a different whisper, one that stirs inside my heart, hopes it could turn into so much more than that.

37
KILLIAN

I peel my eyes open to blinding daylight and wait for the craggy rocks, looming over me, to come into focus. My fingers comb the fur beneath me, and in a rush, I remember where I am.

As memories of last night ripple over me, so does sudden panic, and I sit up.

Brynn.

Rain-soaked skin.

Tangled hair.

Salty lips and the rake of fingernails . . . I peer down at my shoulder and bicep, where three red scratches mar my tattoos, and run my finger over them. *Little Skadi's mark.* I smirk at that.

But as I glance around, the gratification subsides, because Brynn is gone. So are her clothes, and the fire has been out so long, it no longer smokes. My pants, boots, shirt, and vest, all discarded in a heap—a damp heap, I'd guess—and me, naked, are the only remnants of last night. Once again, I find myself alone in here.

I don't know how long she's been gone, or where she went, but my stomach hollows as I consider how much she might regret what happened. How crazy Brynn must think I am. Because gods know, I've done all I can to drive her away.

I laugh at the absurdity of it all. I've been trying to keep the barbed wire that's been taut between us in place so that it's easier to leave her when the time comes. Because I know in my heart that Brynn belongs here, with Leif and Tora . . . Then, I go and do something like this. And the ache to have her again grows even stronger.

"Fucking Killian," I mutter, and rub my hands over my face.

I wait for more self-condemnation to rear its ugly head. But it doesn't. Instead, I notice the tension that's been coiled in my neck and shoulders for days has finally vanished. I've grappled with why and how and what this is all supposed to mean since I first laid eyes on Brynn—been out of my mind with agitation—and this is what it's led to, a proper fucking? One that might be laughed about and forgotten the next day by a man who is not the Reaper. And a woman who is not little Skadi, who has consumed me since she appeared out of nowhere, hating everything about me and my ship. *The woman I must leave behind.*

"Enough." I stand up, knowing I cannot put this off. Nor do I want to. Nothing has changed, not really. The ship will come, it's only a matter of time, and things must be settled before it's too late and Leif hates Brynn as much as he will surely hate me.

I must tell him the truth, whatever the consequence, and pray he is smart enough to listen.

Climbing to my feet, I relish the ache in my arms and legs and in every muscle scored and strained in our cyclone of passionate fury last night. I grab my clothes, definitely still damp from sitting in a heap all night, but I tug on my pants with haste. Then my shirt, knowing I must get this over with.

I tuck the pistol from the trunk into my belt, just in case, and wonder how much time Brynn and I have left before Basher arrives and everything changes.

When I step out into the full wind, I inhale the cool morning air and let it rush over me. *Njord*—sometimes I feel him in the breeze. He bolsters my resolve when it wavers. He fills me with calm, reminding me of my purpose when I start to forget. And Skadi, it seems, has never left me either.

I try not to dwell on how Brynn is feeling about last night as I follow her footprints toward the waterfall. Anticipation hums through my veins, but if it's anxious or hopeful anticipation, I can't be certain.

Until I see her, clinging to the rocks. I feel no anxiousness, only relief as she traces over the red X, and I grin. *If she only knew.*

Her hair hangs long and loose, no longer twisted in haphazard braids. I've wondered before if her sister used to do her hair for her, because she's shit at it. Or perhaps she just doesn't care, and I smile at that.

One of her curses catches the wind as she stretches to trace the last of the X, and I cross my arms over my chest a dozen paces away, watching her. Her determination is commendable, I'll give her that. And while she claims she is lost in the world, now mine feels strangely right with her in it. Confusing and profound, but still, she and I are fated, even if she was only placed in my path to open my eyes to the reality of this unjust world.

Brynn jumps down and dusts her hands off on her pants, finally finished.

"You didn't have to do th—"

"Shit!" She spins around. "Killian! You have to stop sneaking up on me like that."

I try to resist a grin, but it's pointless. "I wasn't sneaking, little Skadi."

Though she would tell me she hates the nickname, her gaze loses its uncertainty when I call her that. It makes me feel powerful to see her pale blue eyes spark to life, and I hate that I've been keeping her guessing for so long.

Needing to touch her, I take her arm, pushing her billowy sleeve up so I can check her knife wound. Last night, I was not careful with her like I should've been, I realize. She acts so tough all the time, it's easy to forget she is not as indomitable as she pretends to be.

"Already scaling walls this morning, I see." I trace my fingertip over her pink, healing flesh, slow and gentle, ensuring it's not overly warm and irritated, and meet her gaze.

Brynn's mouth is slightly parted and she slowly inhales, and nods to the glaring X on the cliffside. "You were right. It was nearly gone."

I stare at it, hating and appreciating that X and all it stands for. "I thought it might be. Thank you." I glance toward our things in the alcove. "You have a habit of leaving me alone in there," I say, and reluctantly, I release her arm. "I thought maybe you'd gone back to Leif's."

"No." Brynn snags the canteen from the sand. "I guess you're not that lucky."

My heart twinges at the comment, even if she says it in jest, because I know I deserve it.

She uncorks the canteen and gulps what's left of the water down. Brynn wipes her mouth with the back of her hand when she's finished and nods to the seaweed lining the shore. "I thought we could take some back to Tora."

I nod, appraising how much washed up in the storm. "That's a good idea, now that they have more mouths to feed." I stare at it for too long, though, and feel Brynn's eyes on me.

"Which Killian do I get today?" she asks, but her sass

sounds equal parts playful and hesitant. "You aren't entirely broody, but you aren't overly playful either."

"The one whose mind is still in that cave, trying to make sense of everything," I admit, and meet her gaze. "About what you said . . . I'm going to tell Leif who I am. He needs to know before he finds out another way and everything is ruined."

"Ruined?" Brynn asks, bracing herself.

"For you to stay here with them."

She blinks, her eyes shifting over my face. "What if they want to leave with you?"

I laugh at that. "You think Leif would, once he knows who I am?"

With a sigh, Brynn shakes her head. "No, I don't think he would."

"But he admires you, little Skadi. If I do this right, you can stay here with them. You *should* stay here."

Her brow crumples, making my chest tighten, and she looks away.

I take Brynn's hand. I can't bare her to think I *want* to leave her here. To think she is a burden to me like I've made her believe a dozen times over.

She stares at her fingers interlaced with mine, but I speak before she can ask more questions I don't know how to answer. "You want to, don't you? To stay here?" I ask.

Brynn bites her bottom lip, eyeing me a second longer. "I do," she admits reluctantly. "More than anything." As disappointing as it is to hear, I can't blame her. It's why I could never ask her to come with me. To give up the only thing she's ever truly wanted.

"Then why fight me on it? You'll have more freedom here than anywhere else, Brynn. You'll be safer too. That's what you want. Even if my family has the best intentions, you won't be happy in New London. And—" I hesitate, because the more I admit to both of us, the harder this will be. "If

I'm honest," I say, "I will worry about you less if you stay here."

Her eyebrows lift. "Worry?" She nods for me to follow her down the beach.

I lift my chin. "Don't look so surprised. I know I'm an ass, but I think it's obvious by now I don't want any harm to come to you. And New London is not a place to be rebellious. If you won't be at my family's estate, I would prefer you to stay here."

"I—"

"Please, don't argue with me," I plead, because I can't be distracted at sea *and* when I am home, worried where she is and what she's doing. If she's alive, or worse—taken as another landowner's property. "I'm serious about this."

Brynn looks like she's trying not to smile, but can't seem to help it as a small one curves her lips. "I wasn't going to argue. I was going to say, I appreciate you saying that. For caring."

Our footsteps crunch the sand until we stop at the waterfall. I take the canteen from her, leaning into the spray to fill it.

"Wow," she says through another grin. "How chivalrous you are this morning," The more I see her smile, the more I yearn for it to never leave her lips.

I shrug, unable to resist a grin of my own. "I have my moments."

The surf ebbs in and out with the waves on the shoreline, and I take a long pull from the canteen before filling it up again.

"I had another thought," she says, though her hesitation is obvious. "It's one I haven't given voice to because I didn't think you would listen, let alone care . . . So, promise you won't be angry with me."

"I will not," I say with a laugh. "Not when you preface it like that."

Brynn rolls her eyes, worrying her bottom lip, and it's all I can do not to stare at it until she finally continues. "Have you ever thought about expanding your efforts?"

I step closer, handing her the canteen.

"I know you are duty bound to your family. But what about taking on a venture of your own?" I open my mouth and she raises her palm to stop me. "Just—hear me out." She reaches for my hand, gaze as devastating to look at as it is imploring me to listen and understand what she's about to say.

I swallow thickly, my fingers squeezing hers of their own accord.

"Your crew knows the sea better than anyone, and there are hidden islands all over the place—land where no one would ever think to look for free people. Just like here."

"Most of these islands are uninhabitable, Brynn."

"But some of them are," she counters. "I saw the map painted on the wall in your navigation room. I didn't know what it was then, but I do now. I saw the X on the ones I assume aren't safe or livable, but there were a handful that were."

I lift my head higher, wondering what else little Skadi saw in all of her peeking around the ship.

"Leif and Tora and Hans," she continues. "They're making it work here. They are happy. If they would offer me a place here, what about others?"

"You are one woman, not ships full of people, Brynn. I doubt they would want—"

"Then forget about Leif. Even if he won't allow it, there are other islands—bigger ones, aren't there? Why not start a colony on one of those for free souls who can live the life they deserve?"

The ferocity in her eyes and the passion in each word—her desperation—stirs something in me. I want to bend to her will as badly as I long to capture that lip she keeps biting with my mouth, and hole ourselves away for whatever time we have left on this island together.

But I lift my palm to her cheek instead, running my thumb over her bottom lip. Her eyelashes flutter closed as her hand covers mine, and she nestles into it.

"I wish things could be that simple," I admit, and I pray to the gods she knows how badly I mean those words.

Her eyes open, boring into me. "But they aren't," she finishes for me, and I hear the ache in her voice as she drops her hand from mine. "I knew it was a longshot."

My hand falls from her cheek, and I clench it into a fist at my side. "You were right before," I confess, glancing out at sea. "My brother relies on the people I bring. And until we figure out how to get him an heir, our family is in trouble. So are all the people on our estate. I can't change course on him—I won't, not now."

Brynn is thoughtful so long, I worry she's retreating from me. From us, whatever we are to each other. I don't want to let her down, but I cannot abandon my brother when I feel I've let him down far too many times to count already.

Finally, she looks at me, her mouth pressed firmly shut and her eyes shifting between mine. I see that ferocity again. That unbridled determination and hurt that she carries with her. The fire that burns in her and in all that she does. She doesn't want to be angry with me; I can see the restraint of it in her gaze, the disappointment and understanding warring with one another. But understanding wins out, because she nods ever so slightly. "Will you do me one favor, at least?"

I dip my chin, hanging on her every word, waiting for her to speak and praying I can give her this one request.

"Will you think on it for the future? Because you're the only one who can manage such a feat."

My shoulders deflate, because I know in my heart she is right.

"As the Reaper of the sea, you wield so much power, even if you've never fully grasped hold of it. Think of what we might accomplish—"

"We?" My eyes widen with surprise.

"I just—I mean, you could give people a choice, New London or . . ." She peers around at the rugged beauty of this place. "Here. The simple life of fishermen beholden to no queen or landowner or chieftain."

"You have all these plans for me," I say, my gaze affixed to hers, wanting her to say the words she dances around. *Needing* to hear them. "Hopes and wishes for my future, and those for your fellow northerners. But how do you fit into all of this, little Skadi?"

With a sigh, she shakes her head. "Honestly, I don't know—"

"Yes, you do. You've been thinking on this for days. So, tell me."

"I—" She shrugs, her shoulders nearly reaching her ears. "I don't know what you want me to say."

"I want you to be honest," I tell her. "I want you to admit where all of this is coming from, because it's not just about everyone else, is it." It's not a question. I might not know what beats in Brynn's heart, but I can feel the charge in the air between us. The undeniable pull to one another, as if the gods themselves are pushing us together, even if they mean to tear us apart by the end of it.

"Peace," Brynn finally admits, and her answer surprises me. "In my heart and mind. To feel as if there's a reason I survived when my sister didn't. To feel worthy of it. You have been placed in my path, Killian. And selfish as it is . . . I know you are the change. And helping you would prove my worth— it would give me purpose."

It's not the answer I expected, or rather, the one I'd hoped for, and knowing I am to blame for her sister's death in the grand scheme of things, is a painful reminder of why Brynn should stay here.

"I'm sorry," I say, and reaching out, I tuck a strand of hair behind her ear. "For the part I played in what happened."

Shock widens Brynn's eyes, and her lips part as if she might say something, but no words follow.

"The truth is," I continue, her hair falling from between my fingers, "seeing the repercussions of my actions, even if they have always been well-intended, is a gruesome truth. One I have been blind to and don't know how to remedy."

Brynn's stormy eyes cloud with tears and she licks her lips. "I—I didn't expect you to say that."

"I can't ignore it anymore," I confess, surprising us both. "But I'm not sure how to change it either. Yet." I run my hands over my face. "I need to speak with Greyson. One of many things to figure out." I don't know if I'm talking to Brynn or myself at this point, but she answers nonetheless.

"Maybe being aware of it is enough for now," she says with a weak smile, and her brow furrows as she seems to realize something. "The queen has inherited an unsustainable reign. I've gleaned that much living with Von. Northhelm is about to implode, and she's running out of ways to keep people happy. Which is why I think she's using your name to buy herself time. So," she says, taking a breath. Brynn looks at me as if she's only just remembered I'm standing here amid all her swirling thoughts. "Like I said, maybe just being aware of it is enough for now. Too much change too quickly, and the queen will get suspicious."

Fear licks up my spine. "Whatever her suspicions, she can never learn about Greyson. It's why she will *never* know my identity." It's a vow, one I will do anything to keep. "I won't put my brother's life, and all that my family has built, in danger. Queen Sigrid can come after me all she wants, but I could never live with myself if—"

Brynn reaches for me. "We won't let that happen," she promises, and I wonder if she realizes she said *we* again. "All of us—your crew . . . They believe in you or they wouldn't follow you. And for what it's worth, I believe in you too. However long it takes, you'll figure it all out, because that's what you do, you help people, like Basher and Tug. Like jumping into the ocean to save me."

I feel the lines in my brow deepen. *"I believe in you too."* My pulse quickens in my throat as I consider a different path from the one that has always been laid before me, weighted with expectations and stipulations. No one has ever believed I could do something because I am capable, only that I *should* because it is my duty.

"For what it's worth, little Skadi," I say, whispering her words back to her. I need Brynn to know how I feel without smirks and bluster. "I see you. Even though you hide behind walls of scarred armor, you *are* worthy, even if you don't think so. Your sister would say the same thing, and I don't have to have met her to know she would wish you to find peace. You are far worthier of it than I am."

"That's not possible," she rasps.

"It is." I run my hand down her arm and take her elbow. Gently pulling her closer, I lean in for a kiss. It's breathtaking and heart-stopping. One of hope and promise I don't quite understand, but I feel it unraveling me as her arms wind their way around my neck, and my hands trail down her back to her hips.

A throat clears, our eyes pop open, and Brynn and I straighten.

Leif is standing down the beach, amusement tugging on his lips. "Sorry to interrupt," he says, drawing closer.

Brynn steps away from me, blood suffusing her cheeks, and I can't help but smile.

"I got worried when you didn't come back this morning. I thought I'd check on you two."

Brynn gestures toward the X. "We were just checking on things, in case the ship comes. We were going to bring back seaweed." She waves toward the lumps of it scattered along the beach. "So much washed ashore last night during the storm." She prattles on, and both Leif's and my smiles grow.

"Good idea," he says. "I can help—" His gaze locks behind me, and I brace myself, knowing all too well what he would see on the horizon as I turn around.

The *Berkano*.

Brynn glances at me, dread filling her eyes, and we both look at Leif. His face changes to something unrecognizable. Not the skeptical intrigue from when he first met us, or the gratitude that shone so bright in his eyes yesterday after he thanked me for saving his life.

His glare shifts to me. "An Englishman?" Leif rasps. I watch as my story replays in his mind, the way it contorts his features from surprise to fiery rage. There is no denying who I am, or at least who I sail with, now that the purple banners fly proudly in the distance.

"I am Killian Blackburn," I tell him. "As I said—"

"Hans was right." Leif's shoulders sag a little and his jaw slackens. I see the wounded look in his eyes as much as I hear it in his voice.

"And you!" He points at Brynn. "You're both liars." He squeezes the grip of his bow so tight his knuckles turn white.

"Leif," Brynn starts, taking a step toward him, but I reach for her arm to stop her. "You don't understand." I step in front of her. It's all I can do not to pull the pistol from my belt.

"I let you into our home," Leif seethes. "We broke bread and—"

"The Reaper didn't kill your family, Leif," Brynn shouts, stepping around me, but I know he isn't listening. Not really. As infuriating as it is to have such violent deeds dripping from my hands that I didn't even commit, I don't fault him for his anger either. "Killian didn't take your servants and slaves," she implores, but it's for naught. "The queen did. Think about it, Leif."

He scoffs. "And I'm to believe you? You, who are sleeping with the devil himself. The Reaper of souls—"

"It's not like that," I tell him.

Leif stares at me. "Your words are poison, Reaper." He's so calm now, I fear he'll crack, and I consider the very real possibility that one of us might be dead in the seconds that follow. I hold still, waiting for the slightest twitch of his fingers on his bow.

"We trusted you, and you used us. You lied." Leif squeezes his bow tighter in his hand, and slowly, I reach for the pistol, worried he'll do something dangerously stupid.

"I will discard my weapon if you do," I say, fingers resting on the grip of the gun. "I did not kill your wife and family. I swear it. Believe me or don't, but Brynn had no part in it."

"I am not a murderer, like you," Leif grits out. His attention fixes on the ship. "Now what? You take us away—"

"They are only coming for me," I promise him. "They know nothing about you, nor will they. I am not in the business of slave trading."

Leif scoffs. "I don't know what you are Reaper, or what you do, only that you are a blight on all of Norseland. The only reason I'm not killing you now is because everything I have left in the world is on this island, and I would not have them suffer as a repercussion."

"And they won't," Brynn promises him.

Leif glares past us, at the approaching ship. It's too big to come to land and will have to anchor out at sea. "But mark my words," Leif continues. "If you come looking for trouble, no matter how many men you have, we will take as many of you down with us as we can."

"We will not come for you," I practically shout, irritation surmounting. "I know it means little, but I give you my word. You and I are not enemies, Leif. No matter what you believe."

He spits angrily into the sand. "No, we are not enemies," he says. "We are nothing." And with that, he stalks away.

38
BRYNN

A quiet reservation befalls us as members of Killian's crew come ashore, Boots, Norik, Tug, and Basher among them.

"Killian!" Tug calls across the water as the tide brings the rowboat closer.

The exchange with Leif lingers, I can feel it as much as Killian can. But I sense a relief in Killian I hadn't anticipated as his crew drifts closer, even if his eyes are taut with tension. It still coils in his shoulders too. I know Leif's animosity is not something Killian can simply brush away like he pretends to do with so many other things, and though I refrain, I want to reach for his hand.

Instead, we wait for the rowboat in silence, our boots kissing the surf.

As his crew rides the tide closer, Basher's expression surprises me. It's not shock or relief to see Killian is alive. It's bemusement I note as she glances between us. It feels as if she can sense all that's happened in the past five days, and I get a bit squeamish under her gaze.

It's only as she jumps into the surf, before the rowboat even touches the sand, that I realize I don't know what Killian and I are to each other, nor do I know how to act.

"You're alive," Norik says, jumping out after Basher. He leaves Tug and Boots to pull the boat into the sand.

"And both of you are in one piece." Basher's teeth are pearly white against her dark skin as she smiles. "That's a surprise."

Killian grins ever so slightly, a secret look passing between him and his quartermaster as he pulls her in for a half hug. Basher's eyes remain on me as she gives him a squeeze and steps away. She doesn't look the least bit surprised to have found her ship captain, whereas Norik seems relieved. He embraces Killian with a backslapping, emotive hug and muttered chuckling. Seeing the two men side by side, and knowing what I do, I appreciate Norik for all he's done. A man who uses his scars to protect Killian. Having been the face of the Reaper and part of the family for so long, I wonder if Norik isn't the most loyal ally and longest friend Killian has ever had.

"So," Basher mutters, eyes on me. "No bloodshed then, captain slayer?"

A blush suffuses my cheeks, remembering the red marks my fingernails left on his body last night, and I clear my throat. "Not for lack of trying," I admit, glancing at Killian.

He smirks, and Basher lifts her eyebrow, seeing everything far too clearly. But when Killian looks at her this time, their silent exchange is indiscernible, and I want to know what I'm missing.

"We need to refill our fresh drinking water before we leave," Norik says, getting down to business as the rest of the crew gather around us. "And . . ." His eyes meet mine. "There's the question of whether or not we want to stay for the night, to prepare a pyre."

My heart sinks. "Phillip?"

Norik purses his lips. "Aye. Bo was with him," he reassures me, and rests a hand on my shoulder. "He no longer suffers."

Nodding, I rally a tight-lipped smile, knowing it's the best I could ask for.

To my surprise, Killian takes my hand. Welcoming the comfort of him beside me, I squeeze his fingers in mine.

"Not to worry," Norik adds. Sympathy and sadness fills his eyes and kindness softens his voice. "We'll mourn Phillip properly, if that's what you want." He looks at Killian for approval, and Killian silently agrees.

I offer them both a watery smile and gratitude.

"Then we have time to stock up on meat while we're here," Basher adds. "The seal on the—"

"No seal," Killian says in his captain voice. It rumbles a little, and he stares at Norik and Basher with warning. "Not this time. We keep to this side of the island."

"Uh-oh," Basher says, hands on her hips. Unlike my hair always coming out of its braid, hers is tightly woven, and only her shirt flutters in the breeze. "What have you done, Kill?"

He huffs, but it's without mirth, and runs his hand over his face. "I'll fill you in after we get everyone off the ship. We'll rest here, tonight only, and set sail for New London first thing tomorrow."

Norik dips his chin, giving me a quirky, purse-lipped smile, then he turns to Tug and Boots, who are playing with the seaweed like children. I smile, watching them in an entirely new light. Like they are all a family. Like they are friends. And it leaves behind a hollow envy I've never felt before.

"Tell me what happened," Basher insists, stepping closer to us as Norik spouts off orders.

"Things have gotten a bit complicated," Killian says.

She looks at me, and even if I know Killian isn't talking about me, I flush under her scrutiny.

"We aren't the only ones on the island," he explains. The wind whips his hair into his face.

Basher takes in my strange clothes for the first time, and her expression pinches with concern. "And?"

"They didn't know who I was."

Basher glances over her shoulder at the ship anchored a league away from shore. "I take it they're familiar with us, then." As Killian nods, it dawns on me that leaving here with the crew is now my only option. I'm no longer welcome on the island.

Despite my letdown, I try to ignore it. I can't blame Leif for his anger, just like I can't blame Killian for what he does, even if I've wanted to since the day I met him. The situation is far more complicated than that.

"Apparently," Killian says carefully, "the Reaper set fire to their workhouse." A shadow flickers in Basher's eyes, and I realize he must be treading lightly on her behalf. "Another horrible casualty in our name." Killian rubs his hand over his face again with another exhausted sigh.

Though I can tell her thoughts are drifting elsewhere, Basher nods in understanding. "Then—" She clears her throat. "Then we do as you say and stay to this side of the island," she agrees. "Unless you think we should be prepared, that he might come this way—"

Killian shakes his head. "No, I don't think so." But still, he looks to me for reassurance.

"I don't think he will either. He has Tank to think about."

Basher's black skin turns an ashy shade of sick right before my eyes. "What?" She grips the lapel of my shirt. "What did you just say?" Her nostrils flare as her fists clench tighter.

I grab her wrists, suddenly terrified. "Tank," I breathe. "His nephew."

Basher's eyes dart to Killian. "Leif?"

The look of surprise on his face is proof that Basher's past is unfolding before us.

A stunned smile consumes her face, her hands fly to her mouth, and Basher's eyes fill with tears. "They got out," she breathes. But as quickly as her smile appears, it vanishes, and her glassy eyes latch onto Killian's. A strangled cry escapes her throat, and Basher staggers backward.

Killian catches her as she nearly falls, tears welling in her eyes, cresting the brim of her lashes.

"It's not possible," she rasps, and shaking her head, Basher squeezes her eyes shut and begins to sob again.

I swallow my own sob of surprise as Basher falls to her knees.

Leif's wife—the servant he married. The one he thought was dead.

Killian pulls Basher into his arms, holding her as she grapples with the truth—the twist in her destiny and the games of the Fates.

The others on shore hurry over, standing around with concern etched on every line of their faces.

Wiping the tears from my face, I shake myself back to the moment. "Basher," I say softly, crouching beside her. "What do you need? Do you want me to go get him—"

"No," Killian says, eyes snapping to me. "He doesn't trust you." Killian takes Basher's chin in his hand and looks into her tear-filled eyes. "You should go to him."

Basher nods, a shaking bundle of nerves, as I help her to her feet.

"Norik, go with them," Killian commands. "Make sure they are protected."

I look at Killian. "You aren't coming? Surely he won't want you dead once he sees you with Basher—once he knows you are the one who saved her life."

He shakes his head. "I have to return to the ship first. I'll be behind you." He's already moving for the rowboat, nodding for Tug and Boots to push it back into the water.

"Killian!" I call, unable to go after him as I hold on to Basher. She wipes her tear-streaked face and looks at me, equally confused.

"Go," he calls back, his voice booming over the wind. "I'll be right behind you."

39
BRYNN

The other side of the island has never felt so far away as Basher, Norik, and I walk in silence toward Leif's cottage. I don't know what Killian is doing, but I have yet to see him coming up behind us, and I'm beginning to worry I might not see him again. I don't know why. There was a look in Killian's eyes that frightened me, though. A determination and resolution in his voice that's had me on edge since he climbed into the rowboat and headed back to the ship.

"It's just over this hill," I tell them, bracing myself for what comes next. Norik and Basher both look at me, and I feel it too. Apprehension, but all for different reasons. Only fleetingly do I consider this might end badly for me. I could be dead the moment Leif lays eyes on me. But I doubt it. Death seems like a cruel joke at this point, always teasing in and out of my existence, whispering its nearness only for it to retreat.

As we crest the hill, I glance behind us again in search of Killian, but I don't see him yet.

"Leif!" Hans calls, and my attention darts to Leif as he steps out of the toolshed. "Was I not clear!" he shouts, and there's only a fleeting moment of ire in his expression as I step closer, because as he scans the three of us for Killian, his eyes fix on Basher.

The skinning knife falls from his fingers. "Koraline?" I see his mouth move, but I hear no words leave his lips.

My heart hammers, seeing her standing there, the wind whipping around her, tugging at her clothes like it's urging her forward. But Basher only stares at Leif, as if knowing he was alive on the island wasn't real until now. Taking the sight of him in. Forcing herself to believe the impossibility.

The immensity of this moment pummels over the thick tension in the air, like the waves pounding against the cliffs beyond us, and suddenly, the wind is charged with relief.

Leif's chest heaves. His eyes are wide, and the confusion and awe make him look like a different man entirely. He doesn't even blink. "Koraline?" he says aloud this time, and takes a tentative step forward. His eyes stray briefly to me, as if he's waiting for an explanation, but I leave the moment to them alone.

He takes an unsteady step closer. "I thought you were dead."

The crack in his voice seems to break his hold over Basher and she runs to him. In a flurry of limbs and muttered comforts, Basher and Leif fall into each other's arms.

Their tears devastate me, and I don't think I've ever known such happiness. Two souls, separated by years of sorrow and grief, finally finding their way to one another again.

Basher nestles against him, clutching onto Leif as if she will never again let him go.

There's a shriek of surprise as Tora runs out of the cottage, the door slamming behind her. All of Basher's hard edges smooth over as she takes Tora and Tank into her embrace.

Norik and I watch the reunion, stunned and humbled.

As Tora fusses over Basher, Leif looks up—looks past me—at Killian.

I spin around.

"Did you know?" Leif asks him, tears streaming down his cheeks. "The whole time?"

Killian shakes his head. "No." He watches Basher with her family, reunited after all of this time, and I notice the rolled paper in his hand.

As Leif sits back on his heels, taking it all in, Killian walks over to him. "How is this possible?" Leif asks him, wiping the tears from his eyes.

"She will tell you everything," Killian says, and holds out the scroll. "But I need you to do something for me."

I step closer, watching the confusion on Leif's face change to one of absolute willingness, whatever Killian's request, as he takes the paper from him.

"It is a map of the islands," Killian explains. "All of them that we've charted."

My eyes widen. I know what this means to Leif and his family—more resources and safer passage. And I know Killian offers the secrets of the Reaper by providing it to him.

"Because the Reaper knows them so well," Leif says dubiously.

"I do," Killian admits. "That's why you know this will be of great use to you."

"What do you want me to do with it?"

"You allow Brynn to stay here with you—"

"What?" I gasp.

"—and any of my passengers who wish to remain on the island as well, and I will give you all the knowledge I have of the Isle of the Lost Winds."

Hans comes up beside Leif, all of us listening with rapt attention to Killian as he barters my future and my dreams. I shake my head. "Killian, I don't want to stay here—"

"Yes, you do," he says, not sparing me a glance.

Hans wipes a stray tear from his cheek. "You said passengers."

"There are twenty-seven passengers on their way to New London. If any of them wish to stay here, I ask that you accept them, whether it is only Brynn or all of them. They will be safe here, and together you can all have your freedom. That is what I want in exchange for this knowledge."

"A colony?" Leif says carefully. "You really are a crazy son of a bitch, aren't you?"

"I would not leave people who have entrusted their lives to me if I wasn't certain it would work. Brynn will help you and Basher see it through. It's her vision. Her plan. I simply have the means to help you make it happen." Killian levels his gaze on Leif, willing him to answer.

Leif unravels the map, studying it as the seconds stretch on, and I find I'm torn. I want to be angry that Killian speaks of me as if I am not standing here, but I also know what he's doing for me, and the weight of such a gift is a heavy one.

"Do we have a deal?" Killian prompts.

Basher and Norik, even Tank and Tora stand around, all of us witnesses to what feels like the second miracle of the day.

And as Leif licks his lips, he nods at me, then at Killian. "I will help you with your colony, Reaper. And Brynn is welcome to stay—of course she is."

The two men exchange a silent understanding, and once their agreement has been made, Killian dips his chin.

Tora throws her arms around Killian, stunning him a moment before he gathers himself enough to answer her whispered gratitude. For as much as I've wished him to be more than the Reaper, it's watching Tora, hearing and seeing her relief, that I *feel* the good that Killian has done, and regret that I wasted any of our time together hating him.

"How do you really fit into all of this?" Leif asks as he comes up to me. His damp, green eyes gleam in the sunlight.

I wipe a rogue tear from my cheek. "I'm just someone Basher took pity on," I admit. And as I recall that day in Basher's cabin, the cross pendant around her neck, the same one Leif has, it seems so obvious.

Leif shakes his head. "I think you are much more than that, Brynn."

His words give me pause, but I don't want to think about me right now. I'm too full of emotion. Instead, I nod toward Leif's family. To Hans and Tora talking with Norik, and Tank inundating Basher and Killian with chatter. "I'll, uh, leave you to your family," I say softly, not wanting to trespass on their happy reunion any longer. Years apart—*mourning* their losses all for nothing—feels too immense, and I can't bear it. So I let the wind lead me away.

40
BRYNN

For a while, I'm not sure where my feet are taking me. Wild grasses bend at my ankles, and the earth is no longer soft beneath my feet as the thermal caves come into sight. With the crew likely setting up camp at the beach, and Phillip's pyre being built, there is no reason for me to hurry back. My heart is too heavy, and with all that's happened today—with all I've learned and all I've felt since last night—I'm not ready.

As I walk toward the hidden pool, my thoughts are a chaos of hope, resentment, and disappointment. Hope that the freedom I've always wanted is possible. Resentment because it still feels out of my control. And disappointment that I will never know the love Basher and Leif do. I've never seen anything like it, never felt it in my core the way I did watching their reunion, with so much love pouring out of them, their lives somehow come full circle.

I climb down toward the water. Not for the first time, I think how strangely fickle the gods are that they would keep Basher and Leif apart, lost in rage and turmoil all these years, only to unite them. Here, of all places.

It's hard to believe there is a purpose for everything—that a higher power, a Christian God or pagan ones, wanted Estrid to die, or at least allowed it. And why? So that I would be on that ship, and all the events from then until now would lead to this? Because Killian never would have jumped in the water and come to this island if it weren't for me. Basher and Leif would never have found one another. And I would never have found true freedom.

Am I the pawn in all of this?

The steaming pool mists with rainbows in the filtered daylight. Too exhausted to pretend I know anything about the gods and their plans, I step to the edge.

I would never have met Killian had I not been taken aboard that ship. But as my heart weighs so heavy I can barely breathe, the true question is clear: has meeting him done me more harm than good?

I'm not sure how long I stand at the water, staring into it, but eventually a chill rakes over me and I realize the cave has filled with shadows. I'm about to leave for the ship when I hear footsteps on the rocks behind me. I squeeze my eyes shut.

"Why did you do that?" I whisper, hating the frailty of my voice.

"Do what?"

I spin around.

Basher's eyes are red and a bit swollen from crying, but there's a glow to her I've never seen. A brightness in her eyes that radiates warmth, and it tugs a small smile across my face. "Why aren't you with Leif?"

She walks up to me and reaches for my arm, pushing my sleeve up to see my knife wound.

"It's healing fine," I reassure her.

She looks at me through her black lashes. "And what about the rest of you?" She drops my arm to my side again, and I tug my sleeve down.

"What do you mean?"

She gestures to the cave. "You're in here alone, looking as if you're heartsick."

My shoulders straighten a little. "I don't look like I'm—"

"Yes, you do. I know it better than anyone." Crossing her arms over her chest, she lifts an expectant brow, waiting for me to answer her, though I don't know what, exactly, she wants me to say.

"Why are you angry with Killian this time?" she finally asks. "I gave you nearly a week to get this sorted between you."

I balk at her. "You what?"

Basher lifts her shoulder as if she's indifferent to my annoyance by now. "You two had some things to sort out, and being stuck here together was the perfect opportunity. With a little time, I figured you'd either get the sexual tension out of the way, or it would blow up completely, and you would hate each other—for real this time." She shakes her head, eyeing me up and down for answers. "But you wouldn't be down here sulking if that was the case, would you? So," she asks again, "what's wrong now?"

"You're right," I admit. "I don't hate Killian." I stare at my fingers. I struck him with this hand—enjoyed it, even. But it was nothing compared to how I felt touching his body last night. "I'm—" I clench my hand into a fist. "I'm not sure what I am."

"Sad," she says softly.

I frown. "Sad?"

She scoffs. "He decided your future for you, and he is not in it," she says as blunt as ever.

Her words sting because she's right, and it did make me sad, even if I know I shouldn't be surprised. We'd all but said the very words earlier at the beach.

Biting the inside of my cheek, I take a deep breath. "He

blindsided me, is all. And he spoke of me as if I wasn't even standing there. As if I didn't have a say in the matter."

"Killian said this place was your idea, Brynn, and if that's true, you *should* stay on the island. It's the best thing for you. So why are you angry with him?"

"I'm not angry," I bite out. "Still, it is no one's choice what I do but my own. Not yours *or* Killian's. I don't appreciate my future being negotiated as if I'm not standing right there."

Basher takes hold of my arms, squeezing gently. "You want to live a life free of men like Ivar and Von Magnusson, do you not?"

"Of course, more than anything."

Her expression saddens a little. "Then you will not find it in New London with men like Greyson and Killian. He knows that, and he saved you from yourself out there by taking the choice out of your hands, because even now, you are torn, and I can't tell what you would do, given the choice. There is kindness in what he did, even if it's not as obvious to you as it is to me. And I know what that cost him."

The blood drains from my face, and I don't realize my heart is thrumming until it's all I can hear in my head. "What do you mean, cost him?"

"I know Killian far better than you, and—"

"Basher."

My gaze darts to the very man, peering down at us from above. His expression is drawn. Sad even.

Basher tilts her head, watching me with far too much amusement, as if she's proven something by coming down here. But I already know I'm a mess, I don't need her to make it worse by casting a wide net of riddles I have to wriggle through. Not when my mind is already reeling.

The instant Basher leaves, however, it dawns on me that I am alone with Killian, and whatever ineptness I felt in his presence before triples.

Killian's gaze never strays from me as he steps over the stones, making his way down to me.

"And what have you come to say?" I ask hastily. "Because I would really like to be alone, if you don't mind."

He stops painfully close, looking at me as he considers something. "I know it's in your nature," he says. "But don't be angry with me." Acutely aware the toe of his boot is touching mine, and he's so close I could lean in and press my lips to his, I take a step back.

"You all but sold me out there, Killian," I tell him, and the hurt bubbles up again, as I realize that's what's really bothering me. "You didn't let me choose. You decided for yourself, like I'm not capable of it."

"It was worse than that, little Skadi," he says, his brow furrowing.

He takes my hand in his and pushes up my sleeve. As his thumb brushes over my runes, a devastating pulse of warmth ripples through my body, and I squeeze my eyes shut, holding my breath for whatever comes next.

"I didn't care."

My eyes snap open. "What?"

"I need you to stay." His voice is low, and he averts his gaze. Good. Because it pains me to look at him and hear such words. "It's what you wanted," he explains. "What you would have chosen before things changed between us. Besides, you promised you wouldn't argue with me about this," he whispers.

I want to tell him I never promised such a thing, but we both knew this was how it was going to end. Even if now that it's real and actually happening, it feels wrong.

"I won't chance something happening to you in New London, like what happened to Basher. Not when I could have prevented it." Killian's voice is delicate, and yet, his words still prick like a new blade in the center of my chest.

He rubs his thumb over my wrist. "You have to stay here, and I have to return." Killian squeezes my hand, his expression pained.

I feel tears on my cheeks, but I don't care. I'm too blindsided that I care what Killian does. That I care for him so much. That he cares for me.

"This is ridiculous," I croak, pulling my hands from his. "I don't know why I'm crying. We were strangers weeks ago. I wanted to kill you—I still do half the time."

A slight smile tugs at Killian's mouth as he wipes a tear of frustration from my cheek.

"Fine," I say, straightening. "I won't be angry, because you're right, I would rather be here than in Briarwood. Especially if your brother is anything like you," I quip, trying to lighten this grayness consuming me. "I doubt we'd get along."

Killian grins so wide, a dimple I've never seen forms on his cheek. "You have no idea, Brynn."

"No idea, what?"

"Greyson," he says, shaking his head with a chuckle, "looks *exactly* like me."

I frown. "What do you mean—are you twins?" I pale in utter shock as he nods. "Oh no," I splutter, emphatically shaking my head. "I most definitely am not going to Briarwood," I agree, more resolute than ever. Not for the reason Killian thinks, but because seeing a version of him every day while he's off on his adventures would be far too painful.

But as our smiles fade and the lightness turns somber once more, I run my hands over my face and exhale a long, steadying breath. "We should get back."

Pulling my sleeve back down my arm, I rally myself to brave the rest of the day and the shipful of people. "I'm sure someone is looking for you."

He reaches for my hand. "No one is looking for me."

I scoff. "You are the captain." I take a step past him. "Of

course they are looking for you." I peer into Killian's eyes and commit their steely gleam to memory.

He tugs me back. "I don't care. My crew will be stuck on a ship with me soon enough. They can survive a few more hours in my absence." Killian stares at my face, but it's not heat or fire I see in his eyes; it's longing and sadness and an earnestness that cuts into my soul, flaying me open. "Can we not pretend it's only us again, little Skadi? Just for a little while."

I can't help my smile, and though I expect and welcome it, my heart flutters as Killian's mouth brushes against mine. His kiss is soft this time. Honest. He inhales me, long and deep. His lips pressing, his tongue coaxing, and as his hand cups my jaw, I wrap my arms around his shoulders as all the apprehension I feel falls away. It's a tender moment, almost sacred, as if it was always meant to be.

Killian's strong arms embrace me, lifting me to my tiptoes. He brushes his nose against my ear. "Brynn," he whispers. My name on his breath sounds like a gentle hum. "Make love to me."

I pull away from him, heart pounding in a wave of panic, but Killian's blue eyes are the most unguarded I've ever seen. The most hopeful.

I lick my lips, willing my pulse to steady and my body not to tremble. I would give him anything at this moment, and leaning in, I kiss him in answer. I don't know when I will see Killian again, if I ever will, and I want all he's willing to give.

Killian's movements are slow as he undresses me, and his lips savor every inch of my body as if he's afraid he'll miss something. They press behind my ear and brush my collarbone. He kisses my shoulder and the backs of my fingers. His touch is featherlight and gentle. His hum of contentment makes my heart sing. And when the last of my clothes fall to the ground, I begin to remove his.

As my fingers trail the waistband of his pants, I kiss him,

tempting words of longing from his lips. No tattoo goes untraced, no plane of his stomach unexplored. And when we are standing with nothing left between us but our impending future apart, Killian gathers me into his arms.

His well-honed body is a gentle, protective shield as he steps into the pool, and I lose myself in the fervid depths of his eyes as he lowers into the water. He submerges us lower and lower into the silky warmth, and I trace over the chills that descend down his neck and over his chest.

As Killian settles against the stones, the water sloshes over our shoulders, cleansing the days and weeks of our tumultuous pasts away, until it's just us.

His hard length presses against me, our chests heave as one, and eyes fluttering closed, I lean into him. I explore his mouth this time, brushing my lips against his. Tasting them. Basking in the sensation of his breath, fanning over me, and the tepid waterdrops trickling down as his fingers graze my cheeks.

Everything about us is different from last night. It's not a frenzy but a sobering goodbye, and as soon as I realize it, my heart aches all over again. All I can think is this may be the last time I am ever in his arms.

Resting my forehead against Killian's chest, I try and fail to catch my breath. "Why?" I whisper, squeezing my eyes shut. I hate how tenuous the word is—how fragile I always feel around him—but I can't help it. I've been unraveling in this man's presence since the day I met him, and I'm completely undone. It's worse than the physical pain I've learned to breathe through over the years, to use as fuel and bolster my will to survive.

But I am not starving or in need of shelter now. Killian is offering me everything I never thought was possible. A life of my own. Freedom. Happiness. And yet, it's still not enough . . . not if a part of me is broken. "Why does it hurt so bad?"

Killian's arms squeeze me more tightly, holding me so close there is nothing but flesh between us. "I don't know," he murmurs, his stubble just barely touching my cheek. He holds me for a while, both of us soaking in the silence. I don't want him to let me go. I don't want us to leave this cave, or for him to get on that ship and sail away. Even if I know he must.

"I'm supposed to hate you," I say in jest, but I can barely muster a smile in my voice.

Taking my face in his hands, Killian forces me to look into his eyes that shimmer with regrets and promises. "I wish you would." His gaze traces the curves and angles of my face, and as his arms wrap around me, Killian turns to sit me on the rocks.

Only this time, when his eyes meet mine again, they are gleaming with unspoken emotion. His nostrils flare as he brings his lips to mine, and he sinks into me. The swell of him fills the most sensitive parts still lingering from last night, and I shiver in pleasure as an indescribable sensation floods through me. It's unearthly, starting at my head and unfurling down to my toes, filling every dark crevice inside of me with light.

My body feels weightless and alive, and as the markings on my arms begin to sing, I feel whole for the first time in my life. I feel special in this moment. I feel worthy of it.

41
BRYNN

One of the female passenger's *lokk* rides the breeze, her high-pitched song echoing far into the distance for all the gods to hear. The drums behind me beat a steady, pulsating rhythm that puts my heart at ease as three dozen of us stand on a cliff, mourning as the fire envelops Phillip's pyre. The flames battle the wind tugging at his linen-wrapped body, and I find I am content.

I wish he could have seen this place, and its beauty and possibility, but I am relieved he is no longer in pain. And I am grateful I did not have to watch him in his final days, even if that makes me a coward.

Three lost on this journey of ours, and I feel their deaths keenly. Knowing Killian and his crew have lost dozens of lives in the past, I think I finally understand the true weight of Killian's burden.

I am ashamed of the words I spat at him when we first met. He is not callous, nor is he immune to the Fates' decision to call the people he's trying to save home. I have seen the fear and anger in his eyes when he is at sea. I know that no matter which halls the poor souls feast at in the afterlife, they stay a mark on Killian's soul forever. That is what his duty to his family and to these people costs him.

Staring at the building flames, snapping in the wind, I reach for Killian's hand. A silent offering. A poor consolation and apology.

He squeezes my fingers in his, perhaps for both of our sakes, and we watch the blaze engulf the pyre, knowing Phillip's soul descends the horizon with the setting sun, to feast with Surg and his son, and the others lost at sea.

42
BRYNN

After a funeral feast of seal and codfish, the communal fire blazes at least two people tall from the pit the camp gathers around. I'm fully sated, having eaten the best meal of my life, and I watch everyone in celebration.

Norik plays the fiddle, Boots bangs on an empty crate and a barrel, and Sonya, Tug, Mikal, Bo, and a few of the other passengers, dance around with abandon.

Everyone else watches. Exhaustion weighs heavy on some of their features. Others wear a mask of somberness. But everyone seems settled in the same relief to be on land and grateful to feel the black sands under their feet, for a little while, at least.

Taking a sip of ale, I watch Leif and Hans on the other side of the flames, their eyes gleaming with drink as they clap their hands in time with the tune. Basher hasn't stopped smiling since easing into an evening of much-needed levity. She and Tora have been lost in conversation most of the night, their smiles reminiscent as Tank nestles deeper into his mother's arms, desperate for sleep.

Tora's eyes meet mine, and a different kind of smile curves

her lips. A friendly smile, or perhaps it's one of gratitude, though I'm not sure why. I've done nothing to ease the broken hearts of their family. That's Killian's doing. He was their savior long before anyone truly knew it.

I meet his gaze across the flames where he speaks with Doc, outside one of the tents. He doesn't smile, at least, not with his lips. His eyes crinkle and flicker with an acknowledgment that makes my insides melt with the want to be in his arms. Not sex. Not love making. Just to be with him once more before he is gone.

Reading my thoughts, Killian dismisses Doc. She strides toward the cooked seal that's long been cold and readjusts her oversized hat. It's pointless in the night, but she wears it, covering half her face, all the same.

Killian prowls around the fire toward me. It's not a look of hunger in his eyes but one of mischief, and taking my hand in his, he leads me away from the group. He collects a few fur pelts, tosses one at me, then takes my hand again, leading me down the beach. Much like the heat of the flames, the sky dances in waves above us. The green-and-blue colors move in time with the laughter growing distant behind us.

"You don't want to dance?" I ask as we come to a hidden spot between two rocks.

Killian's brow lifts with intrigue. "Why, do you?"

I scoff. "Not in the slightest."

His cheek twitches a little, as if I'm so predictable, and he plops down into the sand out of the wind, coaxing me down beside him. I lay the pelts over us, and tension uncoils from my shoulders as I wrap my arm around his chest.

"I've never done this," I admit, watching the stars twinkle between ribbons of color.

"Done what?"

"Been with someone like this."

Killian folds one arm behind his head. "Neither have I," he

admits. "Not like this." He bends his neck and kisses my forehead, and I feel myself curl in closer, like it's the most natural thing. I don't know tenderness—at least, I didn't until today with Killian, and for the third time in the span of mere hours, tears prick my eyes despite my will to deny them.

"Life is easier when there are no expectations or attachments," I explain, even though I don't think Killian needs me to.

"And yet, we chose now to form such a thing," he muses. It's supposed to be a joke, but it makes me think of Basher's words earlier. "Did Basher tell you she knew where we were—that she left us here on purpose?" I ask curtly.

Killian chuckles, but it seems odd for her to have done that. Not to mention reckless.

"We could've been dying for all she knew. Why would she risk that?"

Laughter faded, Killian lies there silent, his chest rising and falling for a few deep breaths. The silence between us starts to feel . . . strange, and rising to my elbow, I peer down at him. My eyes narrow. "What are you not telling me?"

When Killian drags his gaze to mine, it's with guilt.

"Killian?"

"The X," he says.

"What about it?"

"It's a sign to stay away."

My mouth drops open. "*What?*"

"After making these journeys for nearly a century, the crews have procedures in place for just about everything. The X," he repeats, "means it's not safe to come ashore."

"But you put an X on there even before we met Leif." I shake my head, utterly confused. "Did you know he was on the island the whole time?"

Killian laces his fingers with mine. "No, it's nothing like that," he murmurs, and his gaze shifts to mine, glinting with green in the sky's light. "I knew Basher would know what it meant."

"Which was what?"

Killian stares at me, eyes shadowed and guilt-ridden. "I wanted more time."

"What?" I bite out again. "More time for what? With me?" I shove at him, only partially playful. "That makes no sense —none—"

He clasps my face and presses his lips to mine, his tongue languidly coaxing mine in a lazy, delicious kiss. He's distracting me, I know he is. I want to pull away but I can't. Every part of my body yearns for him. So I give in, and kiss him back.

Eventually, when my eyes feel too heavy to open, Killian pulls away. "I needed to figure out what was wrong with me."

Prying my eyes open, I blink him back into focus—his wild mane of dark hair, his gorgeous eyes, his kissable mouth I've all but memorized in the past two days. "What does that mean, Killian?" My head floats with a dozen questions, but really, I just want to be near him and hear the timbre of his voice. It's the simplest of things, yet it eats away at me, knowing that after tonight, I might not hear it again.

Killian kisses me once more, his lips lingering before he breaks away. "I haven't told you something, little Skadi." His thumb strokes my jaw, and I hold my breath. "I've dreamed of you."

"You mean of Skadi," I amend, because he's told me as much.

"No. I mean—yes, maybe—but her voice . . . It was yours I heard coaxing me out of sleep that night she came to me. That night I nearly died, I saw your markings, and I heard your voice, and it's followed me over the years, haunting me in a way I didn't understand. Then I met you, and I wondered if I'd finally lost my mind."

I can't explain the feeling that ripples over me. Disbelief. Awe. A renewed appreciation for the gods, for bringing us together. What Killian says should be impossible, but a part of me feels it too, an inexplicable draw to him.

Killian rises to his elbow and peers down at me. "You saved me somehow, and I don't know what to do with that."

"Is that why you've been so broody?" I ask as it begins to make more sense. "The whole time we've been on this island, you were so angry with me—"

"You hated me," he says passionately. "You wanted to *kill* me. I was trying to figure it all out. Plus, what you've said from the beginning is true. Knowing that I had any part in what happened to your family makes me feel sick inside. It seemed the cruelest twist of fate, especially since I know it was somehow you who saved me, little Skadi. Even if it's crazy. Even if it makes no sense."

"Killian—"

"I just—I needed more time. I needed to figure it out." He rests his forehead against mine and tucks a loose strand of hair behind my ear.

"I'm sorry," I say, because I've thought it a thousand times but I want him to hear it. "I've been wrong about so many things, and I've only made it harder for you."

Killian stares at my arm, at the markings covered by my sleeve. "I've stopped trying to understand it, but I do have one question," he says softly, and he kisses my wrist. "Why do you have them? What do these runes mean to you?" When his eyes meet mine, they are full of wonder and pain at once.

I trace the runes forever etched in my skin. "My mother always told us stories, and Skadi was my favorite one. She was fierce and strong, and I needed her—needed to remember the good things that I was beginning to forget. So, six years ago, I did the only thing I could think of to ensure I never forget them."

"Six years ago?" Killian asks, so low I barely hear him.

I nod.

Killian lies back down, and I watch his profile in the night shadows, wondering how far away his mind drifts. "Six years ago, I could barely stand myself and started spending more time at sea."

"It's funny," I think aloud, knowing it's all twisting threads in an intricately woven tapestry we never get to see until the end of our journey. "I got my runes to be closer to my past, when really, they were a path toward my future. They brought me to you."

Killian's brow crumples a little, and he laces his fingers with mine again.

"Now it's over," I whisper. It's a dismal realization, and I curse the X for not working properly. "I traced that X on the rocks until it was *blaringly* red, so why would Basher come back now?"

"Provisions," he says easily, sounding like a captain again. "They are getting low. It's why we must leave for New London tomorrow."

That brings everything back to reality once more, and with a deep inhale and a heavy heart, I snuggle closer to Killian and peer up at the most brilliantly sea-colored sky I've ever seen. I don't want to make it harder and tell Killian I will miss him when he leaves, because he already knows. And I won't make him feel guilty for leaving, because I know he can't stay. So, I say nothing because his decision is difficult enough.

"I will come back when I can," he says quietly. "That's all I can promise you, Brynn."

I squeeze my eyes shut, holding his promise close. Nodding, I let the silent tears fall from my eyes. For the first time in my life, I don't want to be strong. I want to feel every pang of heartache so that I can remember what it's like to feel at home with someone.

"Will you tell me your mother's story about Skadi?" he asks as the wind whistles through the rocks.

"Only if you tell me yours," I whisper, and lying in each other's arms, I regale Killian with some of my mother's tales of Skadi and Njord's complicated love, torn between land and sea. And he tells me his grandfather's story about destiny, how even gods are not immune to it, and despite their ire for one another, together Njord and Skadi brought prosperity and independence to the just and deserving.

43
BRYNN

Long after morning, when I finally wake with the sun high in the sky, I feel rested. It's only as the breeze burns my wind-chapped face that I miss the press of Killian's body and warmth beside me.

Sitting up, I stare at the empty spot on the pelts beside me. He's gone.

Holding my breath, I scan the horizon. His ship is gone too, and camp is being dismantled down shore.

My heart drops, even though I knew this moment was coming. But now that it's here, I'm angry. He just . . . He took the coward's way out.

But as my chest burns with sadness, a part of me is glad he did, and once again, I realize Killian made the hard decision and tore the scab off for both of us. This time, when the tears threaten to come, I refuse to let them. Because enough is enough.

I climb to my feet, stretching as I tell myself there are far worse things than heartache. I survived before Killian, I will more than survive in this new life he's helped create for me. I will thrive, and I will be happy—I'm determined to be.

Swallowing the lump in my throat, I collect the pelts we'd wrapped ourselves in all night, and make my way to what's left of camp.

I'm surprised to see Bo and Tug have remained behind with Basher and me.

They give me a quick wave when they notice me approaching before they load what appears to be the last of the provisions Killian left for us—crates and sacks of food—onto a supply plank.

Basher steps out of the alcove Killian and I stayed in, carrying the trunk he dug up, and his absence hits me in a fresh wave of sorrow.

I stop at the embers, all that's left from last night's campfire, and fold the pelts to take back with us. "What can I carry besides these?"

Basher sets the trunk down. "This," she says. "I will put the pelts on the carrier, with the rest of the supplies." The fowl in one of the crates squawks as Basher reorganizes the placement of things, tucking the pelts in between a couple of sacks.

Leif finishes collecting what few obscure items have been left on the beach, and all at once, their four gazes shift to me. Bo wipes the sand from his hands onto his pants, Leif tosses an empty mug onto the supply plank, and Tug looks at me, almost wary.

I freeze, glancing between them. "What is it?"

Basher nods to a pile of supplies in the sand. My eyes narrow as I realize they aren't random supplies, but a scroll, a forge hammer, tongs, and a chisel wrapped in a leather carrier that weighs it down in the wind.

I crouch down, picking up Bo's hammer. I'd recognize it anywhere, intricately etched with his father's craftsmanship. I look at him. "I didn't know you'd brought it with you."

Bo shrugs. "I needed a skill in New London. It seemed fitting."

I'd forgotten Bo was given the option to board the ship, so it makes sense he would leave Norseland prepared for his new life. "But that's for you," he says, pointing to the scroll underneath it.

"For me?" I look at Basher, and she nods.

"From Killian," she explains, and suddenly my heart is racing. I stare at it for a moment, watching as the wind bends its edges before I finally reach for it with trembling fingers.

Bo's shadow extends over me as he draws closer, hands on his hips and curiosity in his eyes. All of us stare at it. It's not a scroll so much as a small, rolled piece of parchment, and I unfurl it as I rise to my feet. Scribbled words I don't understand stare back from the page. And as everyone waits for my reaction, my cheeks redden and I clear my throat.

"I can't read," I whisper, shaking my head as I look at Basher. "I don't know what it says."

Leif extends his hand. "Would you like me to read it to you?" He sounds apologetic, though he has no reason to be. "Please," I say, handing it to him in a rush. I want to know what it says more than anything.

I look from Leif to Tug, who stares at the parchment with as much anticipation as I do, then at Basher, wondering if she already knows what it says.

"Little Skadi," Leif starts, and my eyes squeeze shut as the lump grows larger in my throat. "What do I write to the woman who's sworn to kill me? Who hates me beyond measure, but who has stolen the heart I wasn't sure I ever truly had?" My nostrils flare, but as Killian's words soothe my soul, everyone else disappears. "The tools are for the new forge you will need as you make yourself a home. Do me a favor, little Skadi? Keep an eye on Tug for me. And tell him I will take care of Cat. He has my word." I look at the kid whose eyes are as full of tears as mine. Killian, the only father and brother the boy has known for years, gone on this morning's wind. "When

I come back," Leif reads, "I expect he'll have taught you how to swim."

That makes me snort a laugh despite myself, and I wipe the tears from my eyes. When I look at Tug again, a watery smile parts his lips.

"Until we meet again. Ever yours, Killian."

As Tug swallows a sob, I reach for him, knowing he and I will feel Killian's absence most. He wraps his arms around me, and I breathe him in. He smells like the sea, like the wind and the waves—just like Killian.

"He'll be back soon," Tug croaks, trying to reassure me.

"I know," I tell him. I peer into Tug's brown eyes. Study the freckles on his face from so many days under the sun. "It still smarts."

He wipes the snot from his nose with the back of his hand. "Yeah, it does."

As much as I want to sit here and think about what will happen between now and *next time*, whenever that might be, I know it helps none of us. "Well," I breathe, scanning our audience. "I guess we have a lot of work to do while he's away."

Basher snorts. "Teaching you how to swim will be the hardest," she teases, and I can't help but chuckle with the rest of them.

"Killian will bring more people with him next time too," Tug says, his glassy eyes widening with excitement.

Killian never promised that, but I smile with hope. "We better be ready, then."

"Come," Leif says. "Let's get back and settled. I want an evening alone with my wife," he says, his eyebrows dancing suggestively. "We can plan the weeks to come tomorrow."

Bo collects his tools in one hand and wraps his other muscley arm around Tug, mussing the kid's hair. "Maybe Tora can teach you how to cook," he teases, and Tug rolls his eyes as his cheeks beam red.

Basher and Leif exchange a look before the guys lift the supply plank over their heads.

I tuck the note quickly into my vest. "I've never seen Killian like this," Basher confides. "I've never seen him in love. I've never seen him afraid."

"Afraid?"

She nods. "He was as afraid to leave you behind as he was to take you with him." She rests her hand on my shoulder, giving it a squeeze. "He will come back."

"I know," I say as she goes to help the guys. But the question remains, will he be back in months, or will it take years?

The gang trudges through the sand toward the ravine.

"I'll be right behind you," I call after them, and collect the trunk. I stare at the distant X on the side of the cliff that taunts me, and shake my head, laughing. With a final glance at the ocean, at the expansive sea that Killian sails, I wonder what he's doing at this very moment.

I see him as I close my eyes. An image of Killian at the stern of the ship, hands braced on the balustrade as he stares into the horizon.

As a warm breeze passes over me, sending a wave of chills over my skin, I smile.

44
KILLIAN
NEW LONDON

Standing at the stern of the ship, I stare at the glinting town of Lowestoft. A fishing village clustered on the hillside, safe from the tide that rises with every storm, compliments of the Great Turning—or the Shift, depending on which part of the world you hail from.

As the gray skies darken and night sets in, I leave Norik to plan the careening of the ship while we're in port, for there are no safer shores than what we'll find in Lowestoft to clean and caulk the *Berkano* before sailing out again.

Disembarking, I head down the pier for the village, to secure wagons for the passengers' transport to Briarwood first thing tomorrow. But my tasks don't end there. Word must be sent to Greyson, since my arrival in New London is long overdue. In the three-day wagon ride to Briarwood, my brother can prepare for the arrival of his newly acquired tenants.

Tenants. A familiar, admonishing voice would tell me I am fooling myself to call them that.

With the waves lapping around the rocks and pylons, I walk toward land. Fishing and whaling boats butt against the pier as the tide ebbs, splashing over the entrails staining the wood. And as the gulls cry in the dying light, I think of her. Again.

Brynn. My little Skadi, asleep on the beach. She'd looked peaceful for the first time since I'd laid eyes on her, and I didn't have the heart to wake the beautiful imp. Or perhaps I didn't have the courage.

I've never had to say goodbye to someone I care about. Not like that. Not like her. As aggravating as she is intoxicating. So fragile, yet insufferably strong-willed and courageous. Maddening beyond measure but undeniably meant for me.

Climbing the hill to the village, all I can think about is how the days since leaving the Isle of Lost Winds have weighed me down, making me question everything that used to be so certain.

And for the first time in my life, the solid ground feels unnerving. After days on the water, I am here, arrived in my home country, and I want to be out in the water again. Closer to her. To a different sort of life than the one I'm tethered to here.

Guilt chases such thoughts away. My place is with Greyson. I owe him as much. I *want* to be a part of this. To help him. Even if I want to leave the past behind.

"Oye! Move faster, would you!" A portly fish merchant leans over an assembly line in the alleyway, his shouts echoing over the wet slap of fish guts tossed into piles on the ground in the streets. Despite the onset of night, laborers still work, tirelessly as ever, for the Council.

A group of children run up to me.

"Flowers, mister?" A young girl with choppy brown hair offers me a bundle of wilted flowers, probably hand-picked this morning from the cracks in the ground.

"How 'bout a box of matches?"

"What about a sweet orange?"

"Only a coin each!" They talk over one another, and

though they are different ages and heights, the desperation on their gaunt faces and dirty cheeks is the same.

I stop, pulling out the purse tied to my belt, and offer each of them a bill. Their eyes light with absolute awe and my chest aches for them.

It isn't that I've never noticed their plight before—I've been surrounded by it my entire life, here and in Norseland—but I see Brynn when I look at them now. I see a little girl with long brown hair that constantly falls into her cunning blue eyes, and pursed pink lips ready to lash out at me. I want nothing more than to save her from the cruel world that's hardened all her edges and made her live by blade and with unending sacrifice.

The children offer me their goods, but I shake my head, about to continue on, when I hear a chuckle.

"I thought you'd left, Master Blackburn." A constable of sorts strides up, glancing at the children and me with bemusement. His mustache is groomed, his uniform tailored to a perfect fit, and his hands are braced on his hips as if he is someone important.

He's one of the Council's men, placed here to ensure the work they require of this small village is being done. That the constable knows my family is no surprise, even if I don't know him, and I'm about to tell him I've only just arrived, when a strange look befalls him. A look I've seen many times over. A look of confusion as people register that something about me isn't quite right. A look that tells me, I am not the first Blackburn twin the constable has seen lately.

"You've spoken to me recently?" I ask, shoulders tensing. Something heavier than before settles over me as I consider Greyson was only just in Lowestoft.

Recognition lights the man's features. "Ah, the brother," he says. "The giant ship in port should have given it away." The constable chuckles to himself. "Tend to get that a lot, do you?"

"Where is he?" I inquire. The sudden urgency and apprehension I have to see Greyson tenses my neck and shoulders.

The constable nods toward the tavern. "Was staying there for a few weeks, but—"

I make haste as my thoughts swirl. It feels like an entire lifetime has passed since I last saw my brother. And while I always dread going home to look into the troubled eyes of Greyson Blackburn, a part of me doesn't feel whole without him.

Despite my unease, a smile tugs at my lips, and I can't get to the tavern fast enough, praying he's still there.

The moment it's in sight, I hold my breath and fling the tavern door open, stepping inside. Chatter quells in the brine-scented room, mingling with the fragrance of stale ale and a savory hint of stew that makes my mouth slightly water.

The tables are mostly full as I scan the patrons, looking for a familiar face. My eyes lock on a woman with golden spun hair and wide blue eyes that pin me momentarily where I stand.

And then I see him. My more serious self. My twin.

"Brother!" I cheer, and in a swell of relief, I embrace him. His hair is a black mane combed back from his face, and his body is fit and strong as he wraps his arms around me. But he smells like home. Like lemon and hay and leather.

Greyson claps my back, his body sagging a little as he exhales. "Where the hell have you been, little brother?"

"Little?" I chuckle, taking a step back to look at him. This. Us. My brother, whom I resent as much as I trust to tether me to this life. "Two minutes counts for nothing," I say, exaggerating, but when Greyson's severity settles back into place, and I see the weeks, perhaps months of concern crinkling his eyes, I sober once more. "There is much to tell you," I admit, though I have no idea where to start. "And I will. I promise."

Greyson glances at the golden-haired woman on the other

side of the table, still staring at me. Her blue eyes shimmer as if she's mesmerized by the sight before her.

I blink before it dawns on me. "She's with you?" I ask, looking her up and down. She's slender and pretty, but it's her pregnant belly my eyes latch onto.

Greyson has found someone? Or the Council has intervened once again. No. This is something else, something I thought impossible, and yet, she stands there like she belongs, her hands clasped on her belly, shoulders back, and curious eyes assessing every inch of my face.

"You must be special," I muse aloud, unable to hide my shock. I'm not sure if it's awe or relief in my voice. Perhaps it's both.

"Killian," Greyson says, moving to her side. "This is Selene."

"And she's pregnant . . . with your child?" I look at him, unable to swallow the concern forming in my throat. Concern for him. For his heart. Because I don't think he can take much more grief.

"As you can see," she answers, lifting her chin. "And *she* is standing right here," she sasses. This woman is not fainthearted. She is not meek and meager in any way. And imagining her and Greyson together gives me insurmountable pleasure.

Unable to help myself, I laugh, wholeheartedly, and look at Greyson. "Oh, I like her." I glance at Selene. "I like you," I repeat, shaking my head. "Big, brooding Blackburn has a beautiful woman to keep him in check." I can barely believe it as I huff another laugh. "Can I call you sister?"

"Of course," she says, a satisfied lilt in her voice. There's a glint in her eyes that makes me think she isn't only his match, but she is happy. With him. And she's carrying his child.

In two strides I wrap my arm around her, my heart

cinching in my chest as years' worth of burden instantly evaporates.

"You're finally home," she whispers.

I squeeze my eyes shut, nostrils flaring as the pain in her voice, her concern, whether it's for me or Greyson, seeps into me. "You've been missed."

Selene squeezes me tighter before I pull away, and staring at this stranger I've never met yet feel as if I have known all my life, I think, *she's come home.* That Selene, this woman before me, is finally here, with Greyson.

I stare between them, wondering how they've come to be in Lowestoft.

"Perhaps we should get another round of drinks," Selene says, taking Greyson's hand as she rests the other on her belly again. "You aren't the only one who's had a bit of adventure, it would seem."

You have no idea, I think, and looking at my brother's empty ale mug, I snort a laugh. "I'll need something stronger than that."

45
KILLIAN

In my tavern room, Greyson and I stare into the flickering flames burning in the hearth. He sips on whiskey in the high-backed chair beside me, both of us lost in quiet thoughtfulness while Selene sleeps in the adjoining room.

My head hurts as I absorb all that's transpired in Briarwood this past year in my absence, and I mourn the loss of our family and friends Greyson has had to bury along the way.

Running my hand down my face, I lean forward, drink sloshing in the other. "I should have been here," I mutter, regret and exhaustion pulling me into dangerously raw territory. Resting my arms on my knees, I curse. "Draven never would have *stepped foot* on our land if I had been. He wouldn't have dared."

"Had things been different," Greyson says, "I would not have brought Selene into my life." He looks at me. "And Basher —" He stops himself, a confounded expression on his face as if the unveilings of my past few months are wholly unbelievable.

Greyson blinks and the calming blaze of the fire captures his attention once again. "Had you been here, Basher would not have been reunited with Leif. So, it does no good to dwell on what might've been, Killian." Ever the words of an "older" brother. He takes a sip from his glass, then rakes his teeth over his bottom lip. "It's not as if you've been listless either. In fact, you're lucky you are not dead. If not for going overboard, then for the turmoil in Norseland. Or Leif's fury. But then—" Greyson shrugs, his voice low in thoughtful consideration. "The gods have always favored you."

I frown as he continues.

"I have lost faith in them more times than I can count. Yet, you've always been in their graces, and I've resented you for that."

"You resented me?" I scoff, wondering if he's drunk or simply exhausted and not thinking straight.

Greyson leans his head back against his chair with a sigh and stares down his nose at me. "I always thought you had it so much easier than I did. That you could not possibly know loss like I have. But I know that is not true. I was simply too resentful with the pressure I've always had to live up to and all I've had to carry for our father and grandfather, to see how my marrying Rebecca and her passing affected you. And all of that resentment, for what? There is a reason Father chose me for Briarwood and you for the *Berkano*. I could never spend months at sea, like you've always had to. Especially knowing what it has cost you."

"Cost me?" I parrot. If Greyson only knew. I think of having to leave Brynn behind. Of finally finding a reason to want to be better.

"Don't look at me like that," he grumbles.

"You mistake my surprise, brother," I say, voice hoarse as I tilt my head. I wait for Greyson to meet my gaze, so that he will finally understand what has festered between us unsaid all of these years. "I harbor no ill will in your resentments toward me. I've had plenty of my own, unfounded as they may have been. They've led to many regrets." I pick at a blemish on the wooden table between us. "I'm surprised, is all."

Greyson stares at me, a dark sheen to his eyes I've mistaken so many times for disappointment, but see it now for what it is: concern. For me. For whatever this fracture has always been between us.

I glance at the simple gold band around Greyson's ring finger and grin. For the first time since arriving, I am *grateful* to be home. Greyson is well. He is better than that, my brother is happy, and that brings me more peace than I ever dreamed was possible. "Governess, huh?"

Greyson smiles to himself. "It seemed like a good idea, at the time."

"Sounds brilliant to me," I tell him. "What I wouldn't give to have been able to watch her put you in your place a time or two."

Greyson chuckles. "It wasn't pretty, I'll tell you that."

I imagine her dressed in rags with that haughty, straight-shouldered look I've seen her give him a time or two tonight, and I admire her gumption that Greyson so clearly adores.

"You're smirking." Greyson's eyebrow lifts, expectant.

"She reminds me of someone," I confess, and face the fire again.

"The stowaway?"

"Little Skadi," I whisper. Picturing her again fills me with both longing and a sense of peace, knowing she's living a better life on the isles than any I could give her here.

"You've gone out of your way not to mention her more than you've had to," Greyson observes.

My tightly wound emotions begin to unravel as I allow myself to acknowledge them with no ship tasks or distractions. Raking my fingers through my hair, I heave out a sigh. "I'm not sure where to start," I admit.

Greyson pours us more whiskey. "It's not Chauncey's good

stuff," he warns. "But it will have to do."

Smirking, I take a sip from my glass and remember the first time I saw little Skadi, inching her way closer to the edge of the ship—so careful, it was as if she thought the gods themselves might reach out and pull her in. "She's a maddening little devil," I murmur.

"So maddening you smile when you think of her?"

I meet my brother's steely gaze. "As maddening as she is tempting." I shake my head, longing to hear her scathing retorts, and to kiss her pert mouth. The thought makes me smile, sad as it is, and I lean my head back against the chair. "Do you remember my dream?"

Greyson's mouth purses with thought. "Which one?"

"The woman who came to me in the woods."

"Woman? I thought you said it was Skadi—the first of many times the gods have saved your life."

I smirk again and turn my glass around on my thigh. "I thought it was Skadi," I admit. "And it might have been, but it was Brynn's voice I heard. It was her arm I saw." I shake my head, laughing at how impossible it sounds. "I don't pretend to understand any of it, but when I saw Brynn on the ship, something awoke inside me, Greyson. And it's terrifying."

My brother chuckles softly. "Don't tell me you haven't learned the affects women have on—"

I snort a laugh. "You know what I mean. Or," I say, scratching my bearded chin, "perhaps you don't," I confess. "I barely do."

Greyson turns in his chair to fully face me. "You love this woman," he says in astonishment, and crosses one leg over the other. "Whatever role she's played in what you've been through, it is for the better, Killian. You are different. Distracted more than usual, and yet, you're not as restless and itching to fill the quiet with feigned amusement." He dips his chin, eyes narrowing slightly. "Why did you not bring her?"

"This is not the life for her," I tell him, though it pains me to admit it. "She is much like your little governess, dragged through the trenches, yearning for the one thing she's never truly had."

"A choice," Greyson whispers.

"Ah, yes," I say with a smirk. "You do understand." I wag my finger in Selene's direction. "They are very similar, I think."

Greyson smiles to himself.

"Coming here," I start, running my finger over the leather stitching in my pants. "It would not have suited her." I take the last sip from my glass. "Selene knows this life. But Brynn . . . I would never be able to leave her for fear of what trouble that temper of hers might get her in."

"So, you do love her."

I take a deep breath. "Is it possible to love someone after only weeks of knowing them?"

"Only weeks?" he asks. "Or a lifetime?" His expression is contemplative and sincere. There's no jest or mocking in it, knowing how long my dreams have plagued me—how unsettled I've always been. "She has been a part of you since your childhood, Killian. You've been searching for her without even knowing it." He points to me. "You believe in destiny, despite what you claim. And you, more than me, live among the gods, because you've always felt more connected to them. Why would they not put this woman in your path? Especially if she can get through that thick skull of yours when so many others have tried and failed in the past?"

"I'm not sure any of that matters," I tell him. "I belong here, with you and Paige. With the family."

"Do you?" Greyson's gaze cuts through me. "You said yourself, times are changing, brother." He takes a sip from his glass. "New London is not what Grandfather thought it would be, you were right about that. It is dangerous, but we are not weakening. Selene has shown me that much. We have power here, more than I ever realized. So do not worry you will let me or Grandfather down by seeking a life that brings *you* peace. Because I would wish this feeling of happiness a thousand times over for you. You deserve it as much as I do."

Greyson combs his fingers through his hair, searching for his next words. "I know you have regrets, Killian, but don't. Father chose me to manage the estate because I want a family, not because he favored me. I am content to be here, surrounded by these people who I trust with my life. You—you have a restless spirit. You belong out there."

Eyes burning, I stare at my brother and into his earnest expression, absorbing the candor in his voice. Our lives have been a topsy-turvy mess of loss and loneliness. And as we sit here—men, brothers, renegades—it feels as if, for the first time, we are also partners. Equals.

Greyson leans back in his chair, content having said his piece, and lifts his glass to his lips. But my heart is anything but settled. It pumps manically as I allow myself to hope and seriously consider all that's possible moving forward.

"If you truly believe what you say," I hedge, "then I wish to speak with you about something."

The fire crackles as Greyson looks at me, his eyes glassy with satisfaction and drink.

"If I am to continue this crusade, I want to give northerners a choice—Briarwood or the isles." Knowing this impacts my brother's livelihood—in turn his family and the entire estate—I don't say it lightly. "I want there to be more than one choice. I want them to truly *have* a choice."

Greyson's features are inscrutable as he mulls my words over in his mind, and I watch as the charted path of our family's history changes course, sailing toward a different future as he considers it.

Finally, Greyson's mouth tugs at the corner, and he sighs. "Selene would be the first to tell you there are plenty of people in New London who deserve better. If it is a choice you wish to give your passengers, so be it. We will always welcome them to Briarwood, but I agree the choice must be theirs. And—" Greyson's voice tapers away. "Perhaps it is time you built yourself your own army. Not of warriors," he clarifies, waving the assumption away. "But of loyalists who would do anything to protect what they love—their freedom, their lands. I've seen firsthand what a power like that wields."

Imagining such a thing is epic indeed. It's exciting and promising and something to be proud of. And as the possibilities of the future unfold, Greyson and I sit in silence. Contemplating. Strategizing. Planning.

Eventually, I place another log on the fire, knowing daylight is mere hours away.

"Will you do me one favor?" my brother asks, and brushing my hands on my pants, I rise to my feet.

"I guess that would depend how much trouble it will get me into," I jest, and reclaim my chair beside him.

Greyson smiles. "Will you bring your little Skadi here, just once? I want to look into the eyes of the woman who has tamed my brother's restless spirit."

"Tamed?"

He nods. "I never thought it possible."

I laugh, deep and loud. "She is the wild one, not me."

"Then I want to meet her all the more." Greyson grins, so wide it fills his face and his dimple shows beneath his scruff.

I can't remember the last time I saw him smile like that, and eyes blurring with drink and far more emotion than I want to admit, I nod.

"Yes, brother. If she will have me, I will bring her to meet you." Feeling suddenly weightless, I lean my head back, close my eyes, and bask in a sensation that feels dangerously close to happiness.

46

BRYNN
14 MONTHS LATER

As I wrestle the net of flopping fish into the boat, the spray of the ocean is a welcome reprieve from the sun, fierce and high in the sky. Summers on the island, I've learned, are fleeting, and I soak up every minute of it against my arms, neck, and face without complaint.

"Brynn, look!" Just as Bo shouts, a whale breaches the waves a few leagues out.

I hold my breath as the giant sails through the air, sending the cawing birds flying and water swelling as the beast crashes back into the sea.

"That's two today," I call over the sound of the ocean, unable to stop smiling.

Bo nods. "It's going to be a good week for fishing, then."

Our rowing forgotten, we watch the whale surface once more as the tide carries us the rest of the way to shore. The sea is beautiful when it wants to be. Terrifying half of the time, but on days like this, with the sun high in the sky, it glistens and sounds almost peaceful.

"Grab that oar." Bo grunts as the surf splashes over the side of the boat, beckoning us home.

I snatch it before it's lost to the water and tuck it under the mound of codfish, ready to be cleaned and dried to tide us over during the cold months. It's a daily routine in the warmer weeks—Bo and me out here on the water. It gives Leif and Basher more time to tend to the crops that burst to life without the gray of heavy cloud cover, and Hans and Tug more time for hunting and curing meats before the weather turns unfavorable.

Bo jumps out of the boat and pulls us ashore, while I knot the net to haul our codfish bounty over to our cleaning station. The gulls are already circling, waiting for their daily entrail delicacies, and I find myself strangely content to be out at sea.

I try not to think of him, of course, and push images of stormy gray eyes away.

The waves crash around my boots as I jump onto the beach. "Gods," I breathe, arms straining to pull up one of the nets.

"I'll do it." Bo tosses the oars into the sand. His red hair is braided back, like mine, and my cheeks are likely as pink as his from so much sun. "My brawn is the only reason you keep me around anyway, isn't it?"

I laugh. "True. That, and endless amusement."

Bo grabs the larger of the nets for me. His big arms flex as he lugs it over his shoulder, as if he's moving a sack of laundry. "Compliment or insult?" he asks, giving me a sideways glance. "I can never tell with you."

I smirk, refusing to answer, and heave the smaller net onto my back.

"Oh, look!" he says, pointing at the heap of green in the sand.

"Seaweed," I deadpan. "Fascinating." I don't take two steps before his net is in the sand and he's tossing the seaweed at me.

I drop my haul of fish. "What are you, seven?" I hiss, then wag my finger. "No, wait. That's an insult to Tank."

Bo chuckles, and I elbow him in the rib. "Ouch, you're bony," he says, rubbing his side. "And so violent."

"It's in my nature," I admit, and think of Norseland. I try not to for many reasons, but mostly because, once again, I think of Killian. I think of how many months it's been since I've seen him. How the longer it takes for him to return, the more I worry he never will.

"Come on," Bo says. His playfulness turns to a familiar kindness because he knows where my thoughts drift. "Stay focused, would you? Stop playing around. We have a lot of work to do."

I shove his shoulder again as Bo barks with laughter, and we get back to work.

The cleaning station is not much more than a large canopy with net siding to keep the birds at bay, but it works. The breeze carries the scent of fish away, and the fabric top, loud as it is whipping in the wind, keeps the sun off our necks.

Still, Bo and I hurry through our task, cutting off each fish head and disemboweling it to dry. It doesn't take long before it's a competition between us, trying to pass the time more quickly to see who can clean their fish the quickest and get out of there for the day.

Once the codfish are clean and hung to dry, the sun is beginning to lower in the sky.

"I stink," I say, peering down at my scale-covered clothes and fingers.

"You and me both," Bo mutters.

Wiping the sweat from my brow with the back of my arm, I squint out at the water. It shimmers as the waves roll in, blue and cool, even in the summer, I know it would be a satisfying way to clean off.

Bo must think the same thing because we look at each other, grin, and with a peal of anxious laughter, we run for the waves, and my legs won't move fast enough.

47
KILLIAN

Little Skadi runs with abandon toward the shore, laughing as she leaps over a pile of seaweed, through a barreling wave and into the water, diving beneath the surface. I can't help my smile as I watch her, alive like I've never seen before.

Her head breaches the surface before she dives back down again. Coming up for air, she floats on her back, and Bo pops up beside her. She splashes him as they swim in different directions, and the smile never leaves her face.

"Afraid, she is no more," I breathe, and watch as Brynn swims like she is made of the sea, like she is happy, and like this is home.

48
BRYNN

When the sun descends on the horizon, Bo and I head back to the village. It's no longer two cottages and a few outbuildings. With over a year to prepare for whoever else might arrive one day, we've built nine cottages, most of which sit empty. We built a barn that Bo and I can use as a foundry, when needed, and to corral the few sheep we wrangled back from one of the islands, as well as the chickens Killian left us.

With more hands, we planted more fields of grains to harvest once a year. And we cultivated more herbs for Tora's garden. We even have a fox friend that skitters around from time to time, as curious about us as he is comfortable, and feasts on the rodents and rabbits that like to frequent our gardens, so we've gladly welcomed him into the fold.

As Bo and I make our way between two of the cottages, Leif comes around the corner, headed for the toolshed.

"We had a good day," I tell him, drawing closer. "The fish are clean and dry—" All coherent thought evaporates.

Unfamiliar faces unload goods near one of the cottages with Basher and Hans.

I look at Leif, barely able to make my tongue work, let alone tame my racing thoughts.

Leif nods, knowing exactly where my mind is at. "He brought a few people with him."

But as I frantically scour the new arrivals, my palms sweating and my heart galloping in my chest, I don't see Killian.

"He and his crew are setting up camp on the beach, on the other side of the island, like before."

I frown, staring at the empty cottages we've spent the last year building in hopes they would be used on a day like this. "Why aren't they staying here?" *Why isn't he?* I don't ask that one, because the answer terrifies me. But it's obvious, whatever Killian's reason for staying on the north side, it has to do with me, because Leif averts his gaze. Something is wrong. "Leif," I prompt, my voice hard and wary.

When his green eyes meet mine, my stomach hurts and my lungs constrict because I'm afraid to breathe, to ask him what he's not telling me.

"Is he okay?" I whisper.

Leif waves my question away. "He's fine. It's nothing like that, but you should speak with him."

All I can think is that Killian has someone with him, or he has changed his mind about us. Either way, I need to know before I see him. I need to prepare myself. My hands tremble at my side, and I clench them, forcing myself to steady.

"All he said was they were going to set up camp at the shoreline."

I look at Bo, who looks equally perplexed.

"Tug is already over there," Leif adds. "He wanted to see the crew, and Cat, of course."

I stare at the two women and three men bustling about this place like they are coming to stay—something that should make my heart soar because it means all of this has been worth it. The months waiting for Killian. The days that felt like years, and the sleepless nights. The longing. The crying. The doubting. And now this discomfort—this horrible feeling that something isn't right—makes me want to throw up.

"Brynn, you should go to him," Bo says gently.

I blink up at my friend, seeing the concern in his eyes. He's been with me through all of this—from the moment I woke on Killian's ship, determined to kill the Reaper, to now, my heart breaking as whatever truth I'm about to discover gnaws away at this new happiness I've found.

I nod because I know I need to go to Killian, even if my feet refuse to move.

Killian didn't come down to the beach.

He didn't wait here to see me.

He isn't staying at the village, not alone or with me.

Hands clenched at my sides, building anger urges me forward. It forces me to walk—to know what's going on. I deserve that much, at least.

49
BRYNN

The ship mocks me as I get to the beach. It's out there at sea, just as it was before, a looming reminder of what has always stood between Killian and me. And now that he's returned, the elation I thought I would feel curdles in my stomach like sour milk.

This is the safest place to anchor, I remind myself. *He would not want to leave the ship unattended . . .* But as logical as those facts might be, they don't feel right either.

I stop just outside camp, eyeing the tents that billow in the wind. The ropes are all that keep them taut and from blowing away, and the lanterns threaten to extinguish as they swing from their pegs and hooks.

Immediately, I know which tent is Killian's. It's bigger—at the helm of the camp, as a captain's place should be. And it's large enough for more than one person. For late nights scouring maps of the sea . . . and other things.

I stare at the flap of Killian's door, uncertain what I will find inside. I'm more terrified than I have ever been. Changing my clothes was pointless because I'm already sweating again.

Fourteen months. So much can change. *Everything* can change, and I fear that it has.

Norik comes out of one of the smaller tents, his face lighting up when he sees me. "Brynn, the captain slayer." He chuckles, and comes in for a hug. I can't help a smile, even if I am not feeling very jovial.

Norik looks me up and down, then shakes his head. "You look good, kid. And Tug—you did well with him. He's been filling us in all afternoon. I think he's in Boots's tent with Cat. They're likely getting into a bit of trouble." Norik lifts an invisible bottle and pretends to chug it back as he rolls his eyes, making me laugh.

"He's missed all of you very much," I admit. "Wait until you taste his mutton stew. He's had plenty of practice while you've been away. Though, he'll probably be here until you set sail again." The thought sobers me, and Norik must notice because he points to Killian's tent.

"He's in there," Norik offers, and with a clap on my shoulder, he trudges through the sand in the opposite direction.

My smile fades as I force myself closer to my fate. The sand is suddenly thick and arduous to walk through, but I keep going, only stopping when I reach Killian's canvas tent. I hesitate. I listen. But all I can hear is my heartbeat pounding in my ears.

You're being senseless. I chide myself because I have braved much worse than this. And squeezing my eyes shut, I shake out my hands, and with my heart in my throat, I pull his tent flap aside.

Immediately, my breath catches. Killian is inside, alone, his back to me as he bends over a trunk beside his cot. He is windblown, some of his dark hair escaped from the knot at the back of his head, his sleeves rolled up to his elbows, and his pants and boots speckled with dried seawater. Maps and scrolls are stacked on a rickety table, and a few trunks line the sides of his tent.

"If this is about provisions, Norik," Killian says without looking behind him. "I've spoken with Basher already."

I swallow thickly. "It isn't," I whisper.

Killian stills, and the seconds it takes him to turn around feel like an eternity. I nearly die where I stand by the time he is looking at me with those stormy eyes that I've dreamed about nearly every night since he left. That I've longed to see again—thought of more times in one day than is natural. They are just as conflicted as I remember, too, and my heart sinks as I let out a breath.

"Brynn," he says, clearing his throat. He glances around his tent, though I don't know what he's looking for. Or maybe it simply hurts to look at me, the way it kills me to look at him with so much uncertainty.

"Imagine," I say, licking my lips. I can't help the sag of my shoulders as I shake my head. "Imagine my shock to learn you returned." My voice hardens a little. "And that you didn't bother to find me."

Killian grips the sheet of parchment in his hand tight enough to make it crinkle between his fingers. "I did, actually. But you were having a splendid time swimming," he says, smiling a little.

"I was *swimming?*" I practically sneer.

"I didn't want to disturb you."

I glare at Killian, taking a step closer. "Well, thanks for that. But I think *swimming* could have waited."

Killian's eyes shift over my face, and another small smile, sad as it is, tugs at his lips. "You are happy here." He says it like that's a bad thing. Like it makes him sad.

I shrug, uncertain what that has to do with anything. "Yes, I am happy here, Killian."

His lips purse. "Good."

A horribly awkward silence stretches far too long, and I can't stand it. "Will you at least tell me how long you are staying? Or where you've been?"

He tosses the parchment onto the table with a sigh. "It's undecided how long we're staying," he says, exhaustion heavy in his voice. As he rubs his hand over his face, it dawns on me something must be wrong. Maybe things with his brother have worsened.

I take a hesitant step closer. "What happened, Killian?"

When he looks at me, his brow furrows. "How do you mean?"

"Is your brother okay? Did you go to your family's estate?"

Killian lowers himself to the edge of his cot and drapes his arms over his knees. "It's okay, now. But there was trouble while I was away."

"What kind of trouble?"

"The estate burned to the ground—an attack on my brother and his new wife."

My hand flies to my mouth. "Oh, Killian." I want to step closer, but I pause, uncertain I should. "I'm so sorry."

He shakes his head. "They are well now. They have a son, and a new home. It's all been sorted."

"I saw you brought people with you too," I add. "Does that mean you've been to Norseland?"

"No," he says, his brow furrowing slightly as he looks at me. "Not yet. I've been in New London, helping my brother and the tenants rebuild. Spending time with my new sister and nephew." He says the last part, smiling to himself. "And little Paige, of course. Though she is not so little anymore."

That Killian seems content despite his exhaustion makes me glad.

Another moment passes in this strange distance between us, and Killian looks at me. "I'm happy you learned to swim," he says, and there's a glint of amusement in his eyes.

"Yes, well, that was one of your stipulations, if I remember it correctly."

"Good, you read my note then—"

"I've read your note a thousand times since you left," I admit. "Leif taught me how, so I could memorize every single line."

His jaw clenches beneath his beard, as closely cropped and well kempt as ever.

"Killian." I breathe his name, and it sounds like a plea. "What is this? What's happening?"

"What do you mean?" He frowns as if he's completely oblivious, while my heart is breaking, and I don't even understand why.

"I have pictured this moment hundreds of times—I've dreamed of it, of us—and never did I anticipate it would be like this. That there would be fathoms between us." I grip the edge of the table, refusing to cower from my fear. "It's been over a year. So much time for things to change. I just need to know . . . Have your feelings changed? Is there someone else?"

Killian stands. "No." He shakes his head. "Well, yes."

I feel my face fall despite myself.

"No—" he says, stepping closer. He waves his words away. "No, there is no one else. It's not like that." He reaches for my hand.

"Then what is it?" I ask, far too reedy for my liking. My shallow breaths quicken. *I will not cry. I will not cry.*

Killian's jaw clenches, and his eyes fix on me in a way that makes me afraid to exhale. I don't know if he's holding my hand to lessen the forthcoming blow or if he's reassuring me it will all be okay.

"Brynn," he says firmly. "I have spent the last fourteen months doing *everything* I can to get back to you."

"If that's true, why are you acting this way?"

He takes a strand of hair between his fingers that has come

loose from my braids, then tucks it behind my ear. "You have consumed me, little Skadi. Every thought, every single moment, has been measured as a day and week closer to when I might see you again."

"But?" I whisper, because I know what's coming. My heart thuds harder with each shallow breath, waiting.

"You are happy here, and I—"

"Killian," I practically growl. "Yes, I'm happy here, but . . ." The tears breach my eyes despite my efforts, only angering me more. "How can you be so infuriating?" I breathe, and a part of me wants to scream. "Do you not understand that every morning when I wake up, I walk to the northernmost hill to peer into the horizon, praying to the gods that finally I will see you? And I check again every night before I sleep, even when I cannot see a single thing through the fog. I look, always, for you."

My nostrils flare and I avert my gaze. I stare at the ground. At the furs on his bed. At his booted feet. Anywhere but into his eyes that undo me when all I want right now is to hold myself together. "So what if I am happy? I have been waiting for you."

Killian takes my trembling chin between his fingers and forces me to look at him, into the blue tempest that rages in his eyes. I see his torment, even if I don't understand it. And the instant his eyes flick to my mouth, I refuse to hold back.

I kiss him. It's punishing, because how dare he do this to me? How dare he make me wait, only to come back and make me suffer all the more? "You are an idiot, Killian Blackburn," I scold him, anger clipping every word as I climb into his arms. His kisses are as fervent as mine, as desperate.

"I know," he breathes, but I swallow the words as I kiss him again. I squeeze my legs around him, refusing to let go as he falls back onto his cot with a groan.

"I hate you," I tell him.

"I know," he says again. "You should. Because I want to take you away from this place."

I still in his arms and pull back, peering down at him in utter confusion.

He looks ashamed, and as I lick my lips, I sit up and wait for him to explain.

"I brought Nell, Demetri, and the others because they wanted to help—to see for themselves what we want to do with this place. But the only reason I came back at all is to take you with me."

"Where?"

"To Norseland, for others. To the Old Lands, wherever you want to go, to bring them back here." He pushes up my other sleeve, staring at my Skadi markings as he runs his finger over them, tracing the runes as if they're some holy script. They tingle as always when he touches them. "I should go without you. Leave you here to be happy. I realized that the moment I saw you on the beach. It's dangerous at sea. In Norseland. It's safest if you stay here where I know you will be happy. And yet . . ." He brushes my hair from my face, his thumbs caressing my cheeks. "And yet, I want you with me. I don't want to leave you again."

My heart thuds.

"My brother is happy," Killian admits, his thoughts drifting back to Briarwood. "And with that comes an inexplicable relief I never expected to feel. There's no more guilt. No more self-loathing. I've wasted so much time, and I . . ."

"Not wasted," I whisper, covering his palm with mine. "Waiting for me." I smile at him.

Killian's hand falls away from my cheek and he laces our fingers, torn between kissing me and waging whatever war is in that overwrought mind of his. "I want to be happy, Brynn. I want to be better than I was and live the life I was given without looking back." He leans in, his forehead resting against mine.

His breath is warm. He is here, physically next to me, and still mine. It's all I care about.

"I don't want to do it alone," he whispers. "Not anymore."

My eyes flit open. *I am his.* Killian, restless soul and Reaper of the sea, has said as much. "You have a whole crew to help you," I rasp.

A smile lifts his cheek. "What if my crew isn't enough? What if I want my little Skadi?" There's a lilt of hope in his tenor, and my heart flutters. "Someone to keep me straight."

I laugh, wrapping my arms around Killian's neck, and look into his eyes. "That's something I'd be more than happy to do."

He grins. "I know."

"You would be stuck with me on a ship for months," I clarify. "You'd have to see me night and day—"

Killian rolls me onto my back, and a laugh bubbles out of me again. "That's the point, isn't it?" he says, claiming another kiss. "Njord and Skadi, sailing the seas—you and I are woven into life's tapestry by the gods themselves," he reminds me.

"You forget, Captain, they did not quite get along."

Killian smiles. "And your point is?"

I grin.

"Besides," he says, "it depends which story you believe more. Yours, or mine?"

"Reluctant lovers, torn between land and sea—obviously, mine," I tell him.

"I like mine better," he counters, brushing a kiss over my lips. "About destiny and prosperity and—"

Palm against his chest, I push him back. "This is never going to work if we're already arguing about it, Captain."

His eyes dance above me as he pushes against my palms, lowering himself over me again. "I like it when you call me that," he hums.

"Then I'll be sure not to," I tease.

"All right then." Killian sits up, separating himself from me.

I reach for his shirt, wrenching him back down to me. "Fine," I tell him. "I will call you Captain on one condition—two, actually."

He tilts his head, a wolfish grin on his face. "You're already negotiating?" I shrug and wait for him to concede. "Fine. Name your conditions."

"First, I want you to make love to me all night, and no one bothers us. No duty or captain business—Captain."

Killian promises me with a kiss.

"And second," I add, holding him at arm's length. He peers down at me as if I hold the moon. Brushing his hair from his face, I whisper, "You have to promise to take me to Briarwood someday."

Killian sobers a little. His brow twitches as he scours my face, looking for the truth. "You want to go?"

"Of course I do. I want to meet your family—to know all there is about you. To see what you have been helping to build all of your life."

I don't know why Killian is so surprised, but a gleam of utter joy shines back at me. "Then you shall know all of me, little Skadi," he says low and guttural, then glances over me. "And we'll start with inside and out."

I laugh as he braces himself on his elbow, lifts his head, and shouts, "No one is to disturb me until I leave this tent! That's an order!" A few chuckles rumble outside, and my face flares with embarrassment.

Killian wraps his leg around me, his eyes shifting over my face with awe. "I've missed you," he whispers. "And I never want to let you go again."

"Don't worry," I breathe, urging his lips to mine. "I won't let you. And you know me well enough to believe that."

50
BRYNN
THREE MONTHS LATER

The ship dips in and out of waves, the wind rushes over me, and a surge of apprehension fills me as I stare at land dotting the horizon.

It's been over a year since I was in Norseland, lost Estrid, and the gods turned my world upside down. So much has changed, and now I sail for the very place that damned me for so long.

The Reaper's purple sails whip in the wind, punctuating the forthcoming future. Imminent. Unpredictable. Terrifying and exciting all at once.

Despite the plan to bring people back to the island, and the pride I feel in that, a darkness hangs over this place, and as that familiar heaviness settles into my bones, I begin to question if what we're doing is even possible.

"You've been staring at the horizon all morning," Killian says, walking up behind me. "You aren't having second thoughts, are you, little Skadi?" His presence instantly makes me smile, and my eyes close as I hold my face to the wind.

"Never," I tell him, and it's true. Fear has never stopped me from anything, and for the first time in my life, it feels like I'm fulfilling a purpose, no matter the outcome. That I have a reason for drawing breath when Estrid no longer does.

If she could see me now. The thought makes my heart hurt a little, but mostly because I know she would be proud. "But," I tell Killian, "I would be a fool not to be wary of this place. It has taken so much from all of us."

Killian's chest is warm against my back, and he grabs hold of the balustrade on either side of me. "Yes, you would," he admits, and kisses my temple. He rests his cheek on the top of my head, and as the rooftops of Talon Bay come into view, we stand in silence.

"This is where you found Basher," I recall, wondering how different Talon Bay might be than Northhelm.

"The outskirts, yes. But we haven't been here since."

"Why not?"

"Our unpredictability is what helps to stoke the chaos. If the cities don't know when or where to expect us, they can't prepare for our arrival."

"But won't everyone's panic and fear put us in more danger? People are impulsive and irrational when they are afraid. Chieftains will be waiting for you to come for them—they will want to protect their businesses, if for no other reason than to keep the queen's favor."

"There is no hiding this ship, little Skadi." The words roll off Killian's tongue as if he's said them a hundred times. "Our presence would never go unnoticed, despite our efforts. At least in feeding people's fear, we can better gauge what we're up against and plan for the worst. Besides, I have a man in all ports—"

I spin around to face him. "You do?"

Killian nods, a smirk tugging at his cheek. He always likes astonishing me. "We do not arrive completely blind," he says, cocky as ever. "Boots will find the man once we're anchored, and we will know who is the greatest threat to us and who we should set our sights on. It's the same way we found Basher and a few others last time."

"That's how you knew about Von," I realize. "I'd always wondered."

Killian hums in agreement. "This enterprise is so much bigger than just me and this ship, little Skadi. You will see."

"Perhaps that's true. But the bigger your enterprise gets, and the longer it goes on, the more risk there will be. It's only a matter of time before the queen discovers what you're doing," I tell him.

"What *we're* doing," he says, grinning.

"You jest, but—" I shake my head. Killian must already know my fears. If I've learned nothing else, I know he is clever, always thinking of various scenarios and strategies.

Killian nods toward the shoreline. "If the queen is planning the Reaper's demise like you say—it will happen soon. Which means we need to be prepared."

I blink at him, watching the way the sea breeze tugs at his hair. The way his eyes fix on the horizon as he thinks about the future, plotting and planning. I watch the way his mouth purses with thought and the broody silence that overcomes him when the weight of all of this—the people, the ship, his family—settles over him. I'm in awe of him all over again. That he would do this for so long and sacrifice so much.

It's then that I feel true relief to be here. That I can help to share his burden, even if it's only in a small way.

"Others must be brought into the fold," he finally says. "There are others like Leif—men who wish for change, even if they fear it." He pauses. "We just have to find them."

Though I would love nothing more than to change the fate of Norseland, I can't help my reservations. "It's a risk," I warn him, one he already knows but I give voice to all the same.

"Just as it was a risk my grandfather took when leaving Norseland years ago. And every time we've sailed here since."

Killian looks down at me, smiling softly. "But you have shown me that complacency does no one any favors. And if we continue to do this, we must change with Norseland. With Briarwood and the isle colony." He peers into my eyes and smiles, as if he sees a future that makes him hopeful. That makes him happy. "We must find a way to be better. And we will."

"Together," I promise, cupping his jaw in my hand.

Killian nods, eyes searching mine as he leans in and brushes a kiss to my lips. "Together."

THE END

Be sure to read Selene and Greyson's story in *City of Ruin*, a Beauty and the Beast meets Jane Eyre retelling. And finally, visit Norseland for Princess Thora and the huntsman's story in, *Land of Fury*,

All ebooks, paperbacks, and audiobooks are available on my website, and across all retailers.

OTHER BOOKS BY LINDSEY

FORGOTTEN WORLD

(Stand-alones, suggested reading order)

RUINED LANDS

City of Ruin

Sea of Storms

Land of Fury

FORGOTTEN LANDS

Dust and Shadow

Borne of Sand and Scorn Prequel Novella

Earth and Ember

Tide and Tempest

THE ENDING WORLD

SAVAGE NORTH CHRONICLES

(Reading order)

The Darkest Winter

The Longest Night

Midnight Sun

Fading Shadows

Untamed

Unbroken

Day Zero: Beginnings

THE ENDING SERIES

After The Ending

Into The Fire

Out Of The Ashes

Before The Dawn

The Ending Beginnings

World Before

THE ENDING LEGACY

World After

The Raven Queen

For all things Forgotten World, visit the goodies hub:

ABOUT LINDSEY POGUE

Lindsey Pogue is a genre-bending fiction author, best known for her soul-stirring survival adventures and timeless love stories. As an avid romance reader with a master's in history and culture, Lindsey's series cross genres and push boundaries, weaving together facts, fantasy, and romance set in rich, sweeping landscapes of epic proportions. When she's not chatting with readers, plotting her next storyline, or dreaming up new, brooding characters, Lindsey's generally wrapped in blankets watching her favorite action flicks with her own leading man. They live in Northern California with their rescue cats, Beast and little Blue.

For mini-fiction, early access, newsletter signups, and book bundles discounts, check out the Forgotten World series hub.

WWW.LINDSEYPOGUE.COM/FORGOTTENWORLDHUB

Made in the USA
Middletown, DE
05 September 2024